FREELY SEEN IN CAMOUFLAGE

JON J. ESPARZA

LIBRARY OF CONGRESS REGISTRATION: TXU001604083

A GAME OF HORSE
FOR
THE GAME OF LIFE

Jack Avila and his father were in the front yard with a basketball playing a game of HORSE*. Jack dribbled the ball to the edge of the driveway, turned and let the ball go in an attempt to duplicate his father's fadeaway jumper. The ball bounced off the backboard, rolled around the rim, finally careening off to the left. No basket. Jack collected the letter *E*. Game over. "That was close," said his dad. "Jack, let's take a breather. I want to run something by you." Words meant as a pre-collegiate pep talk became seared into a seventeen-year-old's psyche.

"First of all, I can't believe how fast the years have gone by. In just several days, you'll be living in a college dorm, meeting people from every background and from every point on the compass. Don't hesitate to talk to these strangers. And when they speak to you, listen closely. You can learn from their experiences. Imagine college and the years beyond it as going on a long voyage. Walk in the footsteps of your ancestral countrymen. Make yourself a modern day Spanish explorer. Remember Cortés,[1] De Soto[2] and De León,[3] and be like them. Don't be afraid to go into the unknown. Every day in the unknown will provide a clearer picture. Remember Padres Serra,[4] Lasuén[5] and Crespi,[6] and be like them. Challenge yourself to climb steep hills and cross broad rivers. Remember the Spanish crews of the

* *H-O-R-S-E: an American basketball game for two or more persons, played either on a home court or in the school yard. At its core, it is a game of one upmanship where difficult and sometimes next-to-impossible shots are used to eliminate the competition from play. As each shooter misses, he or she earns the next letter in the word horse; and when a player reaches H-O-R-S-E, that person is eliminated.*

Niña, *Pinta* and *Santa Maria*, who carried Columbus to a new world, and be like them. Seek the knowledge and adventure that lies over the horizon. Whatever the distance traveled today, tomorrow's dawn will provide a new horizon. Chase what lies over every day's new horizon and you will enjoy a life of excitement and great fulfillment. Wisely use the time allotted to you by God. I wish you all the best, and good luck to you, Jack."

"Hey, thanks, Dad."

ARISE AND SHINE

LIKE MANY HOMES across the land, the Avila house burst into action early every Saturday morning. Jack and Jane went in every direction to accommodate their three kids, Thomas, Joanie and Suzanne.

"Jane, Jane." *Doggone it, where is she?* thought Jack, as he walked through the upstairs bedrooms. She was nowhere to be found. Downstairs through the kitchen, dining room, living room, den and patio—still no Jane. Jack walked into the garage and there she stood, transferring laundry from the washer to the dryer. Jack thought to himself, *I should have checked here first.*

Jane Keely, Mrs. Jack Avila for the last eighteen years, was a dedicated wife and great friend. She was the quintessential living image of a person with Midwest values. Born in South Bend but raised in Elkhart, Indiana, any Hoosier around the world could point to her with pride. Jane, courteous to all she met, industrious at home and work, gifted in her pursuits and dedicated to the family, was relentless in her attempt to cover all the bases. She gave 150 percent when only 50 percent was required. At 5' 2", petite, with blonde hair and blue eyes, she was an energetic dynamo way beyond her proportions.

"Jane, unless you need me to do something, I'm going to the sporting goods store to renew my hunting license and get ammunition for the upcoming hunt with Uncle Val and then taking off for Tom's scrimmage."

"That's fine," said Jane. "I'm leaving with Joanie in a few minutes for her game."

"See you later tonight," answered Jack.

Jack took off to the local sporting goods store, which was several miles away. When he arrived at the store, Jack walked the aisles looking at the latest hunting equipment. He finally went to the gun and ammunition counter and asked for a box of .308 caliber, 165 grain, boat tail, soft point cartridges. The clerk turned around and grabbed the requested box of cartridges off the shelf. "Can I help you with anything else?" said the clerk.

"I need to renew my hunting license," answered Jack.
"Here's a renewal form. Complete it and give it to the guy at the regis-ter. He will verify all the information. You can pay for the ammunition and the license at the register."

"Thanks a lot," answered Jack. On the first line, Jack filled in the name requirement: Joseph Phillip Avila. Hair: Brown. Eyes: Blue. Height: 5' 9". Weight: 190 pounds. He added his driver's license number and date of birth. Joseph Phillip Avila. He was named Joseph after his father and grandfather. Avila is a name deep in the roots of Spanish history. There were too many Joes at family gatherings. Someone had to change and it would be Joseph Phillip. His father started calling him Jack at six or seven years old. With a name like Jack in the family, it was a true marker that the family had transitioned from Spain to America.

Jack had finished his hunting license application and waited in line. The clerk at the register that day was a young American of Mexican descent with dark complexion and black hair combed straight back. He was friendly and jovial to all customers. He was a great representative for the store, as all making a purchase had to pass by him. Finally, Jack came to the counter.

"Did you find everything OK and was our service good?" asked the clerk.

"Yeah, everything was great and the guy at the gun counter was very helpful," replied Jack.

"That's good to hear," said the clerk. "In regard to your hunting license renewal, I'll need your driver's license." Jack handed the clerk his driver's license. The clerk started to verify the descriptions on the hunting license application, comparing them to the descriptions on the driver's license. The clerk was checking the information when he suddenly stopped. He looked at the hunting license, then the driver's license and then at Jack. 2

He quickly repeated the same actions and stared at Jack. "Avila. Hey, man, you're a white guy," exclaimed the clerk.

"I know. It even blows my mind," Jack said laughingly. Jack paid for the license and ammunition and jumped into the car. He could already feel the excitement of the upcoming hunt. It was time to drive to his son's pre-season high school football scrimmage in Santa Fe Springs.

Jane was already at Joanie's soccer game in West Los Angeles. Joanie, at fourteen years of age, was the Avila's middle child. She was very athletic for fourteen years of age and her coaches loved her for it. She was always assigned the left fullback position because she was left footed. She could rocket a soccer ball upfield past offensive players, who assumed she would make a pass with her right foot. Joanie was never intimidated by the size or speed of an opponent's blow. What Joanie took, she gave back two-fold. Joanie's reputation preceded her and right offensive wings rarely came her way.

This particular game was a league division playoff. A large fourteen-year-old right wing was dribbling the soccer ball past the center part of the field, heading to her right. By going right, she was heading for the left full-back. Joanie Avila was waiting. The offense wing was past center field now, moving unopposed toward the goal. With only twenty yards to go, the wing slowed down, thinking the goalie was the only defender. Suddenly, a speeding shadow approached the wing's left side. The wing instinctively tapped the ball to her right and took off running into the trap. Joanie made a quick circle and ran back toward the ball. Coaches on the other side of the field knew of the collision that was coming. Joanie had played for them at some point in time. With the wing heading for a corner kick, Joanie closed in with a foot on the ball and her other leg between the stride of the wing. When the wing leaned forward and lowered her shoulder, Joanie lowered her shoulder and did not stop. Joanie had the momentum and the angle; so when the collision occurred, the larger wing tumbled off the field. Joanie went after the ball and with her left foot sent it sailing to midfield. Her team went over to the attack. The speedy little fullback had made a point to all watching, *Don't tread on me,* while her sideline erupted.

"Do you believe that? Do you believe that?" said the head coach, as he walked up and down the rows of parents. "That was a beautiful defensive play."

The female assistant coach turned to the head coach and said, "That was a great play and what a transition from defense to offense." The assistant coach then turned around and said to all the parents, "How many times have we seen Joanie turn an offensive player into a pretzel?" Joanie's team went on to win by a final score of two to one.

With the game concluded, Jane approached both coaches and thanked them for their hard work and dedication. "Jane," said the head coach. "You've got to be proud that your daughter plays with such determination. That comes from the inside and not from any coach's instruction."

Jane told Joanie as they walked away from the field, "I'm very proud of you. That was a great play you made, helping to turn the game around."

"Thanks, Mom," answered Joanie.

Jane was thinking while driving home, "If Joanie remains this aggressive, so much for the debutante ball."

Later that Saturday morning, Jack arrived at St. Paul High School in Santa Fe Springs where Tom and his sophomore football teammates were scheduled for a scrimmage. The opposing coaches had known each other for many years, from previous coaching positions as well as from having played with or against one another. They thought this scrimmage would be a good test for both clubs.

During warm-up exercises and offensive and defensive drills, the two teams watched each other. The hard-core fact of tackle football was descending upon them. Whistles blew and there was a quick meeting in both camps. In less than a minute, both head coaches sent players into various positions to test their strengths. Suddenly, players on both teams came face to face with an opponent directly in front of them. Tom had been assigned right inside linebacker. He looked straight ahead at the offensive guard and for the first time saw an unknown face with unknown intentions behind the face guard. It did not occur to Tom that the offensive guard saw the same unknowns. On a quick snap play, the opposing offensive line pushed the defensive line backwards. The opposing team's halfback was almost on the ground when Tom was blasted from behind. It was the classic "cheap shot." Tom slowly picked himself up to see the guard, who played in front of him, walking back to the huddle celebrating with "high fives." The nose guard and defensive tackle asked Tom if he was OK. "I'm OK," said Tom. Tom hovered three feet away from the offensive guard on the next play. As soon as the ball was snapped and before the guard got out of his three point stance, Tom delivered a massive forearm blow into the face mask of the guard. The guard's helmet broke away from the chin strap and the face mask went directly into the guard's face. The next play found Tom in front of the guard. Blood was dripping off the guard's face mask onto the field. Tom got within a few feet of the guard to let him know what was coming. When the ball was hiked, the guard absorbed another forearm blow and rolled backwards into the fullback, who in turn fell sideways and tripped up the halfback. The running play ended up behind the line of scrimmage. One of the opposing coaches had noticed Tom's actions, and sent in a play that would be an embarrassing surprise for Tom. Again, the offensive team came to the line and returned to the same formation. A quick snap call found the defensive team unprepared. Tom rushed forward toward the guard only to see the guard veer right and help double team the nose guard. Tom was met helmet to helmet by the fullback. The play forced both of them to stack straight up and stop in their tracks. The full back had accomplished his mission. Tom was eliminated from the defensive scheme. The play was a "slant" to the left side of the offensive line. Once the halfback squirted past the line of scrimmage, he was on his way to a 70-yard touchdown.

During the course of the next hour and a half, both coaching staffs substituted freely. The main goal was to determine the players' strengths and weaknesses. The conclusion of the scrimmage found both coaching staffs at midfield exchanging handshakes and small talk. They wished each other good luck in the upcoming season and left for their respective teams. The slant play was decisive. Tom Avila's team lost the scrimmage by a score of 7 to 6. Tom and his teammates climbed on the bus for the ride back to West Los Angeles.

Jack picked up Tom at school. They talked about the game on the way home. "Boy, Dad, we really got burned on that slant play," said Tom. Jack hesitated momentarily and then said, "You're right. Your side of the line did get burned. The offensive line of the other team did a great job of blocking on that play. You burned yourself."

"What do you mean?" snapped Tom.

Jack said, "Delivering punishment was more of a priority for you than correctly playing your position. I'm sure their coaching staff saw your actions and realized, with little effort on their part, you could be taken out of the play."

"Great. Thanks, Dad," blurted Tom.

Jack quickly pulled the car over to the curb and turned off the engine. "I'm sure you've heard this from your coaches, but you better listen to me right now," said Jack. "Football is a game of discipline. Once you step over the white chalk line onto the field, you follow the coach's instructions and play your position. If you get hit very hard on a play, that's too bad. The next play requires you to maintain your position based on responsibility and not based on retribution. If you get the opportunity to deliver retribution on a future play, then do it, but not at the expense of your teammates. The team always comes first. It's great to be driven by emotion but it must be tempered by logic. The linebacker position has great freedom of movement that allows and requires you to stop the run or intercept the pass. Emotion without logic can be ineffective. Logic without emotion can be lackluster. Use emotion to enhance your logic as you look across the lines. Let the opponent's circumstances and their formation predict their intentions. Never predict your movement. Make it a personal goal that whatever they attempt to do, you will be there to thwart their plan. Being involved in stopping their plays will make any opposing team respect you more than any cheap shot you could ever deliver. All I can say is, if you can't take it, don't step on the other side of that white line. But if you can take whatever is delivered to you, then do step across that white line with energy, personal pride and determination."

Jack started the car and pulled away from the curb. They had traveled several blocks and had come to a red stoplight. While there, Tom looked at Jack and said, "You know, Dad, you're right. I let emotion get the better of me. During next week's practice, I'll start using more logic."

As soon as Jane returned from Joanie's game, it was time to take Suzanne to her piano lesson. Suzanne differed from the other two Avila kids in temperament and looks. Her idea of a good time did not involve sweat and body contact. She enjoyed reading, a trip to any museum, and learning the piano. Tom and Joanie had sandy blonde hair, blue eyes and a normal white complexion. Suzanne had jet black hair, a lily white complexion, huge blue eyes and naturally red lips. These contrasting colors on her face made many who looked at her go into a trance. It was difficult to look away from her. When Jack looked at Suzanne, it brought back the image of his grandmother from Pamplona. He had seen pictures of his grand-mother, as a young woman, and Suzanne was a miniature duplicate. It was not uncommon for Jane to be at a department store or market and have an unknown woman approach her and say, "Your daughter is stunning," or "absolutely striking" or "I couldn't take my eyes off her."

Two hours after dropping Suzanne off at the piano teacher's studio, Jane returned to get her. On this particular day, Suzanne was very quiet and appeared dejected. "What's wrong?" asked Jane.

"Nothing," was the answer.

"Yes, there is," said Jane. What's the problem?" Jane asked.
Suzanne hesitated and then said, "You and Dad always go to Tom and Joanie's practices and games. You never visit or encourage me when I go to practice."

Jane was caught off guard. Grasping for an explanation, Jane told Suzanne, "Your Dad will let you know why, because he is always very logical."

"How did the scrimmage go?" asked Jane as Tom and Jack walked through the door. "It was close, Mom, but we lost seven to six." answered Tom.

"That was close, so both teams must have been evenly matched," Jane replied. Tom left to take a shower. This was Jane's opportunity. "Jack, you need to talk to Suzanne. She's down tonight," said Jane.

"Down? What is she down about?" asked Jack.
"She feels that we don't participate in her practice or effort. I didn't say much. You've always had a knack of explaining life's situations to these kids. I know you can do it again," said Jane.

"Well, Jane, I hope you're right. Each individual explanation to each individual kid brings its own individual response. I'll let you know what Suzanne has to say. Be back in a while," said Jack.

Suzanne's door was closed, so Jack knocked on the door before entering. He opened the door to see Suzanne sitting up against the headboard of the bed reading a book. She did not acknowledge him as he entered the room. "Mom told me you are disappointed in us," said Jack. "If we have hurt your feelings, it was not intentional, and I know that you know that. Your Mom and I have always treated the three of you very equally. On any given day, one of you may get more attention than the other two, based on the circumstances. That day's circumstances determine who gets attention, not the indiscriminate flip of a coin by me or your Mom. Now, tell me why you are disappointed in us." Suzanne did not initially reply. She kept reading her book. Suddenly, her eyes welled up with tears and she began to cry. "Hey, I'm your dad and I'll always be here for you. Tell me why you are sad," said Jack.

Suzanne pulled out one of the sheets on her bed and wiped the tears off her face. "You and Mom always go to Tom and Joanie's practice sessions. You stay there for hours. With me, you or Mom just drop me off and leave. I guess I don't rate very highly with you guys," sobbed Suzanne.

"We love you very much, and of course you are close to our hearts, but you are missing an important part of the picture," Jack said matter of factly.

"What am I missing?" asked Suzanne.

"Tom and Joanie participate in team sports. They have to deal with different coaches, multiple offensive and defensive players and hostile sidelines. You don't face these obstacles while you learn how to play the piano. You deal with one teacher and yourself. Mom and I don't sit there at your lessons as we could be distractions. You might not try hard, thinking you might make a mistake in front of us. You know what it is like when someone stands over your shoulder while you are reading or writing," said Jack.

"You're right, Dad. I don't like that creepy feeling," answered Suzanne.

"Well, that's the feeling we might bring by sitting off to the side while you try your best. Plus, there is one more important thing for you to remember," said Jack.

"What's that, Dad?" asked Suzanne.

"It's most likely that ten years from now Tom will not be playing football, or Joanie soccer. But ten, fifteen or twenty years from now you will be playing beautiful music on the piano. Tom and Joanie's results seem immediate. Your results will happen in the long term. However long the term, your Mom and I will be there to help you achieve the results you desire. We love you very much," said Jack.

Suzanne was now busy wiping away the tears from her face with her forearms. With the tears gone, the radiant colors of her face came back into focus. She smiled and said, "Dad, I guess I didn't see the big picture, I mean all the family together," said Suzanne.

"That's OK," said Jack. "I'm just glad that we got to talk about something that bothered you. I really hope, as you get older, you will always feel free to talk to me about anything that bugs you, or to review a situation in which you are not comfortable. I love you very much and my door is always open."

Suzanne jumped up on the bed and grabbed Jack around his shoulders and kissed him on the cheek. "I love you, Dad."

IT'S NEVER BOARING

EARLY ON SUNDAY morning, Jack packed his suitcase and hunting gear for a boar hunt in Paso Robles. The children came down
the stairs and met him as he was placing items into the car. "Hey,
Dad, have a great hunt and say hi to Uncle Val for us," said the Avila kids.
At that point, Suzanne came forward and said, "Dad, get a champion."
"I'll do my best to get a champion," Jack laughed to himself. He knew that
Suzanne meant "get a trophy." He then thought, *Don't all champions get a
trophy?* Jack hugged his children and his wife and told them how much he
loved them.

Jane followed Jack to the car. "Please be careful," she said.

"Of course I'll be careful," said Jack. "I love you very much and I'll see
you in several days. I'll call you from Paso Robles."

"Great," answered Jane.

Jack left his house and soon was on his way to pick up his uncle Val
in Ventura. He had driven some distance on the westbound 101 Freeway
when a radio commercial caught his attention. The commercial
advertised full and part time positions with the National
Investigative Department. Jack turned up the volume so as to verify
that what he was hearing was true. When the commercial finished,
Jack stared at the radio. *This must be some radio station's joke,* he
thought. *The NID would not advertise on the radio.*

Jack continued on Highway 101, down the Conejo Grade, past
Camarillo and Oxnard, finally arriving in Ventura. He exited and drove to
his uncle's house. There was Uncle Val in front of the house with luggage,

gun case, and a bag containing salami, crackers and cheese. Jack got out of the car and greeted him: "Hey, Uncle Val, are you set? I'm really excited."

"I'm excited too," answered Uncle Val. "It doesn't get better than hunting in the beautiful countryside of central California."

"No, it doesn't," said Jack. "If you're ready, I'll pack your items and we're off."

"Sounds great," said Uncle Val. "Let's get going." Jack grabbed Uncle Val's bags and gun case and placed them in the car. Uncle Val climbed into the front seat and off they went. Jack quickly merged into northbound traffic on Highway 101. They were on El Camino Real, the Royal Road.

The stretch of Highway 101 between Ventura and Santa Barbara, with the roadside sea level beaches and towering cliffs always provides for a scenic drive. They had not driven far when Uncle Val reached into his back pocket and said, "I just received some pictures from our cousins in Spain. Let me show them to you." He organized the pictures and explained them as Jack drove. "Your mother and I donated the uncles' house to the town. The home was demolished, and in its place a small plaza with a fountain was built. The mayor sent these pictures to show us the results. The last picture is the best. On a wall of a house adjacent to the little plaza, a plaque was erected to commemorate the family." Uncle Val passed the photo to Jack. "That is amazing," said Jack. "We live half a world away and the town recognizes and appreciates our family who left long ago."

Jack and Uncle Val stopped in Buellton. They refueled the car and bought some soft drinks. Once past San Luis Obispo, they climbed the steep grade to Paso Robles. Upon approaching Paso Robles, Uncle Val said, "I've heard there are some good wineries off Highway 46. Let's look for them and I'll buy."

"OK," said Jack.

Jack drove east on Highway 46 and found the wineries. Uncle Val was in heaven as he sampled the various wines and cheeses. Soon, it was time to head back to Paso Robles and check into the motel. After registering with the motel and placing their luggage and gear in the room, Uncle Val placed the wine, salami and cheese in the refrigerator.

"Well, we're here" said Uncle Val. "Is there anything you want to do, Jack?"

"Ed told me, if we got up here early on Friday, he would take us on a Friday evening hunt. He said to be in a dirt lot across the street from the local bar in San Miguel. But in any case, I would like to see the mission, "said Jack.

"No problem," answered Uncle Val. "We have our rifles, ammo, and hunting tags in the car. I'll put the salami, cheese and bread in my back-pack. I'll buy the beer in the bar until Ed arrives."

"Wait a minute," said Jack. "You're the guy who taught me never go hunting by yourself and have a beer only after the hunt."

"That's right, but I'm older now. I know you'll be there to carry me home," laughed Uncle Val.

After checking what they needed, Jack drove the nine miles from Paso Robles to San Miguel. Jack and Uncle Val took the first San Miguel exit. They came to a rolling stop in front of the Mission San Miguel Arcangel, as they gazed upon its dilapidated and ruined edifice. The old ramparts were crumbling and major cracks were visible in the walls of the church. Jack turned to Uncle Val and said, "Does it seem strange to you that a mission named for Michael the Archangel, sent by God to defeat Satan and his legions, has not rallied much support?"

Uncle Val hesitated before saying, "I think you're right." Both of them walked around the mission to firmly implant its condition in their minds.

Uncle Val and Jack drove down the street and waited in a dirt lot across from the local bar. Ed Willis, their hunting guide, had given Jack a description of his truck. Suddenly, a pickup truck flew off the paved road, sending up a large cloud of dirt. The truck pulled up next to Jack's car. When the dirt settled, Jack saw a burly driver, with a large handlebar mustache and wide brimmed cowboy hat. The three hounds in the bed of the truck left no doubt the driver must be Ed Willis. "Are you Ed?" asked Jack.

"I am," was the answer. Ed was an affable guy. He explained where Jack and Uncle Val would be hunting that evening. Ed had Jack and Uncle Val sign the required Waivers of Responsibility. "Have you hunted boars previously?" asked Ed.

Uncle Val replied, "We have hunted boars for years. This is our first hunt with you in this area."

"Great. I'm glad you picked me. You'll have a great time. There are lots of hogs on these ranches. Well, it's time to go. Follow me. We will go approximately 15 miles into the countryside. Then we'll stop at a 10,000 acre ranch and I'll drive from there."

"Sounds great," answered Jack. We'll be right behind you."

They followed Ed through the beautiful countryside east of San Miguel in the general direction of Parkfield. Large and small homes dotted the hillsides. Deer and turkeys could be seen in the fields. At one point, Jack and Uncle Val passed a small group of tule elk. Finally, Ed pulled off the paved road and onto a dirt road leading to a large ranch house. Jack and Uncle Val pulled in behind Ed.

"Get your rifles, ammo and anything else you need for the next several hours. Don't forget your license and tags, as the DFG may check us," said Ed. Jack and Uncle Val got the necessary items and waited for Ed to return from his truck. When Ed returned, he noticed that Jack and Uncle Val had identical rifles. "I must admit that, over the years, I have had identical sets of twins come and hunt, but I can't remember when different people have showed up with identical rifles. What do you guys have?" asked Ed.

"We have Winchester Model 88 lever action rifles in .308 caliber," replied Uncle Val.

Ed continued, "When I was in the Army, our snipers used rifles in .308 caliber. That is a great cartridge." They got into Ed's truck and started driving into the ranch. After two miles, Ed pulled off the dirt road. "I have the Ed Willis Challenge if either of you would like to take a shot. In that small grove of trees on our right is a frying pan, hanging from a limb of the middle tree. It's 400 yards plus change from this spot. Do either one of you want to take a shot?" asked Ed.

"Whoever takes a shot at anything from 400 yards, anyway?" said Uncle Val.

Jack looked off into the distance and asked Ed, "What group of trees are you talking about. There are several groups on our right."

"Look at the three trees at the mouth of that small canyon," said Ed. "There is a frying pan hanging from the middle tree."

Jack spotted the three trees and said, "This is a case for nine power," and turned the scope ring from three to nine power magnification. "I see the frying pan in the scope," said Jack. "What the hell, I'll take a shot." Jack opened the truck door to use it as a brace. He slipped the leather sling around his right arm and elbow, found the frying pan in the scope, and then pulled the rifle lever down and up, placing a cartridge into the chamber. Jack knew the calibration of his scope. Elevation at 100 yards was accurate on the bull's eye. Windage at 100 yards found the bullet drifting less than one inch to the left. Ed positioned himself on the front hood of his truck looking through his binoculars. Uncle Val leaned on the rear of the truck looking through his binoculars. Jack took a deep breath and exhaled. He found the pan in the scope. He moved the crossing reticles several inches above the center of the pan. He then moved to the right of the center of the pan and slowly started squeezing the trigger. The sharp recoil pushed Jack away from the truck door, but he quickly recovered to look through the scope and see the frying pan swinging wildly.

"Did you hit that goddamn thing?" exclaimed Uncle Val. Ed just looked through his binoculars.

"Congratulations, Jack. There is a journal in my glove compartment. Just grab it and pass it over to me," said Ed. Jack opened the glove compartment, found a small booklet and gave it to Ed. Ed started going through the pages. "Well, let's see," said Ed .This is my thirty-second year as a guide and I have been on over 7,000 hunts for hogs in this area. Jack, you are the twenty-sixth hunter to hit the frying pan on his first attempt. Ninety-eight percent of all hunters don't even take a shot at the pan. I know what a difficult shot it is, not only because of the distance, but the filtered light coming through the tree limbs makes the pan seem to appear and then disappear."

"You're right about the filtered light coming through the tree limbs," said Jack. "As I looked at the frying pan through the scope it seemed that a slight breeze started the pan swinging from right to left and just before the rifle fired, the pan started to turn at an oblique angle"

"Whatever the circumstances, that was a hell of a shot," said Uncle Val.

"Well, thanks, but I just did my best to hit the pan," replied Jack.

Jack and Uncle Val climbed into their truck and followed Ed deeper into the countryside. Ed stopped at several sites where he thought hogs might be grazing but no hogs were found. At a fork in the road, Ed suggested that Jack walk down the road alone and Uncle Val would go with Ed. "Nothing personal, Ed," answered Uncle Val, "but I would rather be with my nephew. We've done a lot of hunting together over the years and this is another occasion for us to be together."

"That's not a problem. You and Jack follow this road," said Ed. "Be very quiet as you approach the upcoming crest. There is a pond as you descend the small hill on your left. At this time of the evening, hogs will leave the barley fields to get water. I'll check out other watering areas," said Ed. Uncle Val and Jack left Ed's truck.

Jack and Uncle Val walked down the road speaking in muffled tones and every so often checked the direction of the wind. "I heard what you told Ed about us hunting together," said Jack. "A lot of hunts come to mind. How about the duck hunt at Uncle Pete's ranch where I almost 'bought the ranch'?"

Uncle Val responded by saying, "Jack, you have always shown good sense and insight but on that particular day, you were a stupid fool, almost losing your life for a duck. You were lucky that I was on the ranch that day," said Uncle Val. "You violated the first rule of hunting: Never go hunting by yourself."

"You're right," replied Jack. "That brings to mind when I went on the bear hunt and I got my ass kicked," said Jack. "The guides estimated at the end of the hunt that I had walked ten to twelve miles up and down the hills and canyons, with no paths, of the Sequoia National Forest.

Uncle Val chuckled. "I remember you walking the small path out of the forest with the guides and dogs. One of the guides told me that your hunt had been one of the most difficult in recent years. "Physically, you looked OK, but I remember you talking to yourself."

"That's what I meant about getting my ass kicked," said Jack. "I've always been logical and determined but after all the hiking and wandering through the forest, I was talking to myself. I was so excited when we came across the small path, which led us back to the main road." Jack asked Uncle Val as they walked down the road, "How's your hip?"

"It's sore, but the doctors who have examined me tell me to live with it. It's part of getting older," replied Uncle Val.

Jack and Uncle Val started heading for the trees at the top of the road, occasionally stopping to pluck blades of grass and toss them into the air to determine the direction of the wind. It was time to be quiet, stay downwind and continue toward the trees. Each footstep had to be calculated, as a step on fallen twigs, leaves or branches could alert hogs below the crest that danger was approaching. They came up behind the trees and peered down the hill to the watering hole. No hogs were there.

A minute later, Ed came driving down the road. He turned the engine off fifty yards away and walked to the crest. "Did you see anything?" asked Ed.

"No, there was nothing here," replied Uncle Val.

"There were no hogs at the other two ponds. Let's get in my truck and we'll check out some barley fields," said Ed. They had gone only a mile when Ed turned off the engine and coasted forty yards down a hill. They exited the truck, careful not to slam the doors shut, and walked to the tree line. When they gazed beyond the trees, twenty to thirty hogs were grazing in the barley field. Ed turned to Jack and Uncle Val and whispered, "We can get within fifty yards of where they are grazing. This field sits on a small plateau. You can't see it from here, but there is a ravine that goes around the field's perimeter. Let's go. It will be an easy shot. Who's going first?" asked Ed.

"Well, if it's going to be easy, I'll take the shot," said Uncle Val.

"OK, follow me," said Ed. They walked into the wind, and as Ed had predicted, they stood forty yards away from the grazing hogs. Uncle Val got down on one knee, braced the rifle, aimed and pulled the trigger. A medium-size hog in the middle of the group fell down and then immediately got up and started running. It ran through the field and disappeared into the ravine. "You hit hard," Ed yelled as he looked through his binoculars. "Let's go get it." All three walked through the field to see the hog at the bottom of the ravine, motionless. "Good shot," said Ed. "I'll go get my truck and I'll be right back."

"Well, Uncle Val, you got a nice hog. That was a great shot, as it's getting dark," said Jack.

"Yeah, aiming at dusk into the barley, it was a little hazy," replied Uncle Val. He had taken a few more steps, when a rock that he stood on came away from the dirt, and he rolled thirty feet down the ravine and ended up by the hog. Jack slid down the ravine with his rifle all the time pointed at the hog, in case it was wounded and decided to fight. When he reached the bottom of the ravine, Jack pushed the hog's head with the muzzle of his rifle. There was no movement. Jack put the rifle on the ground. "Uncle Val, are you OK?" asked Jack.

"My hip really hurts, almost as if it's on fire," said Uncle Val.

"Everything will be OK. Ed should be back here any minute," said Jack. Ed returned to the scene but saw no one. He looked down into the ravine and caught a glimpse of Jack and Uncle Val. "Hey, Ed!" yelled Jack. "Uncle Val hurt his hip. We're right next to the hog."

"I'll bring my truck to the top of the ravine and toss you a rope," yelled Ed. Ed drove the truck to the edge and threw a rope into the ravine. "Jack, I want you to cut through both shanks of the hog's back legs. Tie a good knot and then climb back up the ravine. Be sure to bring the rifles with you. Val, when Jack gets up here, he will direct me. I want you to grab the hog's front legs and hold on to them. The other end of the rope is tied to my front bumper. I will back up very slowly. The hog's body will be like a sled and pull you along." At that moment, Jack arrived at the top of the ravine. "Jack," watch your uncle. If all is OK, keep your arm up. If I am going too fast or he stumbles, drop your arm and I will stop. Are you ready, Val?" yelled Ed.

"I'm all set. Get going!" yelled Uncle Val. The hog acted just like a sled and less than a minute later, Uncle Val popped over the top of the ravine. As soon as Uncle Val reached the top, he lay down and grabbed his hip. "I think I'm really screwed up this time. I feel like my hip is out of the socket," Uncle Val said.

"Put your arm over my shoulder and I'll help you to the truck," said Jack. While Jack helped Uncle Val back to the truck, Ed was busy field-dressing the hog.

They had reached the truck when Uncle Val yelled, "Stop! Stop! My leg won't bend."

Ed came over immediately. "Val, can I help you?"

"My leg won't bend. I can't get into the truck."

"Take your time," said Ed. "Go slowly so we can help you." After a minute, Jack and Ed lifted Uncle Val gently off the ground and placed him into the front passenger seat.

"Are you comfortable?" asked Jack.

"Actually, I feel OK. Thanks, guys, for helping me. I can now stretch out my leg," said Uncle Val.

Ed finished the field dressing. Then they drove back to the ranch house, where Ed placed Uncle Val's hog in a cheesecloth bag and put the carcass in a cooler. "Do you want a beer or water?" asked Ed.

"No, that's OK," replied Jack. "What time do you want us to meet you tomorrow?"

"Meet me at 4:15 tomorrow morning at the gas station off the second San Miguel exit," answered Ed. Ed drove Uncle Val and Jack back to Jack's truck on the ranch. Ed would spend the night on the ranch and meet them in San Miguel in the morning.

Jack and Uncle Val drove the twenty miles, in darkness, back to Paso Robles. When they arrived at the motel in Paso Robles, Jack draped Uncle Val's arm over his shoulder to support him in walking back to the room. "I'm OK. Let me lie down. Oh, man, that hurts," exclaimed Uncle Val as he entered the room. Uncle Val lay down on the bed and said, "That's better. Having my leg straight out makes my hip feel better."

"Good", replied Jack. "Now, what do you prefer, Advil or merlot?"

Uncle Val laughed and said, "First available, but I'm hoping you find the merlot first." Jack turned around and produced a glass of merlot.

"I'll be right back," Jack said. He left the room and went to the local Bar-B-Que. He ordered chicken sandwiches and fries and then returned to the motel. They ate the sandwiches while they reviewed the afternoon.

"You made a great shot on that pig," said Jack.

Uncle Val hesitated as he was eating his sandwich, then put the sandwich on his plate and looked at Jack. "This was my last hunt, Jack. My hip has hurt for a long time. I'm in my early seventies and there comes a time in everyone's life when they must deal with reality. I can't hike for miles anymore. I have great memories and pictures of you and me on hunts over the years, but, I'm sad to say, this is the 'end of the line' for me."

"Come on," said Jack. "There is a long way to go."

"No, there isn't," answered Uncle Val. "I'm giving you my rifle."

"I'm not going to take your rifle," said Jack.

"Jack, you must take my rifle or I'm going to throw it off the Ventura Pier," said Uncle Val.

Jack yelled, "What the hell am I'm going to do with two identical rifles, in identical calibers, with identical scopes? Come on, Uncle Val, be real."

Uncle Val remained calm and said, "Jack, I am being real. I can't go on this type of hunt anymore. You need to take my rifle and keep it in the family. Tom may want to use it and may enjoy the outdoors as much as you and I have done over the years; and, besides, if you ever go on a grizzly bear hunt, you'll need a rifle in each hand."

Jack sat across the room, quiet and reflective. After a minute, he responded. "I've always respected your comments about hunting, and life in general. I'll take the rifle and all the memories associated with it. Thank you very much."

"Memories go in many directions, Jack," said Uncle Val. "I have great memories of you and me walking through meadows and over hills. I also have those scary memories of the two of us wading across rushing streams and getting stuck in muddy ponds. This is the challenge of hunting and everyday life. Always persevere and move forward."

"I guess you're right," Jack answered. "I'll wake you in the morning. I'm getting very tired," said Jack.

"Me too. I'll see you in the morning," replied Uncle Val.

The 3:30 a.m. wake up call came as a clap of thunder. "Oh, man," said Jack, as he jumped out of bed, slipped on his jeans and shirt and grabbed his socks. "Come on, Uncle Val, we need to get going."

"I'm not going," was Uncle Val's answer. "I can't go; my hip feels like it's welded tight. You go and have a great time. I'll go to the motel's jacuzzi later. Sorry to let you down."

Jack replied, "You're not letting me down. You have to do what's best for you and take care of yourself. I'll be OK." Jack put on his boots, grabbed the ammo and his side arm and took off on the dark highway to San Miguel.

He met Ed at the gas station off the second San Miguel exit. He pulled over to find Ed in the cab of his truck with three hounds in the truck's bed. Ed got out of his truck expecting to greet both Jack and Uncle Val. As Jack got out of his vehicle, Ed asked quickly, "Where's your uncle?"

Jack told him, "His hip was so sore he couldn't get out of bed. He decided to stay at the motel."

"I'm sorry to hear that. But grab your gear; we need to get going."

"Sure," said Jack, returning to the vehicle to get what he needed.

As Jack climbed into Ed's truck, Ed asked," Where's your rifle?"

"Well, Ed, this is a two-day hunt, and since this is my first day with you, I brought my .44 Magnum pistol. If I don't get a shot this morning, I'll use my rifle in the afternoon. I've done this before, and I realize when hunting, circumstances always change. How close can we get for a shot?" Ed hesitated and said, "If all works well between wind, terrain and stalking, we can get within feet. It's an outside chance but it may work. I don't want to brag, but I have gotten hunters very close over the years."

"You're not bragging", said Jack. "You are telling me your capability and I appreciate that."

"Well, Jack, jump into the cab. We should get going. We need to be on a different ranch before dawn," said Ed.

Ed drove the several miles to the ranch. Once past the barbed wire gates, they drove the narrow and ruddy roads. Always driving slowly and looking left and right with their binoculars, Ed and Jack gazed at the distant hills and ravines. At one point, Ed turned off the engine, slowly coasted down the hill and put on the parking brake. When they got out they could see hogs in the distance. The animals were far away. As Jack and Ed returned to the truck, the dogs jumped up in the bed of the truck and their noses went in one direction, their eyes fixated on a distant object. They had been trained not to bark until given a command. The dogs were huddled together. Ed saw them and peered into the distance. Suddenly he spotted what the dogs had seen. "Jack, jump in and don't slam the door. I'm going to coast down the hill. There is a huge hog right down the road. He's jet black and must weigh at least 350 pounds. From this point on, we need to whisper."

Ed drove a short distance before placing the truck in neutral and coasted down the hill. He headed away from the road so as to approach the hog from downwind, and stopped the truck at what he thought would be the best vantage point. While Jack and Ed had moved, so had the large hog. The hog was grazing lazily on a small hillside, almost sixty yards away. It was too far for a pistol shot, but it would have been an easy rifle shot. The hog had not realized that Jack, Ed and the hounds watched its movements. After a couple of minutes, Ed said," I think I can get us closer. There is a small canyon that leads to that hillside about half a mile away. If we can get there and the hog is still on the hillside, I'll set the dogs loose and they might bay it up. Let's go."

Ed and Jack climbed into the truck, mindful to be as quiet as possible. Ed drove through the small canyon and emerged only forty yards away from the hog. The dogs were already straining their chains but made no sound. "What do you think? Can you make that shot?" asked Ed.

"I can't. It's too far," said Jack. "I was thinking around twenty yards. I've done it before."

"OK," replied Ed. "I'll turn the dogs loose and maybe the hog will stay right there. Here we go." As he approached the back of the truck, the three hounds jumped wildly but remained quiet. Ed unchained their collars and the dogs waited for their command. Ed whispered, "Look," to the dogs and pointed to the hog in the distance. Their eyes and noses locked onto the hog. Ed whispered again to the dogs, "Go." The dogs bolted out of the truck bed and, for the first time, barked and yelped as they hurtled toward the huge hog. From this point on, the dogs were like heat-seeking missiles. No other animal, be it another hog, a deer, raccoon or badger that crossed their path, would distract them away from the pursuit of their quarry. They would be relentless in following the scent. Like so many objectives in hunting, Plan A immediately failed. The hog took off to disappear over the crest of the ravine, with all three dogs in hot pursuit. Ed and Jack immediately took off after them.

Ed could climb the steep hills and descend the ravines as if some invisible staircase existed. Jack continually slipped and fell, stumbling to one knee in his attempt to keep up with Ed. As they came to the top of a very high hill, Ed said, "We need to listen for a minute." He gazed into the distance. "From where we are standing, there are two canyons that come into this ravine. The barking of the dogs makes me think they are veering left. So we'll go down this canyon to intercept them."

After several more ravines and hills, Jack and Ed reached a new peak and stopped to listen, but they heard nothing. Jack turned to Ed: "Well, what do you think?"

"Either, we went left and the dogs remained where they are, or they moved farther to the right. We need to go back the way we came," said Ed. As before, Ed glided up and down the hillsides while Jack slipped and fell. They had walked half a mile when they reached a cliff. They could hear the dogs in the distance. Their barking echoed eerily through a canyon. Jack could only think of the haunting sounds of banshees, as if danger beckoned. "We're going down that canyon right now. Let's go. We need to hurry," said Ed.

As they descended the steep hill, the baying of the hounds became much louder. Ed and Jack were almost upon the hog and the dogs, when all four animals bolted away. Ed placed his hands on his hips and put his head down in exasperation. Jack looked to his left and stared into the distance. Suddenly, the sounds of the animals were very loud. They had not gone far and Ed and Jack ran to the location. The hounds had pursued the hog into a five-foot-deep by six-foot-wide dry wash and were now farther into the wash, where the walls rose to ten or twelve feet high.

"We need to load our pistols and it's time to talk turkey," said Ed. "You can remain here and wait for the dogs to tire and return, or you can follow the hog and hounds down the wash; but it will be very dangerous and I need to remind you of your signed Waiver of Responsibility. If you do want to go down the wash, I will be slightly to your right and behind you. I'll do everything possible to support and provide for your safety. It's your call," said Ed.

Jack's response was, "Let's go, Ed. If I turn around now, I'm not testing myself."

Ed and Jack, each with a loaded .44 Magnum pistol extended in their right hands, slowly turned the corner and proceeded down the narrow wash.

They had gone only twenty to thirty feet around the corner when loud barking and grunting came their way. "Look out!" yelled Ed, as the hog turned into the wash. Ed jumped up to grab the large roots of a manzanita tree extending into the wash. Jack also jumped to grab the roots, only to have them snap. Jack was coming straight down on his back. Just before he landed in the wash, the calves of his legs brushed the rump of the hog; then he hit the ground just in time to be trampled on his face, arms and chest by the pursuing dogs. Jack never lost his composure and kept the pistol straight up in the air with his finger away from the trigger.

"Are you OK, Jack?" asked Ed.

"I'm OK, but I think I have a rock embedded under my right shoulder blade. There's something there," said Jack.

The animals running through the narrow wash had created a small tornado of swirling dust. Suddenly, Ed yelled, "Jack, look out!" Through the dust came the image of the hog. Jack, still on his back, did what came instinctively. He pulled his legs up, tucking his knees under his chin to protect his vital organs. Jack pulled the hammer of the pistol back and put his finger within a hair's diameter of the trigger. He would go for the "boiler room" shot. With the .44 Magnum extended and held in both hands, the range would be less than three feet. Though dirt in his eye partially obscured his vision, Jack followed the image as it came through the cloud. As it started to pass him, he placed the muzzle of the pistol close to the rib cage, only to see the head of one of the dogs emerge from the dust. *Oh, my God*, thought Jack. *What a horrible mistake that would have been!* The dog made two circles around Ed and Jack and then started running down the wash. The dog had gone a short distance when it stopped. It was panting heavily and looked back at Ed and Jack as if to say, "Hurry, and follow me."

Ed told Jack, "We need to go now."

As they traversed the wash in the opposite direction, the terrain rose in elevation, coming up to ground level with thick high brush and manzanita. They approached the hog and the dogs with Ed saying, "This is the end of the line. The hog will fight the dogs until the dogs give up. With this heavy brush, we will not find the animals until we come into the clearing with them.

Ed and Jack started walking through the high brush, careful to stay upwind and not step on fallen branches. They had gone only another thirty feet, when they all of a sudden found themselves on top of loud grunting and howling. Ed pulled Jack aside and said, "Get ready for a broadside shot. I'll watch the dogs. When I say "Now," you shoot. Do you understand?"

"Got it," replied Jack. Jack cocked the hammer of the pistol keeping his finger away from the trigger. Ed pulled the high brush back to reveal a movie director's dream. Ten feet in front of them was the huge hog fending off the dogs. The hounds darted in and out, from left and right, from front and back. *Amazing*, thought Jack, observing the instinctive coordinated probes of the dogs. Yet regardless of the direction, the hog met the dogs head on. Jack lifted his pistol and held it with both hands extended in front of him, hoping the hog would turn sideways.

Twice a dog's head popped up into the line of fire as it howled and charged the hog. Suddenly, one of the dogs charged the hog on the hog's right side. The hog turned to its right and caught the dog with its tusks. There was a loud yelp as the dog became airborne, doing cartwheels in front of Jack and Ed. Another dog's charge made the hog turn right, presenting the broadside shot. Ed yelled, "Now!" As soon as Jack heard the letter *N* in the word *Now*, he pulled the trigger. The recoil pushed the pistol upward and sent shock waves through Jack's ears. When he brought the pistol back into the line of fire, there was no hog. Jack lowered the pistol to see the dogs tugging at the hog, which was lying on the ground. He sat down on a large rock, head in hand and pistol off to the side. Ed just stood there in silence. It was time to regroup. After a minute, Ed said, "Now the hard part."

Jack stood up, put the pistol into his shoulder holster and said, "Ed, I'm guessing that we have several miles back to your truck and there are plenty of hills and ravines between us and that truck."

"That's a pretty good estimate," said Ed. He proceeded to field dress the hog. When he had completed the process, Ed placed a dragging strap around the hog's rear legs. "Are you ready?" he asked.

"I'm set," replied Jack. They both grabbed the strap and started dragging the hog behind them. The dogs walked proudly alongside, every now and then sniffing at the hog.

Two hours later Ed and Jack arrived at the truck. The hog was placed into the bed and the hounds jumped in, ready for the ride back home. Ed climbed into the driver's seat and said, "I want to congratulate you."

"Why?" asked Jack.

"You took a chance on the frying pan and actually hit it. Most guys would never have made it as far today as you did. They would have told me to stop and take them back to some easier hunting spot. You just kept going. And even after taking a bad fall, you hung in there until you got the hog."

"Well, thanks, but I kept going as it is part of the challenge," replied Jack.

They drove to the ranch house and, after arriving, Ed placed the carcass into a meat cooler. Jack paid Ed and thanked him for his hard work and for making the hunt exciting. Then Jack got into his vehicle and drove back to the motel in Paso Robles.

When Jack walked through the motel door, Uncle Val looked at him and said, "What the hell happened to you? You're here to hunt pigs, not to wrestle with them. Jack's face was covered in dust and there was a slight cut on his upper lip. His shirt was dark and wet with sweat.

"It's a long story but I got a huge hog. I might have it mounted," said Jack.

"How did you get the cut on your lip?" asked Uncle Val.

"I'm not sure," said Jack, "but I think it might have happened when the hog came around the corner of a wash. I jumped up and grabbed some manzanita roots growing through the bank, but they snapped and I fell flat on my back just in time for the dogs to run over me. I think one of the dogs used my nose as a starting block to get better traction. Whatever, it was a great day. I'd better call Jane and let her know I'm OK." Jack dialed his home phone number, knowing Jane would be waiting.

"Hello," said Jane.

"Hi, it's me. I'm back from hunting. Uncle Val and I got great hogs. The one I shot was a monster, so I may have it mounted. I could go for years and never get one that would be this large," said Jack.

"I'm happy for you and Uncle Val. So the hunt went smoothly?" asked Jane.

"Do you want a generic answer or a descriptive answer?" asked Jack.

"Come on, Jack, we've been married a long time; so spill the beans," said Jane. "Well, OK. Uncle Val shot a pig on Friday afternoon but he rolled down a ravine, hurt his hip, quit hunting and gave me his rifle. I fell flat on my back in a dry creek bed just in time to get run over by the dogs, almost shot a dog, then watched a dog do midair cartwheels after it got caught on the tusks of the hog, and then I shot the hog from ten feet away as it was fighting the dogs."

As Jack described the hunt, Jane put her head in her right hand anticipating the oncoming headache. "Jack, does it occur to you that you have three great kids, and, I might add, a great wife? Maybe you should consider doing what regular men do, like golfing, tennis or join a cycling club," said Jane.

Jack could hear the concern in her voice, and he smiled as he replied, "But Jane, if I do what regular men do, then that would just make me regular. It's more fun to be unique."

"That you are, Jack," answered Jane.

"Besides," said Jack, "I thought the only time in life when it's good to be regular is the consistency of your need to use the restroom."

"Jack, you can make a point without getting rude," replied Jane.

"I'm not trying to be rude. I'm just trying to think it all the way through," Jack responded.

"I'm glad both of you had a great time. Please drive home carefully. I'll see you later. I love you," said Jane.

"I love you very much and I'll be careful," said Jack.

The next morning Uncle Val and Jack left Paso Robles and drove to the ranch outside San Miguel. They took their hogs out of the meat cooler, placed them in Jack's vehicle and headed home. They drove through San Miguel to Highway 101 and went south, quickly passing Paso Robles. They had driven several hours and were approaching Santa Barbara. Uncle Val said, "If you don't mind, I'd like to get a bite to eat."

"Fine with me," replied Jack. "I'm hungry myself." He exited on State Street. As they drove toward downtown, they saw the entire area festooned with Spanish flags. "Amazing," said Jack. "I never expected that the people who chronicled and explored a third of the current United States by land

and sea, the people who gave names to rivers and mountain chains, who founded missions, towns and cities and whose influence would eventually become the names of States would be remembered or celebrated anywhere."

Uncle Val turned to Jack and said, "I think it was here in Santa Barbara that the last Spanish flag in California was lowered. Maybe that's why the flag flies as an important part of this city's history."

"Maybe so," was Jack's answer.

After lunch, Jack drove back onto Highway 101 and headed south along the beautiful coastline. Jack dropped off Uncle Val at his home in Ventura in less than an hour. "Hey, Uncle Val," said Jack, "it was another great time together."

"It was," answered Uncle Val. "Promise me that you'll take care of my rifle."

"Of course I will," replied Jack. Jack helped Uncle Val unload his gear and then took off to West Los Angeles. He had not driven far when he heard the same advertisement as before coming across the radio, an ad soliciting part time jobs with the NID. He looked at the radio and thought, *Maybe this is true.*

Upon arriving home, Jack was ecstatic to hug his family and they to hug him. "How was the hunt?" questioned Tom. "I want to hear all the details. When I get older, I want to go with you and Uncle Val."

Jack hugged Tom and said, smiling, "One day you will."

Last, but most importantly, was Jane. "I love you, Jack, and I'm glad you had a great time," said Jane.

"It was fun, but I missed you a lot," replied Jack. "I was very lucky the day I found you. Now I need to unload the hunting gear into the garage and get cleaned up." Jack quickly placed his clothes, ammunition and the two rifles in the garage. Then he went upstairs to shower and get dressed. By the time he arrived back downstairs, Jane had dinner prepared and on the table. As the family sat down to eat, Tom said, "Dad, tell us the details of your hunt."

Jack recounted the long hike, how the manzanita root had snapped and how his feet had grazed the rump of the hog as he fell. He then went on to explain the scene of the dogs and hog fighting and the close proximity of the shot.

"That is so great, Dad," said Tom. "I can hardly wait to go."

Suzanne, with a frown on her face, said, "Dad, you're a meanie."

Joanie hesitated for a moment, then said, "Dad, you need to go talk to someone. I think you need some help."

Jack started laughing and asked, "What kind of help?"

"Mental," Joanie replied.

Jane, also laughing, remarked, "I've been telling your dad that for years."

When dinner concluded, Jack asked his wife, "Do you need any help with the cleanup? Otherwise I'm going to put all my stuff away."

"Go ahead," replied Jane. "The kids can help me."

Jack went into the garage, placed his clothes into the washing machine and put the ammunition onto a shelf. He grabbed some old towels and his rifle cleaning kit; then he placed the rifles on the towels and began to clean them. He applied solvent to a small patch of cloth held in place by a fixture at the end of a cleaning rod and ran the rod up and down through the barrel until he determined it was clean. He did this procedure on both rifles. Then he wiped the surface of each one with solvent to remove any dirt and moisture, using a hand towel to wipe away any residue.

Leaving the garage, Jack walked upstairs. He placed his rifle into a gun case but discovered there was no additional room for another rifle. He looked at Uncle Val's rifle and decided to put it in the attic. As he covered the rifle with a towel, Jack thought, *What am I ever going to do with this thing?*

Closing the attic door, Jack went downstairs and met Jane.

Having checked that the kids were in their rooms doing homework, he said to her, "Jane, I heard that ad again, from the NID, looking for people for part time positions. What do you think?"

"What do you mean, what do I think?" she replied. "Why don't you call the telephone number? I'm surprised you even ask. I remember when we were dating and I didn't quite know you that well, some of your college buddies told me you should have been a spy. They weren't joking with me. College tuition isn't that far away, and our kids will be there soon. The extra money will be handy. What the heck! Next time you hear the ad, just call."

"Jane, your Midwest common sense and insight always hit the mark," said Jack. "Thanks for your everyday support."

"Well, of course I support you, but don't hesitate to make a simple phone call. Just do it," Jane responded.

"I will," replied Jack.

PEEP SHOW

J ACK RETURNED TO the office the next day to review construction contracts and customer activity. The dispatchers gave him a recent list of customer orders. He met with "the prez" to check sales and rentals in the various company locations; then he made a list of places he would call on for the remainder of the week and spent the balance of the day visiting jobs and offices in the immediate vicinity.

Jack's first stop the next morning was a job in Long Beach at Anaheim Street and Walnut. A lot of company equipment was at the work site and Jack had brought the crew donuts. The men took a break to eat the donuts while Jack spoke to the foreman. "Thanks, Jack, for bringing the vitamin D pills. These guys love this stuff."

"It's my pleasure. You have always been a great customer and your business is much appreciated."

"Thanks," answered the foreman. "By the way, Jack, have you been hunting lately? I remember you brought me some hot sausages after one of your hunts. They were great."

Jack started laughing and said, "I just got back from Paso Robles. How much longer will you be here?"

"I'll be at this site for another two weeks," said the foreman.

"The meat should be processed by then so I'll bring you some."

"Great," beamed the foreman. "I can almost taste them right now. Thanks, Jack." Jack started to make a remark, when the foreman interrupted him and said, "Jack, you should have been here a couple of days ago. There were two hookers walking around here and they were good looking."

Jack replied, "I've seen prostitutes in this general area for years. They just seem to come and go."

"Yeah, it's weird," said the foreman. "They w ere h ere o ne d ay b ut w e haven't seen them since."

"Take that as a good omen," answered Jack.

The foreman laughed a nd said, "That's go od ad vice. Ho pefully, I'll see you in a couple weeks with the sausages. I've got to get back to the job."

"No, problem," answered Jack. "I need to get going myself." Jack got into his truck and left the job, but by now traffic had clogged all the main streets. Jack's next stop was in Signal Hill, so he maneuvered through residential and side streets, finally arriving at Ohio and Pacific Coast Highway.

He was met by a solid line of cars. There w a s a t r affic ac c ide nt one block away at Temple and Pacific Coast Highway and all movement had been brought to a halt. Jack had intended to make a right hand turn but there was nowhere to go. Cars had come up behind him on Ohio, so the option of backing up was gone. *Great*, thought Jack. *I can pick any combination of streets in Long Beach but I pick an intersection with an accident. OK, calm down; listen to talk radio and accept the situation.* Jack had been sitting there for almost ten minutes when something caught his eye. Approaching on the slight incline to his left was a sight to behold. A white woman with brown hair, a pageboy haircut and statuesque figure was walking up PCH. She wore light blue pumps, a matching mini skirt and a red and white striped off the shoulder blouse. She was a living poster for the Fourth of July. As she got closer, Jack noticed that she had very large breasts that jiggled and swayed with every step, indicating that she wore no bra. She started to cross the street in front of Jack, smiled and said, "Do you date?"

"No, I don't," answered Jack.

She was almost in front of Jack's truck when she made a ninety degree turn and came up to his window. "Are you sure you don't date?" she said with a wider smile. Before Jack could answer, she continued, "Has anyone ever told you what beautiful blue eyes you have?" Her breath hit Jack with a strong mouthwash or alcohol smell.

"As a matter of fact, I have been told that before," answered Jack. "The only problem was he was drunk and I'm straight, so nothing was going to happen."

At that moment, she bent over and placed her hands on her knees to come face to face with Jack. "Well, I'm a she, not a he, and I'm very straight," she said. Jack went to respond but hanging down in front of his face were huge 44D-cup breasts. All was revealed except the very tips of her breasts by the off the shoulder blouse. After a moment she asked, "Does the cat have your tongue?"

"No," replied Jack. "It's just always been hard for me to stare and talk at the same time." Jack went on to say, "I don't get it. You are very attractive. Most women wake up every day hoping they could look like you. Plus, you have a good personality. Why are you out here?"

With Jack's remark, she put her head down between her arms as to face the pavement below. She raised her head and told Jack, "I'm an alcoholic and I can't beat it."

Jack had not realized that he was an inadvertent participant in a peep show. Two workers in a Public Works truck looked back to see the dangling breasts. "Damn it, Floyd," said the laborer to the foreman. "We're out here all the time. How come we never see a woman who looks like her? I was in a supermarket yesterday and the cantaloupes they were selling weren't as big as those knockers."

Floyd just shook his head and said, "Every dog has his day and today is that dog's lucky day."

Two women carpooling to work observed the conversation at Jack's truck, and the driver remarked, "What a disgusting man. How horny must he be that it doesn't bother him to deal with a prostitute in front of all these people?"

The passenger replied, "What a pig."
In an adjacent car, two other women were also carpooling to work. The passenger said, "I really like her pumps. They're very cute. I wonder where she got them?"

"They are cute," replied the driver. "If you look closely, they are one or two shades off from exactly matching her skirt."

"I didn't notice that at first, but now that you bring it to my attention, you're right," responded the passenger.

The c a r b e hind t h em f o und a v e ry d i ligent m o ther s i tting r a mrod straight in the driver's seat with both hands clenched on the steering wheel.

She gazed straight ahead at the stalled traffic through black rimmed glasses. She was taking her son and three classmates to the local parochial school. The boys, wearing navy blue corduroy pants, white shirts and matching navy blue ties, sat in silence. Suddenly, one of the boys in the back seat yelled, "Hey, check out those buns!"

"Oh, man, yeah!" yelled another boy. All eyes in the car went right, including the mother's eyes. With the woman bent over face to face with Jack at his truck, the bottom curves of her buttocks were showing below her uplifted mini skirt. The mother was mortified for two reasons: the first was for the public display of indecency; the second was the realization that her thirteen year old son and his friends were referring to female derrières as "buns." Her mortification turned to anger. "That is obnoxious. I want you to be quiet and look straight ahead," she demanded. The boys did what they were told, almost. They remained quiet, faced straight ahead, but their eyes veered right.

After making the remark "I can't beat it," the woman regrouped and started to continue walking on PCH. She passed the front of Jack's truck, then made an immediate right turn and leaned through the passenger-side window. She was crying as she said, "Why did you tell me how pretty I am? Do you know how long it has been since a man told me I'm pretty without asking for something in return?" Her grief now turned to anger. She grabbed several items, including Jack's wallet, and glared at him.

Jack went on to say, "You are very pretty but you don't have to believe me. When you get home tonight, just look into a mirror. You will see what I see and what most women would hope to see. Now, you need to put the items you grabbed back down where you found them. I know that you are not a thief." She hesitated and then threw the items in her right hand onto the floor of the truck. She wheeled around and started walking along Pacific Coast Highway toward Temple. Almost simultaneously traffic on PCH began moving, as the Long Beach Police and tow trucks had cleared the intersection of the accident. Jack turned right on PCH and had driven a short distance when the NID ad came on the radio. *That does it*, Jack thought. *I'm going to call.* Arriving home later that evening, Jack told Jane, "I heard that ad again. I'm going to call."

"Go for it, Jack," said Jane.

PRELUDE

JACK ARRIVED HOME early the next day and dialed the toll free number. The call was promptly answered by a female voice, with the immediate question, "Why have you called this number?"

"I called this number based on radio advertisements for part time positions with the NID. Do I have the right number?" asked Jack.

"Yes, you do," she replied.

"What's the next step?" asked Jack.

"I need your name and address. We will send you an application. Based on the evaluation of your answers, you may or may not be requested for additional information," was her reply. Jack gave her his correct full name and mailing address. "You will receive an application within the next five business days. Thank you for calling," and she ended the conversation.

Jack looked at the silent phone receiver and said, "OK." He turned around to see Jane enter the kitchen. "Well, Jane, I called the NID and they will send an application. I guess you can say that the train has left the station and I'm going for a ride."

Jane nervously smiled and inquired, "Where do you think you are going?"

"I don't know, but even if it is a short ride, it will be interesting," answered Jack. "Do you want strawberries in your glass of wine?" asked Jack.

"Sure, that sounds great," answered Jane.

A week after the telephone conversation, Jane found a large brown envelope in the mail addressed to Jack. The envelope displayed no return address. That evening, as their children did their homework, Jack and Jane opened the envelope and reviewed the enclosed questionnaire. Although Jack was the sole applicant, certain information was required on Jane's background. They provided their true names, address and Social Security numbers. It was required that Jack and Jane provide bank account numbers, credit history, extended family, relatives and personal references. Personal references also included a list of neighbors. Current employment and prior employment history was required. Another section of the form requested foreign languages spoken, hobbies and any personal affiliated organizations.

Jack and Jane reviewed the form and their responses late into the night to ensure their accuracy. "What do you think?" asked Jack.

"I think we have answered all the questions directly and in all honesty," was Jane's reply.

"That, we have," responded Jack. He sealed the preaddressed return envelope. "I'm going to mail the application tomorrow."

"I'm tired," said Jane.

"Me too," agreed Jack. "Let's hit the sack. Tomorrow will arrive soon."

Jack's first appointment was a meeting with a contractor at the Long Beach Airport. When the meeting concluded, he drove to the large regional post office on Redondo Street and mailed the questionnaire. As it was sliding down the mail chute, Jack thought to himself, *Bombs away!*

Several weeks had elapsed, when one evening Jack returned home and played the telephone recorded messages. One message requested a reply to an 800 number in regard to an application. Jack visited several job sites the next day and then stopped at a public telephone. He called the 800 number and was greeted by the same female voice. The voice requested Jack's name and the reference number listed on the cover page. It offered Jack multiple dates to come to the office for an interview. He agreed to a day and an hour and upon confirmation, Jack was given an address. He arrived home that evening and told Jane about the arrangements he had made.

The next two weeks would go by quickly for Jack. Through company office reviews, job site visits and construction meetings, the upcoming interview was foremost in his mind. On the Friday of the second week when Jack came home, he approached Jane. "Well, tomorrow is the day, and now that it's here I'm excited", said Jack.

"I'm glad you're excited, but I'm nervous," was Jane's reply.

"I'm looking forward to it," said Jack. "I remember my dad telling me not to be afraid of the unknown, and tomorrow's meeting is the unknown. Whatever happens, though, will provide a clearer picture."

THE INTERVIEW

J ACK LEFT EARLY from his home on that Saturday morning. The ultimate mistake would be arriving late for such an important appointment. He found the address on Wilshire Boulevard, right off the 405 Freeway and very close to UCLA. Jack parked and with some trepidation entered the building. He took the elevator to the floor with the designated office number and went to the appropriate door but found it locked. After several knocks, Jack heard the electronic retraction of the door's deadbolt and pushed the door open. He entered a small waiting room with no one present. He looked around and saw a glass sliding window, but nobody was sitting behind it at the desk. The office had several seats and a table with some magazines. Jack seated himself in one of the chairs and noticed a dark cupola on the ceiling, evidently concealing a camera. He sat there momentarily and was reaching for a magazine when a male voice came across a speaker and asked him for his full name and the reference number in the letter. Upon confirmation by Jack of this information, the voice said, "I'll meet you shortly."

A tall white man came through the door and introduced himself as Agent Cunningham. He asked Jack to follow him to an interview area. Once there, Agent Cunningham introduced Jack to Agents Richardson and Wilcox. The three agents sat behind a large desk, while Jack sat in a chair before them. Jack thought to himself, *So this it is what it's like to sit in front of a tribunal.* Two large prints were behind the agents. The print on the left depicted two Labrador Retrievers in a duck blind. The print on the right depicted two German Shorthaired Pointers flushing quail.

Agent Cunningham had served four years in the Air Force. Agent

Richardson had served two years in the Marine Corps, while Agent Wilcox had served twenty years in the Navy. Agents Cunningham and Richardson were white; Agent Wilcox was black. Jack would be answering to three men committed to service, country and personal integrity.

Agent Cunningham opened the interview. "Your name is Joseph Phillip Avila but you go by the name of Jack. Is that correct?"

"Yes, it is. I do prefer that you call me Jack," replied Jack.

"We will call you Jack," was Cunningham's response.

The next few minutes were filled with the common exchanges of any interview: "You grew up in this town, went to high school there and college over there." Everything Jack would mention had already been confirmed. Agent Wilcox now intervened. "Jack, you have declared on your application that you have an undergraduate and a master's degree from two universities in Los Angeles. Is this a true statement?"

"It is," replied Jack. "I have signed releases for you to verify."

"Thank you," said Agent Wilcox. "We have used your releases to determine that your graduation statements are true."

"Jack," interjected Agent Richardson. "You have noted on your application that your hobbies include hunting, fishing, military history and especially the Second World War."

"I have a large World War II collection that I started as a kid," Jack stated.

"If everything works out OK, I'd like to see it someday," responded Richardson.

"Certainly," Jack said with a smile.

Richardson enquired, "Jack, since you have such an interest in military history, did you ever spend time in the military?"

"No, I did not," replied Jack. "When I left college, the military was a volunteer organization. I guess you could say that I volunteered to go a different way."

"No problem, Jack. It wasn't a trick question. We appreciate your candor," said Richardson.

Agent Wilcox then remarked, "You have listed that you can speak Spanish and German. Is this statement true?"

"Yes, it is," replied Jack. "I learned Spanish by listening to my grandparents and German at college."

Agent Wilcox asked, "Did you decide to learn German because of your interest in World War II?"

"Not really," answered Jack.

"What does 'not really' mean?" asked Wilcox.

"Well, I had always gone to Catholic schools and never had an elective class. I was all the time told the class to take and that I would have to do my best. When I went to college, a counselor told me to pick classes from certain categories. I randomly picked classes. The same counselor asked me if I was going to take French or German. I asked her if I had to pick one right now and she told me I could decide right before the college semester started. I was too naïve to realize I could have picked one of fourteen languages. Right before school began, there was a movie on TV called *The Enemy Below*. It was the story of an American destroyer chasing a German U-boat in the Atlantic. The Germans in the U-boat were rattling away in German, and it was then I remembered the counselor telling me I must take French or German. I thought, *Well, since I must pick one, I'll pick German. Next time I see the movie, I'll understand what the U-boat crew is saying.*"

"Let me get this straight," said Wilcox. "You decided to learn a foreign language based on a movie?"

"That's right," answered Jack with a smile.

It was only a matter of time till the conversation moved into the realm of being "politically correct." The ice was broken by Richardson.

"What is your position on affirmative action?" asked Richardson.

"I'm a great believer in affirmative action," was Jack's reply. "I believe that every individual should affirm to improve himself or herself and then take the appropriate action."

Jack's direct reply made the agents hesitate and look at each other. Agent Richardson was the first to respond. "What's your view on minorities in America?"

"It doesn't bother me," blurted Jack.

The agents were again taken by surprise and quickly assessed Jack's application. Agent Wilcox then responded. "Oh, I see. Are you responding that way because you have a Hispanic last name?"

"Hispanic?" questioned Jack. "No, I'm Catholic, and in America, Catholics are a minority when measured against all other Christian denominations." Before any agent could respond, Jack said, "The word *Hispanic* means "having a direct association with Spain." My grandparents came from Spain and they would have been considered Hispanic. But they would have rejected that title. They would tell you they were Spanish. As for myself, I am not Hispanic. I was born and raised in America. I believe the category of Hispanic is the fraudulent attempt by somebody somewhere to forge an ethnic group by the common use of the Spanish language. I was in Ensenada years ago and found Chinese shopkeepers. They spoke Spanish and were citizens of Mexico, but the bottom line was they were Chinese. Bernardo O'Higgins,[7] one of the great liberators of South America, was of Irish descent. Does a Mayan Indian disappear from history because he or she now speaks Spanish? I once watched a World Cup soccer game between Italy and Argentina. The Argentine roster had almost as many Italian names as the Italian team. Were the Argentines of Italian descent no longer Italian because they spoke Spanish? How about a black Cuban or a black Puerto Rican? Are they neither black nor Cuban or Puerto Rican but Hispanic because they speak Spanish? And while I'm on the subject, let me give you guys a tip: Never call a Cuban a Puerto Rican or a Puerto Rican a Cuban unless you can run real fast. Both of their cultures have a lot of pride and they expect you to recognize their histories. The bottom line is this: who wants to claim title to a generic description that does not recognize or describe who you truly are?" The agents starred at Jack in silence.

Cunningham then asked, "OK, Jack, if you don't believe in the word *Hispanic* for a category, then what do you suggest?"

Jack replied, "I use background or color to paint the picture of the individual. But to answer your question directly, if you want to refer to white people as whites and black people as blacks, then it is only logical to refer to brown people as browns—which I suppose, in the big spectrum of things, isn't that big a deal. I mean they do it in Cleveland."

Cunningham retorted, "They do what in Cleveland?"
Jack looked at Cunningham and said, "You've never heard of the Cleveland browns? Hey, man, they're famous. They even named the football team after them."

Wilcox and Richardson started laughing. "Hey, Mike, he got you on that one," said Wilcox.

At that point, Cunningham chuckled, smiled and said, "I guess he did."

Jack moved forward in his chair and replied, "I'm not trying to get anybody. I want you to know what I believe. What's the right slot for a brown European and a white South American? How about a Eurasian Buddhist with a Dutch last name? The color of your skin does not automatically associate you with a person of the same skin color across the room, across the hallway or across the street. Do you teach the X's and O's of a basketball play or do you teach the letter and number combinations of an element on the periodic table? Maybe you work on car engines or maybe you work on crossword puzzles. Is it archery or astronomy that you prefer? On any given Sunday, will you be found in a church or in a casino? I don't know and neither does anybody else, because skin color cannot answer these statements and questions. Only you, by your daily behavior, can prove who you truly are. Hopefully, it is a behavior based on decency and goodwill extended to all people you encounter." Jack continued: "I don't believe in categorizing human beings along ethnic, religious, economic or whatever type of criteria. It implies to me that humans can be divided into groups and they will instinctively roam in packs and herds. Animals roam in packs and herds. Throughout history, when humans have reduced themselves to roaming as packs and herds, they have become animals."

The agents looked at each other and said nothing. They looked down to review Jack's application.

Richardson was the first agent to go through the application and asked, "Jack, are you some type of philosopher?"

"Not at all," replied Jack. "In fact, philosophy was one of the two classes I dropped in college."

"Why's that?" asked Wilcox. "Well, maybe it was me or maybe it was the professor, but the only thing I got out of philosophy as presented in college was that it clouded clear thinking. Let me give you an example." Jack quickly looked around the room and saw the portrait of the pointers flushing quail. "Let's suppose I could grab one of the quail in that picture and as I pulled it forward it came to life. Then imagine I placed it on your desk and it just stood there and looked around. Now, by any measure of common sense, one would say that a quail is a bird. It's at this point that I found college philosophy to be bogus. I could not accept a premise that since I only believe what is in my belief system to be true, then it must be true that what I see is a cow and not a quail. Or, as I relish in my hubris being smarter than all others on this planet, I know that it is a dog. Don't call me narcissistic because I'm right and you're wrong about it being a rabbit. Well, if you left that quail long enough on your desk, it would eventually take a dump. And you know what you would find? You wouldn't find a cow patty because it's not a cow. You wouldn't find any dog stools, and "Why?" you ask. The answer is simple. It's not a dog. No need to get up and look for a dustpan and a broom to sweep the rabbit pellets off your desk. There won't be any. It's not a rabbit. You know what you will find? You'll find bird shit, which is irrefutable evidence that the creature on your desk is a bird and confirms your original common sense evaluation."

The agents laughed. Richardson, smiling, said, "Jack, I want to personally thank you for this informative and enlightening philosophical discussion. I now feel that I have a much better grasp on the works of Aristotle and Socrates."

"No problem," answered Jack.

Agent Wilcox asked Jack, "You are applying for which part time job?"

"Well, I thought I could do surveillance for you," was Jack's reply.

Agent Cunningham leaned forward in his chair to almost cross the desk and calmly said, "Surveillance? What do you know about surveillance?"

"Actually, nothing and that may be a wrong choice of words. I guess what I mean to say is that maybe I could be an informant," said Jack. There was silence in the room.

Jack continued, "I've been to the large homes and manicured properties of celebrities and in the narrowest of alleys in gangland and everywhere in between. I've been cursed by weirdos and thanked by the homeless for the smallest amount of change. I see a lot of crazy things out there."

"So, what do you see?" asked Wilcox.

Jack answered, "I work in the construction industry. Construction crews are everywhere and virtually innocuous. Unless they pose a specific inconvenience to you, they are no more visible than your neighborhood fire hydrant.

They ebb and flow based on the requirements of the job. They may be on your street or in your neighborhood for days, weeks or months. The crews are part of the everyday landscape and do not arouse suspicion. I remember the crew working off Normandie, or maybe it was near Arlington, with an active crack house around the corner. Even though the crew was there for weeks, it did not diminish the traffic coming to the house."

"How, do you know that?" asked Cunningham.

"There were people coming and going all the time. Anyone from gang guys to guys in white shirts, ties and wing tips, to guys in Hawaiian shirts and flip-flops. The house was two stories with all windows having bars. There were three doors to the house. The back ground level door was protected by a large Rottweiler, held in place by a massive chain. Another large Rottweiler sat on the landing by the upstairs back door, also held in place by a heavy chain. The dogs were the perfect alarm system. They would charge, snarl and bark loudly at anyone who came close, notifying anybody inside the house that an intruder was nearby. The only way to approach the house and avoid the dogs was at the heavily barred front door.

"Did you notify the police?" asked Cunningham.

"No, we did not," replied Jack.

"Why didn't you?" asked Cunningham.

"I spoke to the job superintendent about it over the course of the job and we looked at it as a novelty—like there's a crack house over there. If we could observe the house over a long period of time, how could the police not be aware of it? The only thing missing was large neon lights flashing CRACK HOUSE, CRACK HOUSE over the roof in the middle of the night"—Jack moved his hand left to right to coordinate with the words CRACK and HOUSE.

"Let me ask you a question," said Wilcox. "If you are proposing to observe certain activities during business hours, are you going to tell your employer what you are doing for us?"

"I've thought about that scenario. I would have to tell the company unless you could facilitate the situation," answered Jack.

"What does that mean?" questioned Richardson.

"I cannot deceive my employer, but if you could rent or purchase items from the company, then I could make a legitimate sales call on the location of that equipment and look around for you. I would not be wasting the company's resources by going to a job where their equipment was being utilized. After all, they are being paid for their equipment."

"Who's paying?" asked Richardson.

"You are," replied Jack. "To rent the equipment is cheap, and as I mentioned previously, construction crews are everywhere and do not arouse suspicion. I can, or you can, purchase a vinyl magnetic mat with a fictitious company name but a real 800 phone number, which would be answered in your office should anyone ever call, which would be rare. I would remove my employer's magnetic vinyl mat only when I went to a site where the equipment you obtained from them was located. Believe me when I tell you I can go anywhere, and as long as any construction equipment is there—whether it be myself or someone else—there will be no suspicion." The agents did not respond, almost as if they were digesting Jack's remarks. Jack reached into his pocket and pulled out several sheets of paper. He unfolded them and placed the sheets on the desk before the agents. "I took the liberty to bring the price sheets of companies whose equipment can be considered everyday stuff and placed anywhere."

The agents now looked at each other and Wilcox asked, "Do we have any additional questions for Jack?"

Richardson and Cunningham both responded, "No."

"OK, Jack," stated Wilcox. "In a few minutes you will be interviewed by Agents Taylor and Williams to determine your stated language skills. Thank you for your application and for attending our interview."

Jack replied, "I do appreciate your time and consideration. Thank you for speaking to me." The agents left the room.

Jack sat waiting for approximately fifteen minutes. Then two agents entered the office and introduced themselves. Agent Williams spoke fluent Spanish. His father was a member of the United States diplomatic corps, who had spent years in South America. Agent Taylor had been in Naval Intelligence and had served in Europe. He had taught German at the Advanced Language Institute in Monterey, California. Both men were affable and created a relaxed atmosphere. They reached across the desk to shake Jack's hand and thank him for applying. "Well, Jack, why don't you explain to us how it came to be that you stated on your application that you can speak and understand Spanish and German?" asked Williams.

"My grandparents came from Spain. When they spoke to my parents and when I was around them, I just seemed to absorb words, phrases and sentences," answered Jack.

"How would you rate your Spanish today?" asked Williams.

"Actually, I understand everything, but it takes me a minute to think of the right words and verb endings when speaking," Jack replied. After a few moments he added, "I do OK."

Agent Taylor now interjected, "What made you decide to learn German?"

Jack hesitated and then answered, "A movie."

Agent Taylor stared at Jack and said, "Did I hear you correctly— you decided to learn a foreign language based on a movie?"

"Yeah, it's a long story, but that's the truth," replied Jack.

"OK, so how would you rate your German today?" asked Taylor.

"There are dialects of *hochdeutsch* and *süddeutsch*, but my particular dialect is "desperate *deutsch*," said Jack.

Agent Taylor, somewhat irritated, asked, "What the hell does 'desperate *deutsch*' mean?"

"It means if you put me in Germany or Austria tomorrow, I could speak, understand and survive everyday German. I might use the incorrect article or the incorrect genitive or accusative endings, but they would know what I'm talking about," explained Jack. "Don't ask me to participate in a fast or technical discussion because I'll be lost."

"That's fair," replied Taylor. "How is it that you have maintained your German language skills so many years out of college?"

"Well, there are two reasons," said Jack. "The first was my college teacher. Her name was Gabriele Hagel. *Hagel*, in German, means "hail" and is not to be confused with *heil*. She was like a hailstorm when she came into the classroom, almost blowing the classroom door off its hinges. She was from East Prussia, and imposed a strict, almost military, discipline on the class. Actually, I admired her intensity, as she always kept you on edge to make you do your best. When I left college, it happened by accident that I worked with people originally from Germany. I would speak German to them everyday."

"That's good," answered Taylor.

Agent Williams interjected: "We want you to answer similar words in English, Spanish and German. For example, if I ask you in English for the word *knife*, we want you to answer in German, *Messer*, and in Spanish, *cuchillo*. If we ask you in Spanish for the word *airplane*, we want you to answer in English and German the words for *airplane*. Do you understand the concept? We are not trying to trick you, but only to assess your language skills."

"I understand," replied Jack. The session began.

"Airport."

Jack answered, "*Flughafen, aeropuerto.*"

"*Calle*, street, *Strasse.*" "*Hund*, dog, *perro.*" "*Amarillo*, yellow, *gelb.*" "*Bauer*, farmer, *granjero.*" "*Rifle*, *Gewehr*, *rifle.*" "*Mesa*, table, *Tisch.*" "*Kirche*, church, *iglesia.*" This exercise continued for some time. At the conclusion of the session, both agents made notes on the sheets of paper before them. Agents Williams and Taylor exchanged small talk between themselves. They both looked at Jack and smiled.

Williams said, "Jack, we haven't had this much fun in a long time. It's rare that we are ever involved in an interview, as most applicants only speak English."

Jack laughed and rejoined, "Well, so far so good. At least you have been able to understand my `desperate *deutsch*' dialect."

"Not at all, Jack," replied Taylor. "Your pronunciation of words has been very good. *Ist alles klar?*"

"*Ja, alles ist klar,*" answered Jack.

Williams now took over. "Jack, if I ask you a phrase in Spanish, answer in English. If I ask you a phrase in English, answer in Spanish. If Agent Taylor asks you a phrase in German, answer in English. If he asks you a question in English, answer in German. *Entiendes?*"

"*Yo entiendo,*" replied Jack.

"Ready?" asked Williams.

"I'm ready," said Jack.

"*Que hizo esta manana?*"

"What did I do this morning?"

"*Donde estan los caballos?*"

"Where are the horses?"

"Azucar."

"Sugar."

"Hey, wait a minute," Jack said. "I thought you were going to ask me phrases."

"My mistake," replied Williams. *"A que hora es la fiesta?"*

"What time is the party? Hopefully, in five minutes or less," commented Jack.

Taylor asked, "Where is the pharmacy?"

"Wo ist eine Apotheke?" Jack answered.

"Bringen Sie mir eine Gabel."

"Bring me... I'm trying to remember, *Gabel* is either fork or spoon. I'll guess a spoon."

"What is your name?"

"Ich heisse Jack."

"Sind Sie ein Amerikaner?"

"Yes, I am an American, and by the way, very proud of it."

The session continued with Taylor and Williams alternating phrases for another five minutes. Then it suddenly ended as Taylor and Williams looked at each other and then at Jack.

Williams spoke first. "Your Spanish comprehension is very good."

Taylor then interjected, "You're right, Jack. If you were dropped in Germany tomorrow, you could get around with no problem. You did very well."

"Thanks," responded Jack.

Taylor then said, "We have one more test regarding your foreign language speaking ability." He pulled out a folded document from a drawer in the desk. "You previously mentioned in your application that you grew up in Southern California and are very familiar with the Greater Los Angeles Area."

"That's true," replied Jack.

"Have you ever been to Disneyland?" asked Taylor.

"Of course. You can't grow up in Southern California and have never been to Disneyland."

Taylor then completely unfolded the document in his hand. "Jack, this is an Auto Club road map of Los Angeles and Orange counties. I want you to take us from this office to Disneyland, in German. I will follow your directions on the map as you speak. Take your time and let me know when you're ready."

Jack sat in his chair, thinking of the way to Disneyland, trying to gather his thoughts and remember the way there. He looked at the wall above the agents and said, "*Machen Sie das Fenster auf.*"

Taylor put down the map and stared at Jack. "I asked you to take us to Disneyland and your answer is 'Open the window'?"

"Oh, I'm sorry about that," replied Jack. "Whenever I need to be creative or do any problem solving, I tell myself, *Machen Sie das Fenster auf*—you know, as in 'Open the window to your mind.' I had an incident in my college German class regarding that phrase and problem solving."

Taylor asked, "I'm interested in how it came about. Is it a long or short story?"

"I'll do my best to explain and be as concise as possible. I need to warn you that my friends tell me I make a short story long and a long story intolerable," said Jack.

"Go," answered Taylor.

"Well, this will sound crazy, but part of the reason was a Pledge Brother when I joined a fraternity. I was at a party right before school started; he came up to me and introduced himself. His name was Bill Fenster. We talked for a while, and then he told me his last name meant window in German. He asked me if my last name had any particular meaning. I told him I thought it meant one who came from the city, or the vicinity, of Ávila in Spain, but I wasn't really sure. Late in my first semester, my German teacher was going around the class giving instructions in German that necessitated some type of action. For example, "Bring me a pencil," or "Show me your watch." She always called the student's name at the end of every phrase, so you had to focus on every question. In a moment of distraction, I suddenly heard, "*Fenster auf, Herr Avila.*" I looked up to see her blue eyes locked on me. In that moment she had struck me with her lightning, but I should have known better. After all, she was from the land of lightning war. I could feel my face turning red as I looked around, and the entire class was looking at me. My mind started racing. I was thinking, *Fenster, Fenster, Fenster.* Then I thought, *Fenster, Bill Fenster, Bill Window.* I was thinking *auf* means 'action' or 'open.' I looked at the classroom window and it was closed. I walked over to the window and opened it. I turned around and looked at her as she said, '*Sehr gut, Herr Avila.*' It wasn't until the class ended that I learned the entire phrase. That's why, whenever I need to do quick thinking, be creative or do problem solving, I tell myself, '*Machen Sie das Fenster auf*—Hey, Jack, open the window to your mind."

"If you knew your teacher was that intense, what could have possibly distracted your concentration?" asked Taylor.

"I really don't remember," answered Jack. "But there was a girl named Kathy in the class. She had big green eyes, a great figure and always wore short skirts. She sat in the row of desks on my right and two desks up from where I was sitting. If she had turned a little sideways, that would have done it."

"Interesting," said Taylor, "but it's time to go to Disneyland."

Jack blurted, "*Fahren Sie west in die Strasse Wilshire bis der Autobahn 405. Sie müssen süd in die Autobahn 405 gehen.*"

Taylor leaned over the map and followed Jack's directions with a pencil. Williams looked over Taylor's shoulder.

"*Wann Sie in die Autobahn 10 ankommen, müssen Sie ost in die Autobahn 10 gehen. Bleiben Sie in der Autobahn 10 bis der Autobahn 5. Sie müssen süd in die Autobahn 5 gehen. Fahren Sie ungefahr 25 Milen. Die Ausfahrt ist für* Disneyland Harbor *Strasse. Biegen Sie rechts ein. Sie werden* Disneyland *finden.*"†

Taylor smiled and looked up at Jack. "That was very good. You made some grammatical errors, but I followed you across Los Angeles, all the way to Disneyland. Let me confirm what your teacher said years ago: *Sehr gut, Herr Avila.*"

"Thanks a lot," acknowledged Jack.

Williams asked Jack, "Can you take us from Disneyland to San Diego and specifically to Sea World?"

"*Yo puedo,*" answered Jack. "*Regresa para el 5 Autopista y vas sur pero te*

---

† "*Drive west on Wilshire to the 405 Freeway. You must go south on the 405 Freeway. When you arrive at the 10 Freeway, you must go east. Remain on the 10 Freeway until you reach the 5 Freeway. You must go south on the 5 Freeway. Drive approximately 25 miles. The exit for Disneyland is Harbor Street. Turn right. You will find Disneyland.*"

quedas en el 5 Autopista todo el camino hasta San Diego. *Sale donde dice* Sea World Drive. *Y vas al oeste y vas a encontrar* Sea World."‡

Like Taylor, Williams had been following Jack's directions with a pencil across the map. Upon arriving at Sea World, Williams and Taylor again looked at each other and then at Jack. Williams spoke first. "Your language skills are very good, especially when considering you do not speak these languages on an everyday basis."

"Jack, thank you for coming here," interjected Taylor. "This concludes today's interview." Both agents walked Jack through the office door and into the parking lot. "You'll be informed at a later date if there is any continued interest on our part," said Taylor. As Jack got into his vehicle, Taylor walked up to him and said, "Maybe we'll meet again. *Auf Wiedersehen.*"

Jack replied, "*Vielleicht. Bis später.*"§He started his vehicle and drove away.

When Jack arrived home, Jane was anxious to know all about the interview. "Well, how did it go?" she asked.

"I don't know for sure but I think I did OK."

"Why aren't you sure?" Jane enquired.

"They covered my background, education, job, my outlook on various subjects, and then I ended up with two who tested my language skills. I could have blown it anywhere along the line. A guy named Taylor told me I would be contacted if there was any further interest on their part."

"Interest in you for what?' asked Jane.

"I don't know. We never got that far. But, you know, I took a chance by going and did my best to answer their questions honestly. Whatever happens, will happen."

"You're right, Jack. Time will tell," said Jane.

---

‡ *"I can. Return to the 5 Freeway and go south and remain on the 5 Freeway all the way to San Diego. Exit where it says Sea World Drive and go west and you will find Sea World."*

§ *"Perhaps. Until later."*

A WORKING VACATION

JACK WAS DRIVING south on the 405 Freeway the following Tuesday. It was his intention to visit contractors who were using the company's equipment in the Carson area oil refineries. He had exited on Wilmington Avenue when the president of the company contacted him and said, "Jack, you need to go to Oceanside right now."

"Oceanside. What are you talking about?" asked Jack.

"George Friessen just called. He claims our equipment is not working properly and he's going to back-charge us for all the delays on his job associated with our equipment. If anybody can calm him down, it's you. You have had a very good relationship with him over the years. Do the best you can and let me know."

"I will," said Jack. "I'll let you know when I get there." Jack turned around on Wilmington Avenue and entered the 405 Freeway heading south toward Oceanside.

He arrived at the job site in less than two hours. He saw George, approached him quickly and said, "I'm sorry, George if———"

George blasted Jack: "Don't come here and apologize! Apologies don't pay for down time. Apologies don't prevent money coming out of my pocket."

"Well, George, if a piece of our equipment failed you, then nothing I can say will change the circumstances. I won't have an answer until the company can evaluate what happened with the equipment."

Suddenly, George broke into a hearty laugh. "Jack, I've known you a long time and I didn't mean for you to drive down here. When we started this morning, your equipment did not operate properly in the first thirty minutes. I was 'hot' and called your office. I guess I forgot to call back when all went smoothly. I do appreciate your coming to Oceanside, as I know you cover the L.A. area. You proved today what you have always proved to me, that you value me as a customer."

"George, you've always known that you are a valued customer with us and any problem you would encounter would receive an immediate response," said Jack.

"Thanks for coming down here, and when we finish we'll use your equipment back in Los Angeles," said George.

"Thanks," said Jack. "That means a lot to me."

Jack called the office and told the Prez what had happened and that all was OK. He then decided to buy a bottle of orange juice for the drive back to the Los Angeles area, so he pulled off the highway into the parking lot of a mini market at Pacific Coast Highway and Seagaze. There was a non descript brunette, with long hair, braided in pigtails, standing by the ice machine, as Jack walked into the market. He purchased the orange juice and headed to his vehicle when the woman at the ice machine said something about "change". Jack spun around to face her and said, "I'm sorry, miss, I don't have any change."

He was almost at his truck when the woman forcefully stated, "That's not what I said."

Jack turned to face her and said, "I'm sorry. I must have misunderstood. What did you say?"

In a very slow and deliberate voice, she said, "I asked you if you would like to exchange." She stared at Jack.

"I'm sorry but I don't understand what you mean," was Jack's reply.

She calmly went on to say, "If you give me twenty dollars, then I'll give you me. Do you want to exchange?"

Jack did not know what to say, so he began walking toward his vehicle. He started to open the door and then quickly walked back to the brunette. "How do you know I'm not the police?" he asked.

She smiled and told Jack, "I saw you get out of your truck, and besides, you have an innocent naïve look about you."

"Well, in all honesty, I've been told that before," replied Jack. "Wait a minute, how do I know you're not the police?" he asked her.

She chuckled and said, "Give me thirty seconds in your truck and I'll prove it to you. Cops cannot expose themselves. I'll show you some of my assets and they're really big."

For the first time, Jack noticed the great bulges stretching the threads of her T-shirt. "Do you mind if I ask you a personal question? Are you a local and here all the time?" queried Jack.

"No," she answered, "I'm from Phoenix. It's too hot in Phoenix this time of year, so I come here for five to six weeks. I refer to my time over here as a working vacation."

Jack's next question to her was, "Are you working on your working vacation like I think you are?"

"Let me make it very clear to you. A working vacation for me is having a lot of sex in California. Anytime, anyway. You pay, I play."

Her blunt answer hit Jack like a knockout punch. For a moment he felt dizzy and was aware of the heat on his face from flushing red. His knees also seemed to wobble. Jack was thinking, *Should I walk, should I talk, or just lay down in the parking lot?* After regaining his composure, he asked her, "So, you spend five or six weeks in Oceanside?"

"Oh, no," she replied. "I'm only here for three or four days. I start in San Diego. I work on El Cajon Boulevard between the 805 and 15 Freeways and on El Cajon Boulevard from the San Diego State area all the way down to where El Cajon runs into the freeway. I also spend time over by the Sports Arena. When I leave San Diego I come here, but only for several days, and then I go up the coast a ways to Beach Boulevard. I hang out on Beach Boulevard between the 22 Freeway and Lincoln. From there I go to Los Angeles."

"Hey, that's the area I'm normally in," said Jack.

"Well, if you have a change of heart, you can find me on Sunset Boulevard. I'll be on Sunset between Western and Normandie or on Sunset between La Brea and Gardner. But my favorite place is the covered bus stop bench at Sunset and Cherokee," she said.

"Why's that?" asked Jack.

"The bench is covered and provides a nice shady spot. I just sit there pretending I'm waiting for a bus. In any case, whether I really am on a bus or in some guy's car, I make for a very enjoyable passenger, if you know what I mean."

"I know exactly what you mean," responded Jack.

"When I start heading back toward Phoenix, I spend several days in Pomona. I hang out on Holt Avenue between Garey and East End. I've been doing this so long, I remember the street names I visit once a year."

"Well, all I can say is have a great vacation," said Jack.

She quickly answered, "I will. I always do." Jack was getting into his vehicle when the brunette shouted, "Hey!" He turned to face her. "If you're ever in Phoenix, you can find me on Van Buren Street, not too far from downtown."

"Thanks for that info," said Jack. "If I ever visit Phoenix, I'll keep you in mind." Jack returned to his truck. It was time to get back to work in Los Angeles.

He had driven only a few blocks when he stopped at the red light at Pacific Coast Highway and Surfrider. Four Marines, with beach chairs and towels, were joking with each other on the corner. They were almost directly in front of Jack's vehicle when Stevie Wonder's song "Always" came on the radio. *Very appropriate*, thought Jack, *that a song titled "Always" and bearers of* Semper Fidelis *be at the same place at the same time. No, it's more than very appropriate. It's actually very good.*

Two hours later, Jack was back in his sales territory visiting offices and jobs. Toward the end of the day, he scheduled stops that pointed him home. Jack walked into his house to find the normal situation. There was Jane in the kitchen, diligent as ever, chopping lettuce, boiling pasta and stirring mushrooms in a wine sauce. Jack always told her that nothing could beat her Midwest cooking. "Where are the kids?" he asked.

"The usual," answered Jane. "Practice, practice and practice. Football, soccer and piano. I'm lucky. Other parents had to car pool tonight. How was your day?" asked Jane.

"Well, first thing this morning, I had to go to Oceanside," Jack told her.

"Oceanside. What the heck were you doing down there?" asked Jane.

"George Friessen is a very good customer. He called the main office screaming that our equipment was defective and he was going to claim all back charges against the company. Thirty minutes later, the equipment worked just fine but he didn't call back. I made the trip for nothing, but he did appreciate that someone from the company did showed up. Then, I went to get some orange juice at a store and was approached by a hooker. She was from Phoenix but doing her thing in California."

Jane slowly stopped stirring the mushrooms and turned to face her husband. "What is it with you? Are you some type of hooker magnet?" she asked.

"I couldn't help it," answered Jack. "She was very chatty and just kept talking and talking. It's nothing new. My job takes me into great areas and into shaky areas. You've heard my hooker stories for years, but I don't think anything has beaten the area around Baseline Street off the 215 Freeway in San Bernardino. The prostitutes could even be found in some of the residential neighborhoods."

"I do remember you telling me about some of those areas," said Jane.

"Maybe, I should write a book and title it `Hooker Hangouts' and make a million bucks. What do you think, Jane?"

With a very sarcastic look on her face, Jane replied, "Jack, what a wonderful idea! I'll be so proud of you when I'm at a PTA meeting and other women tell me how much their husbands enjoyed `Hooker Hangouts.' And I can hear our kids right now, when someone at school asks them, `What does your dad do?' `My dad wrote "Hooker Hangouts," would you like my autograph?' I've got a better idea. Why don't you first write a book titled `Jack Avila—Lowlife at Large,' so when you do write `Hooker Hangouts' you will already have given the reading audience a reference that you are some kind of dirt ball?"

"Actually, `Lowlife at Large' has a nice ring to it," replied Jack, "`Jack Avila—LL at L.' Anyway, you know I was joking, but your points are well considered."

"I certainly hope so," said Jane.

THE REVIEW

T HE AGENTS WHO had interviewed the previous week's applicants came together to review the applications and provide their input. Also present at the meeting was Agent Franklin, a clinical psychologist and well respected member of the agency. Jack Avila's application surfaced as the third to be reviewed. Agent Franklin smiled and said, "Aw, yes, Mr. Avila," as he passed the transcripts of the interview to the three attending agents.

Richardson saw Jack's name on the application and said, "I remember this guy. He's the fellow that taught us if you see bird shit it must be a bird." All the agents started laughing at Richardson's comments.

"Yeah, he did make that remark," agreed Franklin. "Upon all initial reviews, everything Avila stated is true. His educational background meets our requirements. Avila has been employed by the same company for years and he is a stable family man. He has no criminal background, only a traffic citation from years ago. So, what do you guys think? You spoke to him face to face. I'm going by a transcript and a tape recording."

Wilcox said, "I thought he was some type of smart-ass trying to impress us. His answers were all over the map and evasive. As the interview continued, I began to see the logic in his answers. He always gave examples to support his reasoning."

Cunningham interjected, "My impression was that he was smart but kind of a wiseguy."

Agent Franklin leaned forward and placed his arms on the desk and stated, "He was provoking you."

"What do you mean, he was provoking us?" demanded Richardson.

"He was provoking the three of you and, for that matter, all who would listen to him think. When you asked him about minorities, he answered that he is a Catholic. He was telling you that any group, whether it be religious, racial, political or whatever, can be a minority based on the demographics of the question or one's beliefs. His grandparents came from Spain, but he rejected the term *Hispanic* as applying to himself. He was telling you that one's identity is freely self imposed and he identified himself as an 'American.' He told you that he did not categorize people by skin color. He does not believe that skin color is a common denominator to predict values, behavior or allegiance." Franklin continued, "This guy came here with a plan, which he presented very well. I called on some of the items on the price sheets that he left with you. The stuff is cheap to rent or purchase. I don't know about you, but Avila put a 'bee in my bonnet.' He said that construction crews are everywhere, everyday, but rarely noticed. Now I see construction crews all over. I even saw three or four guys with hard hats working in an alley by my house in Santa Monica. Am I the only one, or did any of you remember anything he said?"

Richardson hesitated and then said, "I don't believe I'm going to tell you three the following, especially after my initial comments.

"I was visiting my brother and his wife over the weekend. I took my seven and eight year old nephews for a walk to the neighborhood park. As we were walking through the park, we approached a pond and I thought I saw a couple of ducks sitting by the water. Then I thought, *They are only ducks if I believe they are ducks. Wait, they can't be ducks, since I truly believe they are swans. They must be swans, since no one knows me better than myself and my evaluation confirms to me they are swans.* As we walked by, one of the birds let go of a load. I recognized the load on the ground as duck shit, so at that point I knew I was really looking at a duck." Everyone in the room laughed.

Wilcox went next. "You know, he did say something that I remembered."

"What's that?" asked Franklin.

"Well, I was reading this year's preseason report on the professional football teams. You guys know what a big Oakland Raiders fan I am. I was thinking that maybe this year, just maybe, on the side, I'd pull for the

Cleveland browns. You know—they're famous." Again, the room erupted in laughter.

"How about you, Cunningham?" asked Franklin.

"Funny you should ask," replied Cunningham. "I was talking to my kids the other day, when I told them it was always important to do the right thing. I told them to affirm to themselves to always do the right thing and then take the appropriate action. As soon as I said that, I thought to myself, *Did I just make that up or was I quoting that Avila guy?*"

Agent Franklin went on to make additional remarks. "There have been workmen on Wilshire, Veteran, Bundy and Santa Monica for a long time, not far from this office. It never occurred to me—or did it to you?—that someone in those crews could be monitoring our movements. I never thought about it, but after listening to Avila, it may be possible."

At this point, Wilcox stated, "Maybe there's more to this guy than we know."

Agent Franklin sat up in his chair and said, "Avila was saying that his experience over the years has proven to himself that construction crews of any sort are part of the everyday landscape and, to use his own words, 'no more obvious than your neighborhood fire hydrant.' I was never in the military, but isn't the best camouflage to be freely seen?" Wilcox, Richardson and Cunningham offered no response.

"Well, you've heard my comments," continued Franklin, "and I may be way off base in regard to my opinion. Go ahead and complete your portion of the evaluation form. You have done this before, so it's nothing new. I'm telling you right now—and it's OK if your impressions conflict with mine—but I am recommending that we let him go."

The three agents at the table were quiet. Wilcox was the first to speak. "He seemed to be a good guy, and after listening to everyone's input this afternoon, in his own way there was something Avila said that made an impression on each one of us."

Cunningham interjected, "There were several candidates we interviewed last week, but Avila is the only guy I remember. It's too bad you feel that we should let him go."

"No, no, no, that's not what I mean" said Franklin. "When I say 'let him go,' I mean turn him loose. Turn him loose across Los Angeles. He probably knows and has seen more than he has revealed. That's O K. It is the concept he presented that we must acknowledge. Complete your evaluations on Avila based on your initial impressions from the original interview and today's review. If, upon your independent review, you come to my conclusion, it is imperative that one of you contact Avila and inform him of the ensuing process." Franklin then stood up and left the room.

The agents looked at each other.

Wilcox said, "Well, what do you guys think? There's something about Avila that we all remember."

"You're right," said Cunningham. "The more we talked about him, the more what he said made sense."

Richardson went on to say, "Everything this Avila guy said was logical, especially about work crews being everywhere but never arousing suspicion."

"Isn't it weird that we are discussing somebody who walked in here and left an impression on us regarding people and everyday life?" Wilcox remarked. "I almost mentioned philosophy, but you know where he went on that subject. Did we say or ask anything that made an impression on him?"

"That's a good question," replied Richardson. " I'm not sure and w e may never know. The bottom line is that I think we are all of the same opinion as Franklin: Let's give this guy a chance."

"Agreed," chimed in Cunningham. "If we are in accord about submitting a favorable review, then one of us needs to call Avila and inform him of the long evaluation process."

"I'll do it," said Wilcox. "While I'm dialing his number, I'll be thinking of the Cleveland browns."

"Yeah, that was a good one," said Cunningham, as he, Wilcox and Richardson laughed.

Jane Avila was reviewing homework with Joanie when the telephone in the kitchen rang. "Hello," Jane said.

"Am I speaking to Mrs. Avila?" asked Wilcox.

"Yes, you are. With whom I am speaking?" asked Jane.

"Good evening, Mrs. Avila. I am Agent Wilcox and I was part of the NID group at your husband's interview last week. We would like Jack to return next week or the following week at his convenience. We want to speak to him at further length. I hope you will keep this conversation between yourself and Jack."

"I will and I'll have Jack return the call as soon as possible," said Jane.

"Thank you very much," responded Wilcox. "Please, let me give you my direct phone number."

"Sure," Jane replied. "Let me quickly grab a paper and pen." After a moment, Jane returned to the phone and said, "Go ahead." She jotted down the number. "Thank you very much for calling and I will give your number to Jack when he returns."

"Thank you, Mrs. Avila, and again, my name is Agent Wilcox."

Jack returned home that evening, put his keys and wallet away, and went back into the kitchen to give Jane a hug. Jane looked at her husband and said, hesitatingly, "You had a call this afternoon from an Agent Wilcox. He was part of your interview last week. Do you remember him?"

"I remember the name," Jack responded. "There were several guys at a general interview and then a couple who reviewed my language skills."

"Whatever." replied Jane. "He wants you to call him. He gave me a direct phone number and would like to set up a review with you at your convenience."

"That's exciting," said Jack.

"I'm scared," Jane expressed.

"It will be OK," answered Jack. "I'm only responding to an inquiry based on an interview. It can't be that important, and even if it is, I would not make a decision without your input. You know that."

The next morning, Jack called the telephone number given to Jane. The phone rang twice, then Jack heard a voice state, "Wilcox."

"Agent Wilcox, this is Jack Avila. I'm returning your call."

"Thanks, Jack, for the quick reply. We would like you to return to this office, as we'd like to review additional items with you. Is it possible for you to come here in one or two weeks? We would need no more than a couple hours of your time."

"Let me check my schedule and I can then give you a firm date and time," answered Jack.

"That will be fine, and we do appreciate your prompt response. Thanks, again," said Wilcox.

Later that day, Jack reviewed his upcoming schedule. Then he called Agent Wilcox and informed him of a date and time when he could return to the office.

"No, problem," answered Wilcox. "We'll see you then and if anything necessitates a change in your schedule, just let me know."

"Thanks," said Jack, "but as of right now, I'll see you on the day I just mentioned." There was no answer and Jack put down the telephone receiver.

Upon returning home later that day, Jack told Jane of the upcoming date.

"What do they want to review with you?" asked Jane.

"I don't know. I didn't even ask. I only know that I'm returning to their office on this date." Jack showed Jane his note from the telephone conversation.

"So, what do you think?" asked Jane.

"I don't know what to think. But, when I meet with them, I'm sure all the cards will be on the table. They are not the type to skirt around an issue."

Eight nights later, Jane brought up the subject again. "Tomorrow is your follow up interview. Aren't you scared?" she asked.

"I'm more apprehensive than scared. I'll probably be dreaming or thinking about it all night. Like a lot of events in life, the anticipation of the event brings more anxiety than the event itself. I'll be OK. After all, they called me, so they must have some interest or maybe they just want to clarify something. I'll find out tomorrow. Jane, don't worry about it. Get a good night's sleep," said Jack.

"OK, I'll try," replied Jane.

The next day, Jack returned to the office on Wilshire Boulevard at the appointed time. Agent Wilcox met him at the door. "Thank you for the quick reply and punctual arrival," said Wilcox.

"No problem," was Jack's reply. "I'm in sales and if you don't respond quickly, or if you're not punctual, you won't be in sales very long."

"I can relate to that," said Wilcox. "We want to review some items with you, so please follow me." Jack followed Wilcox into the same room where his initial interview had been conducted. When Jack sat down in front of the table, he recognized Cunningham and Richardson. The new face behind the table waited for Wilcox to sit down and then said, "Hello, Jack, I'm Agent Franklin. Thank you for returning."

"No problem," replied Jack.

Agent Franklin then began to speak. "Jack, we have done a cursory review of your background and statements you made to us. To date, we have found everything you stated to be true. Should everything work out, at some point in the future we would like to speak to you regarding a few of your observations that we found to be of interest."

"That's great," said Jack. "Please let me know what you found of interest so I can tell my wife. She thinks I'm totally boring." The Agents smiled and laughed.

Agent Franklin continued, "The verification of everything in your background will take many months. It is imperative that you and your wife not reveal this investigation to anyone, including your children. Unless you receive a specific request, do not contact this office. Sorry to sound mysterious, but this is a normal operating procedure."

"I understand and respect your candor," Jack rejoined. He looked at the four faces behind the table but there was no response. "Is that it?" asked Jack.

"That's it," replied Franklin.

Wilcox got up from behind the table and told Jack, "Please follow me." He led Jack to the main office door and said, "Thanks for coming. Maybe it'll work out and we'll meet again."

"Thanks," said Jack, as he walked out of the office and down the hallway.

Upon arriving home, Jane was surprised to see her husband come through the door so early. "What happened?" asked Jane. "Was the meeting cancelled?"

"Not at all," replied Jack. "It was a very quick meeting. They mentioned there was an interest in me, but the evaluation process would take many months. They asked me to keep today's meeting confidential. It's OK to tell you everything, but no one else. They also told me that there is not to be any communication with them unless they contact us."

"So, what's that mean for us?" asked Jane.

"That's a good question, Jane, and I don't know the answer. Maybe it's a test to determine our endurance or to maintain their request or to test our patience. I really don't know. Whatever the case, we'll carry on with our everyday lives. Believe me, after speaking with them, I'm sure they won't hesitate to get back with me if they have the inclination to do so. Tomorrow it's back to work, kids' homework, practice—the usual. Only time will tell with those guys," said Jack.

"I guess you're right. You usually are," said Jane.

FIRST ASSIGNMENT

MANY MONTHS HAD ensued since Jack's interview and there had been no contact in either direction. To Jack, the interview seemed to be a long ago dream. One evening Jane and Jack were in the kitchen, when the phone rang. Jack answered it: "Hello."

"Am I speaking to Jack Avila?"

"Yes, you are," responded Jack.

"Jack, this Agent Wilcox. How are you?"

"I'm OK," replied Jack. "Thanks for asking."

Wilcox went on to explain. "Jack, we would like you to return to our office. We want to review some items with you, but I'm not at liberty to describe them over the phone. When can you come in?"

"Based on my current schedule, I can return to your office next Tuesday," said Jack.

"Perfect," replied Wilcox. "Approximately, what time?"

"How about between ten and eleven?" Jack asked.

"Sounds good," said Wilcox. "I'll let the staff know."

Jack arrived at the appointed time and date. Wilcox met him in the waiting room and then escorted him into the interview area. As Jack walked into the office, he recognized Cunningham and Richardson. Off to the right were Taylor and Williams, but Jack could not recall their names. He only knew them as the agents who had reviewed him in Spanish and German. "Jack, have a seat at the desk. We're waiting for one more individual. He should be here shortly," said Wilcox.

"No, problem," replied Jack.

Agent Franklin entered the room moments later. He took his place behind the desk and said, "Thank you for returning, Jack. You may not remember me but I am Agent Franklin."

"I must admit I do remember your face, but I didn't recall your name," said Jack.

"That's fine. I know many people in this office who prefer not to recall my name," answered Franklin, as the others behind the desk laughed.

"Jack, you were here over six months ago. We have verified your statements and all other items based on your signed release agreement. You came here in response to a part time position. Normally, a part time position refers to some type of clerical job, which will release agents into the field. We want to offer you a different proposition," said Franklin.

"What's the proposition?" asked Jack.

Franklin looked to his right and left, as if to make eye contact with the other agents behind the desk before saying, "Jack, what you said about work crews being everywhere but never arousing suspicion made sense. The agency has sent individuals around construction sites to verify your observations and found them to be true."

"So what do you have in mind for me?" asked Jack.

"Jack, we want to take advantage of your knowledge. Because of your job, you are able to venture into all the crevices of Los Angeles. We have been given approval to work with you. We will supply you with magnetic mats for your vehicle. You pick a name to place on the mat, as you are familiar with company names in the Los Angeles area. We have already selected an 800 telephone number, which will be answered in this office with the company name you select. We will also supply you with business cards. Pick a personal name to be printed on the cards. Upon your supplying a fictitious company name, we will establish accounts with your employer and the other companies you suggested. Get back to us as soon as possible with a fabricated company name and all will be set in motion," said Franklin. "We will review a compensation package with you, which we believe to be fair. Basically, as you see incidents around the city, make a note and inform us. We may have an interest based on what you see. If we do have an interest in what you report and ask you to follow up, your time clock will start." Jack stared at the panel in silence. Before he could make a remark, Franklin continued: "Look, Jack, you took a chance to come here and apply for a part time position. We have verified everything you listed in your application and we have interviewed various people about you. After speaking with you and evaluating where you grew up in this city, your educational background and language skills, and what you have seen and learned through your job, we would consider you to be a valuable asset. We want you to become our roving eyes and ears around Los Angeles. What do you think? Would you consider such a position?"

Jack looked at the faces behind the desk and the thought crossed his mind, *Don't be afraid of the unknown.* "On the surface, I accept your proposal," Jack replied.

"Good," answered Franklin. "One of the things we discussed about you was that you could not deceive your employer. If you had the moral character not to cheat your employer behind his back, you revealed that you would not cheat us. OK, Jack. Provide us with a company name and all will be set in motion. As a point of clarification, under no circumstances will you be armed. You will not have the authority to carry a weapon or a concealed weapon by stating that you are working for us. You will be prosecuted to the fullest extent of the law if you are found to be carrying a weapon. When everything is established, and it will happen very quickly, we want you to look for something you mentioned."

"What's that?" asked Jack.

Franklin responded, "In your initial interview, you mentioned a crack house operating near some construction site that you called on. When we give you the OK, and should your employer have equipment in the general area you remember, then look for that house. Does anyone have any questions?" He looked at the agents sitting at the desk. No one spoke. "Jack, do you have any questions?" asked Franklin.

"No, not really," answered Jack.

Franklin looked at Jack and said, "Everything will be ready in about two weeks. Thanks, Jack."

"Thank you for the opportunity," replied Jack.

Wilcox came quickly around the desk and escorted Jack to the front door. As Jack exited, Wilcox said, "You know, Jack, the last time I saw you, I mentioned that maybe we would meet again. This time I can tell you, I'll see you soon." Wilcox closed the door behind Jack as he left the office.

Jack walked down the hall as if in a daze. *Unbelievable*, he thought. *These guys are giving me a chance. They admitted that they have trust and confidence in my judgment. Maybe because they found everything I told them to be true. How ironic that my first assignment—and perhaps the greatest test they will give me—to see how I will respond, came from my own words at the interview.*

The next week, Jack reviewed the names of construction companies and contractor associations. He fabricated a company name that would not conflict or be misconstrued with an existing company and phoned the agency with his selection. He was contacted two days later and notified that the magnetic mats were available. Jack returned to the Wilshire Boulevard address on Saturday. He was met by Wilcox, Richardson and Franklin.

"Have a seat, Jack," said Franklin, seating himself behind the desk with Wilcox and Richardson. "Here are the magnetic mats with the name you suggested. Take these business cards. We have established accounts with all the companies you suggested, including your employer. All accounts are under the company name on the magnetic mats. The 800 number on the mat and on your business cards will be answered in this office. You will receive instructions from Agent Wilcox and any questions you may have should be directed to him. Should Agent Wilcox be out of the office or incapacitated, you will report to or hear from Agent Richardson. Do you understand?" asked Franklin.

"I do," answered Jack.

At this point, Wilcox took over. "Jack, when you have a legitimate opportunity to be in the area of the crack house you mentioned, we want you to look for it. It may no longer exist. Regardless, let us know what you find."

"I understand completely," answered Jack.

"There is no time frame and don't do anything foolish. Let us know what you find. Am I clear?" asked Wilcox.

"Quite," Jack nodded.

"Remember, Jack, that you are part time and basically a volunteer. We cannot order you on what to do," continued Wilcox. Here are the mats and cards. Never guess what to do or hesitate to call and ask questions. Are we on the same page?" "We are," answered Jack. "If I find the crack house, I'll let you know. I'm hoping to talk to you soon about it."

"We are too," answered Wilcox. "Don't do anything foolish," he repeated.

"Believe me, I won't do anything foolish. My wife would get really upset with me and that would be hell for a week," said Jack.

Wilcox and Richardson laughed. Wilcox answered, "I hear that."

Jack knew the way and left the office.

A week later, while reviewing contracts in the company office, Jack found a contract in the Jefferson Park area. He quickly recognized the address to be not very far from the crack house location, if he remembered correctly. The next day, Jack called in at the job site listed on the contract. After a brief visit with the foreman, he drove down Normandie Avenue trying to recall where the crack house had been. *Was it off Normandie, Western or Arlington?* Jack was driving south on Normandie when a certain landmark caught his eye. He turned right on one of the numbered streets and drove through the neighborhoods. After twists and turns, he found the house, west of Normandie, south of Vernon and north of Florence. The large Rottweilers maintained their positions at the doors. Jack nonchalantly drove by the house and pulled over a block away so that he could observe the building from a distance through the rearview mirror. A man was approaching from the far street corner. The Rottweilers charged at him as he came close to the house, then backed away as the man was greeted at the front door. The man left in less than two minutes. This was the scenario that Jack remembered. Jack drove away, convinced that the crack house was still in operation, and several miles down Figueroa Street he pulled over to the curb to think about the situation.

OK, thought Jack, *what are you going to tell them? Do you have a plan, or do they have a plan for you? If you present a plan, maybe you can preempt them, prove your capability. Alexander proved his capability to his officers when he untied the Gordian knot.*[8] *Think of a plan with contingencies. Then think of additional plans with additional contingencies and with contingencies for the existing contingencies. Think it through before you call them. Was it von Clausewitz*[9] *or Frederick the Great*[10] *who wrote, "To be defeated is understandable. To be surprised is unforgivable"? Don't let yourself be surprised under any circumstance. It would not look good if you had to honestly list on a future résumé that you failed an assignment because you were surprised, and consequently had to admit at some future interview that you would have been "canned" by Frederick the Great. Be creative and plan it well. You've done it before.*

He grabbed the rearview mirror and leaned forward. When the only objects in the mirror were his own eyes, he muttered to himself, "*Machen Sie das Fenster auf.*"

Jack pulled away from the curb and drove south on Figueroa Street.

"WHAT'CHA DOIN' HERE?"

IN THE NEXT several days as Jack did his job across Los Angeles, he contemplated the course of action for the crack house. He thought about the layout of the contractor's job in the area and felt confident his plan would not arouse any suspicion or interfere with the crack house's operation.

Jack called Wilcox and left a message. Later that day, Wilcox returned the call. Jack answered the phone: "Hello."

"Jack, this is Wilcox. How are you?"

"I'm doing OK." Before Wilcox could continue, Jack said, "This is the plan. I need you to call my employer and order this piece of equipment. This is the delivery address. Ask them for an approximate delivery hour, and if no one is there—and I won't be there—tell them that your company will accept full responsibility. My employer may hesitate, as this is your first order, but you must assure them that all will be OK, and it will be OK. Order ten steel traffic plates from this company and twenty delineators from this other company."

"What's a delineator?" asked Wilcox.

"It's the orange cone or pole that guides street traffic through construction zones," Jack replied. "Have my employer deliver the equipment between seven and eight in the morning. Have the plates and delineators delivered between nine and ten in the morning. I'll be there to meet the delivery people with the plates and delineators and to sign for these items with my "company" name. I'll also direct them where to place the plates and delineators."

"If that's it, check with me tomorrow," said Wilcox.

"Thanks," answered Jack. "I will."

Jack called Wilcox the next morning on Wilcox's direct line. The telephone rang and Jack heard, "Wilcox."

"Agent Wilcox, this is Jack Avila. I'm following up with you based on our previous conversation."

Wilcox went on to say, "Jack, we're all set. I called your employer and the companies with the plates and cones. Delivery is this Thursday at the times you requested."

"That's great," said Jack.

"Jack, remember my guidelines and do not violate them under any circumstances," emphasized Wilcox.

"I promise to follow them," Jack replied.

Jack drove toward the house on Thursday morning. He visited a contractor using his employer's equipment only a few blocks away from the crack house. When he left this location, Jack drove into an alley, removed his employer's magnetic mats and placed the Agency supplied mats on the truck. Then he climbed back into the truck and drove off. Within a few minutes, he turned on the numbered street, passed the crack house and pulled over on the right side of the street. This was the opposite side of the street from the house. Jack parked several houses down from the crack house, as his objective was to observe who came around the corner. He could not see the house in the side or rearview mirrors. The piece of equipment ordered from his employer was already on the site. The company with the plates and delineators arrived twenty minutes later. Jack left his truck to instruct the drivers where to place the plates and the delineators, and when the delivery was complete, Jack signed the contracts using his agency name and returned to his truck.

A white man came around the corner within minutes. He wore black slacks, a white shirt, black tie and loafers. Jack sat in his truck pretending to read a newspaper. As the man approached the house, the dogs charged toward the fence and were only held back by the established length of chain. The Rottweilers continued to bark and snarl until the man entered the house. He left very shortly afterwards and headed back down the street and turned the corner. Approximately twenty minutes later, three black men came from around the corner. All were tall and two were wearing bright blue bandanas, while the third man had a shaved head. One of the two men wearing bandanas was broad shouldered, overweight and had his shirt hanging over his belt. The three men were laughing and joking with each other. One of them pushed the overweight man, and as he stumbled, he extended his left arm to brace his fall. His outstretched arm pulled his shirt up to reveal a nickel-plated pistol in his waistband. *Oh, my God, he's armed!* thought Jack, as he pretended to look straight ahead and keep reading the newspaper.

The three men were continuing toward the house, when the one with the shaved head noticed Jack. "Who's that guy in the truck?" he asked. The other two men looked back at the truck. The large one who had fallen down in the street said, "Yeah. Who is that guy? I'll check it out. You guys go ahead."

Jack, reading his newspaper, suddenly noticed the interior of the truck's cab go dark, as if a cloud had come between the earth and sun. He looked to his left and saw the large black man standing next to the truck motioning up and down with a clenched fist and index finger pointing down. Jack quickly recognized the semaphore: Roll down your window. Jack rolled down the window and said, "Can I help you?"

The large man leaned down to look at Jack face to face. He asked, "What'cha doin' here?"

"What am I doing here? I'm supposed to be here. I will be meeting a contractor and if he isn't here in ten minutes, I am to start taking measurements on my own," answered Jack.

With a frown on his face, the man said, "Measurements for what?"

"A utility company is doing a study for the City of Los Angeles. Depending on the results of the study, the city may run all telephone and other utility lines underground. That would mean the elimination of the telephone poles in this area," said Jack. The large man looked at the telephone poles. Jack continued, "A geotechnical firm will arrive in one or two days to take soil samples. That's why the steel plates are here. They will 'pothole' or drill holes through the asphalt to determine the soil type. At the end of the day, should the holes still be there, the company will place the plates over them, so no one trips or some car doesn't hit the hole and get a blowout."

The man, with a skeptical look on his face, said, "Can I borrow your camera?"

"I don't have a camera," said Jack.

"Just checking," said the man. People in this neighborhood don't like having their picture taken. Most of them have a real short fuse." At this point, the large man pushed Jack back into the cab with his left hand and looked inside the truck. He saw brochures, fliers and other promotional items. He pulled back from Jack and the truck cab and said, "It's cool. You do what you got to do, man."

"That's why I'm here," answered Jack.

The large man turned away and went across the street in the direction of the house. Jack leaned back in the seat and thought, *Maybe I just dodged a bullet, literally and figuratively. Maybe my decoy spread of equipment, plates and delineators gained his confidence, just as my spread of goose decoys at Uncle Pete's ranch gained the confidence of the geese and eventually brought them down.*

Jack waited ten minutes, then he got out of the truck, reached into the rear of the cab and grabbed a measuring wheel, several different colors of spray paint and a paper notepad. He went to the corner closest to the house and, walking with the measuring wheel, began noting imaginary measurements on the notepad. As Jack walked down the street, he periodically stopped and sprayed, in various colors, the prevalent cable and utility companies' initials and abbreviations.[11] He maintained the charade, even as he passed the crack house, careful not to glance in its direction. He continued walking with the measuring wheel, noting false measurements and spraying initials on the street. until he was half a block away from the truck. He was about to head back to his vehicle when it occurred to him, *If I get the truck and drive it down the block, I may arouse suspicion from one of the guys who has a weapon. I should leave the truck here, so as to imply really doing a job and being naïve.*

Jack turned around and went on down the street, taking measurements as before, till he reached the corner. There he nonchalantly turned right and found three cars on the left side of the street and four cars on the right While keeping up the pretence of taking measurements, he was actually sketching rectangles on his notepad to simulate the position of the automobiles, noting their description and license plates. Then he walked on down the block, away from the cars, with the measuring wheel in front of him.

Fifteen minutes later, a white BMW convertible parked on the street. A white man dressed in slacks, wearing a white shirt, a multicolored tie and black wing tips, got out of his car, turned the corner and walked toward the house. Jack headed back to the car area, pushing the measuring wheel, and made an additional rectangle, noting the new car's description and license plate. As he left the area, he could hear the dogs barking ferociously and knew this was a signal that the executive type had approached the house.

Jack purposely walked the surrounding intersections, making fake utility abbreviations. In less than ten minutes, he saw the man wearing wing tips leave the house and return to the BMW. As he was leaving, Jack placed an X in the rectangle representing the BMW and wrote "house" by the rectangle, to indicate that the driver of the vehicle had visited the crack house and the car had left the street.

As Jack walked down the street, he heard a man and a woman speaking and looked up to see a man leave a nearby house, get into a car on the left side of the street and drive away. Jack returned, pushing the measuring wheel. He determined which car was now gone from his original map and wrote "local" by the rectangle as he placed an X through it; then he sprayed a utility company marking where the local's car had been, as if it were part of the original plan. Jack had walked a block away, when he heard voices and laughter. He looked up to see the three black men, including the one who had approached him while he was sitting in his truck, turning the corner. He noticed the three men stopped to look at him, but he continued to make bogus notations on his notepad.

"Look at that geek out there," said the man without the bandana. "He looks like some goddamn puppet moving around."

"Yeah," said the man with the pistol. "He does look like some puppet." They laughed and walked to the parked cars. Jack walked in the opposite direction so as not to face the men as they drove away. He continued to make utility markings.

After they had gone, Jack returned to the area of the parked cars and compared them to the original map of rectangles denoting descriptions and license plates. The c ar n ow m issing w as a s ilver C hevrolet I mpala. Jack put an X through the rectangle. Then he placed the measuring wheel over his shoulder and walked back to his truck, threw the wheel and paint cans into the cab and drove away. Stopping in the same alley, he replaced the fake company magnetic mats with his employer's mats, then drove down Normandie and pulled into a gas station. He went to the corner pay phone and dialed Wilcox's toll free number. The phone rang and he heard, "Wilcox."

"Agent Wilcox, this is Jack Avila. I went to the crack house today and walked away with some info."

"Jack, please don't tell me you did anything foolish," replied Wilcox.

"Not at all," said Jack. "I set up a construction site and the neighborhood fell for it. I made notes and I'll review them with you. You need to call off the rental equipment."

"That's easy," replied Wilcox. "When can you return to our office?"

"My employer has an order for a delivery three blocks from your office on Monday. Is Monday OK?" said Jack.

"That will be great. I'll see you then," answered Wilcox.

Early on the following Monday, Jack visited several contractors in the vicinity of Wilcox's office. Around midmorning, he parked by the building on Wilshire Boulevard, entered the lobby and dialed Wilcox's four digit extension.

"Wilcox," answered the voice.

"Agent Wilcox, this is Jack Avila and I'm here in the lobby," said Jack.

"Don't move. I'll be right down," said Wilcox. Wilcox entered the lobby, grabbed Jack and took him back to his office. "So what happened?" asked Wilcox.

"The fake job site worked out great. It allowed me to move freely in the area without raising any suspicion, especially with the guy with the pistol and his two buddies."

"Jack, what are you talking about? Didn't I tell you not to instigate any conversation?" said Wilcox.

"Yeah, you did and I didn't," Jack replied. "I mentioned to you previously that all people approaching the house always came from around the corner. The guy with the pistol was coming down the street with a couple of other guys and one of them pushed him; as he fell down I saw a nickel-plated pistol in his waistband. This fellow then came up to the truck and asked me what I was doing. I told him I was there to do a job and explained what I would be doing and how the equipment on the street would be used. He pushed me back into the cab but then left when he determined that all seemed OK. A few minutes later, I started spraying utility company markings and measurements in various colors on the street, jotting down the false markings on my notepad in case anyone else asked what I was doing." Jack recounted the details of his experience and at the end concluded, "To make a long story short, here is the BMW description and plate number along with the Chevy Impala description and plate."

Wilcox listened to Jack's story and studied the diagram with a stoic look upon his face.[12] "Did you see the three black guys leave in the Impala?" asked Wilcox.

"No, I was down the street and heard them talking. I did not want to look directly at them. When I heard one of the cars leave, I returned to the area where the cars were parked and checked my map. The car now missing was the Chevy Impala," said Jack.

Wilcox stared momentarily at Jack and then started dialing on his phone. He waited and then stated, "This is Wilcox. If you have a minute come down here. I want to review something with you. Thanks."

Richardson entered the room several minutes later. As he walked in, Richardson saw Jack sitting in front of Wilcox's desk. "Hey, Jack. How are you? Good seeing you," said Richardson.

Wilcox turned to Richardson and said, "Jack set up a construction site by the crack house he mentioned in his interview and he is here reporting on what he observed. While Jack is here, can you run these license plates and let me know what you find?"

"No problem," answered Richardson. He took the BMW and Impala descriptions and plate numbers and left the room. In less than twenty minutes, he returned and sat down next to Wilcox. "The BMW is registered to a guy who lives in the Wilshire District," said Richardson. He glanced quickly at Wilcox and then stated, "The license plates on the Impala do not match. They belong to a Toyota Camry in Studio City. The plates were reported stolen three weeks ago."

Wilcox nodded his head up and down as if to indicate he was digesting the news. "Very good, Jack" said Wilcox. "Let me know how many hours you have logged into this project. Get back to me promptly."

"Will do," replied Jack.

"We will give this info to the local jurisdiction, namely the LAPD, for the final resolution. It is imperative that you mention this situation to no one. Do I make myself clear?" asked Wilcox.

"Very clear," answered Jack.

Within days, the crack house address, along with the BMW and Impala license plates, had been sent to a unit of the LAPD. LAPD units randomly drove through the area of the crack house, disguised as utility company workers and residents in older model cars. One LAPD officer driving alone, in a mock utility truck, noticed the Impala with the stolen plates around the corner from the house on a Wednesday morning. In a maneuver imitating Jack, the officer started making utility company markings with various colors of spray paint on the street. As he was spraying by the Impala, he quickly placed a magnetic tracking device under the left rear wheel well. He made several additional markings on the street before returning to his vehicle. In the next several weeks, the Impala would consistently go between the house in Jefferson Park and an address in the South Central area of Los Angeles. A plan was put into place.

OPERATION DOG CATCHER

L APD MOVED QUICKLY on the situation. In a meeting between VICE Division and SWAT Team officers, it was determined that a coordinated operation on both locations would provide the best results. No one would be allowed to escape one location so as to notify the other site. A plan was formulated and after additional reviews of both targeted areas, from street and aerial surveillance, the plan was named Operation Dogcatcher. LAPD waited for the perfect opportunity, knowing it would present itself shortly.

The Santa Ana winds, the strong winds that blow from the desert areas across Los Angeles to the Pacific Ocean, became the determining factor. LAPD SWAT teams moved within two miles of both locations during the second night of the Santa Ana winds. After coordinating time and movements, the larger SWAT team took up positions within several blocks of the crack house in Jefferson Park, while a smaller SWAT team moved close to the house in South Central. Two officers slowly approached the crack house. The time was 3:10 a.m. on a Saturday morning.

The two officers, dressed in black tactical gear and armed with air rifles loaded with tranquilizer darts, approached downwind from the house. Their scent from downwind would not alert the dogs. The officers' deliberate and methodical footsteps were hidden by the noise of the leaves and debris driven down the streets by the violent winds, while tree limbs bristled and snapped. The officers headed for two prearranged sites. They made their way toward two trees, only fifteen yards from the dogs. At 3:28 a.m., one of the officers, looking through his laser scope, placed the crosshair dot behind the shoulder of his target. His target was the dog by the ground level back door. He slowly squeezed the trigger. There was a burst of air. The dog yelped, looked at its side, turned around and went back to sleep. At 3:30 a.m., the second officer looked through his scope at the dog sleeping on the upstairs landing and pulled the trigger. The dog jumped up and scratched its side with its left hind leg. It stopped scratching and gazed into the darkness, but detecting nothing, lay down and went to sleep. The darts had found their marks.

Within minutes, the dogs were no longer in sleeping positions. They were sprawled on their sides with their tongues hanging out of their mouths. The officers stepped out from behind the trees but the dogs made no movement. The house was now vulnerable, as the four legged sentries had been removed from their posts. The SWAT team at the South Central house was now notified by radio to prepare themselves. At precisely 3:45 a.m. the three doors of the crack house in Jefferson Park as well as the front door of the house in South Central were smashed off their hinges by officers using small, hand held beam battering rams. At both locations, officers wielding flashlights and service weapons ran through the houses barking orders and obscenities to intimidate anyone from making any movement. Five individuals were found inside the Jefferson Park house. They were immediately handcuffed, separated and detained for questioning. SWAT Team officers searching the house found heroin, marijuana and methamphetamines. SWAT officers arrested three individuals at the South Central house. The officers found the same contraband at this house. One of the men detained at the South Central house asked to speak to the highest ranking officer. One of the officers left and shortly returned with his captain.

"I want to make a deal," said the man.

"What's the deal?" asked the captain.

"If I give you information, can you help me? Will you let me go, or speak to someone on my behalf?"

"Before we go any further, I must inform you of your rights." The captain read the rights from a notecard. "Do you fully understand what I have read?" asked the captain.

"I do," said the man.

"I can't let you go, but I can tell a prosecutor that you were helpful and that may mitigate your circumstances. I cannot promise anything," said the captain.

The young man sobbed and began to speak. "I know an auto body shop that is really a chop shop and belongs to an auto theft ring. This is the address," said the detained man.

In an hour's time, LAPD had a warrant issued by a judge, for probable cause on an auto body shop in North Hollywood. LAPD personnel waited in a doughnut shop across the street from the auto body shop and in several parked cars on surrounding side streets.

At 8:00 a.m. the owner of the shop opened the front door and went inside. This was the prearranged signal, and all LAPD personnel scrambled from their positions and entered through the front door of the shop. The owner was immediately arrested. Officers found autos in the rear of the shop in various stages of being dismantled, along with stolen license plates. As employees entered the shop, they were immediately arrested and read their rights. The individual workmen were taken away in different vehicles so they could not coordinate their stories.

A complete analysis was made of the crack house in Jefferson Park, the smaller house in South Central and the chop shop in North Hollywood. When the review was completed and had been documented by those involved, the final report was given to Captain Morales. As Morales had previously worked with the NID, he had been directed to notify the agency of the results. Captain Morales dialed Wilcox's telephone number.

"Wilcox," answered Agent Wilcox, as he picked up the telephone.

"Agent Wilcox, this is Captain Morales with LAPD. I wanted to call you and notify you of the results of your tip regarding the crack house in Jefferson Park. Info on the Chevy Impala with the stolen plates, upon additional surveillance, led us to another house in South Central. Both houses were raided early Saturday morning, leading to multiple arrests and great quantities of marijuana, heroin and methamphetamines being confiscated. Also, one of those arrested at the house in South Central asked for "mercy" and gave info regarding a chop shop in North Hollywood. That location was raided later Saturday morning and additional arrests were made. A large chop shop operation was shut down. Tell your agent he did a great job."

"Thanks for calling. I'll be sure to let him know," Wilcox replied as he placed the phone down on the receiver. He thought to himself, *Tell our agent what a great job he did. Now, that's a good one.* Wilcox sat there momentarily to regroup his thoughts. He called Richardson and Cunningham and asked them to come down to his office. Almost as an afterthought, he called Agent Franklin's office and left a message. Several minutes went by; then Franklin returned the call. "Can you come to my office?" asked Wilcox.

"No, problem," answered Franklin. "I'll be right down." Within ten minutes, all of the agents were in Wilcox's office.

"I had a call today from Captain Morales with LAPD," said Wilcox. "It seems the Chevy Impala with the stolen plates that Jack noted on his diagram led to another house in South Central. The crack house in the Jefferson Park area and the house in South Central were raided simultaneously early Saturday morning. Both locations had large amounts of various drugs. After the raid in South Central, one of those arrested came forward and, in a plea deal, confessed to knowing of a chop shop. Later Saturday morning, LAPD obtained a warrant and went to the location, where they found a chop shop in operation and made additional arrests." Wilcox concluded, "Morales told me to tell our agent what a great job he did," and he looked at the other agents. There was complete silence in the room.

Richardson was the first to speak. "I feel pretty damn good. How about you guys?" Before anyone could respond, Richardson continued: "Some guy came to our office, talked about construction sites, and for whatever reason, we decided to give him a chance, and, man, did he deliver! Now I know how it feels to be a coach; it's the bottom of the ninth, two outs, two runners on base, you're behind by one run and you decide to send a rookie to the plate. You want to see what he is made of. He gets thrown a fast ball and he knocks it out of the park."

Cunningham said, "Jack hit it hard, didn't he?"

"Yeah, he did," said Wilcox.

Agent Franklin, observing the remarks of the other men, folded his arms across his chest, leaned back in his chair, smiled and said, "Aw, yes. Mr. Avila. And in regard to Mr. Avila, you need to get his log and make sure he is paid promptly. We gave Jack an assignment and he delivered."

"I'll get with him, review his log and move it along quickly," said Wilcox.

22 JUNI
EIN TAG SOLLTE SICH MAN ERINNERN

JUNE 22
A DAY ONE SHOULD REMEMBER

Jack left his house in West Los Angeles very early on this day. He would be in the Hollywood area for most of the morning. For many years, Jack had visited Orthodox Christian churches. This day, Jack stopped at a Russian Orthodox church in Hollywood, with the intention of lighting a candle. He entered the church, made a donation and selected a candle. As he started to turn away, an elderly man behind the counter asked him, "Why do you come here?"

Jack turned back to face the man. "Why do you ask?"

The elderly man said, "I've seen you here before and I know that you are not Orthodox. You are Catholic."

"By the sign of the cross?" asked Jack.

The man hesitated and replied, "Yes."

"I make the sign of the cross to signify that I am a Christian," said Jack.

"So, why do you come here?" asked the man again.

Jack replied, "Why do I come here or why did I come today?" Before the man could respond, Jack said, "I visit Orthodox churches as they are the other half of the original great and apostolic Christian Church. If Christ extolled the disciples to go amongst strangers and teach all nations, then how could I not extend a hand to my Orthodox brothers and sisters in Christ? I came here today because today is the twenty second of June." A shiver went through the elderly man, as that date had great meaning for him. "I've come here today to light a candle to commemorate the great effort and sacrifices of the Russian people during World War II, or what you would call the Great Patriotic War. Victory in Europe could not have

82

been achieved without the extraordinary determination of the Russian people."

The elderly man could only stare at Jack. *Is what I see and hear true or am I dreaming?* the man thought. *Is it truly possible, that an American Catholic Christian has come here, on his own volition, to remember millions of Russian Orthodox Christians?* The elderly man reflected into the past, when as a young boy in Smolensk, the city was bombed by the Luftwaffe on the first day of the German invasion of Russia, June 22, 1941. Jack turned around and placed the lighted candle in the holder and started to leave through the double wooden doors. The elderly man said, "Thank you for coming." Jack smiled and exited through the doors.

He had gone only a short distance, when he came to the intersection of Hollywood Boulevard and Western Avenue. He looked to his right to see a family studying a map. They all wore short pants and backpacks. The father wore a tank top, sandals and black socks. Jack thought to himself, *It must be a group of "dem feriners."* Knowing the neighborhood could be dangerous, he decided to help them. Jack parked the truck on Western and walked toward the family. They were still looking at the map when he approached them and said, "Can I help you?" All five were startled and looked at Jack. One daughter, with brilliant reddish, almost orange, frizzy hair and piercing green eyes, turned to the others and made a remark. Jack recognized a word and asked, *"Sind Sie deutsch?* (Are you German?)" The family seemed momentarily immobilized, with all eyes trained on Jack.

"Yes, is that OK?" answered the redhead.

Jack's response was, *"Willkommen in die Vereinigten Staaten.* (Welcome to the United States.)"

After a brief hesitation, the father began to speak. *"Wir sollen das heutige Datum in unserem Notenbuch bemerken. Heute haben wir ein Wunder gesehen. Wir haben ein Amerikaner kennen gelernt der eine zweite Sprache spricht. Der Wunder ist, dass er deutsch spricht.* (We should mark today's date in our journal. Today, we have seen a miracle. We have come upon an American who speaks a second language. The miracle is that he speaks German.)"

The father had spoken too fast for Jack to understand; so he again asked, *"Kann ich Ihnen helfen?* (Can I help you?)"

At that point the redheaded daughter intervened and said, "My name is Imelda. I can speak English but my family cannot."

"My name is Jack," answered Jack.

Imelda continued, "This is my father, Robert." Jack extended his right hand, as did Robert, to shake hands. "My mother is Anni, my brother is Erik and my sister is Katrin."

"Very good," acknowledged Jack. "Imelda, maybe you can help me."

With a puzzled look on her face, she said, "How can I help you?"

"*Bitte, kann ich mit Ihnen mein deutsch uben?* (Please, can I practice my German with you?)" asked Jack.

Imelda smiled and said, "*Warum nicht?* (Why not?)"

Jack reviewed the landmarks highlighted on their map. After organizing the sites in his mind, Jack looked at them and said, "*Kommen Sie mit mir.* (Come with me)" They followed Jack, and after he removed all his sales literature from the back seat and placed it into the bed of the truck, the family got into the vehicle. He drove them to the tourist area of Hollywood Boulevard and they climbed out of the truck, knowing exactly where to go. Jack parked his truck and returned to find the family. He was excited for them just to see the family caught up in their own excitement. Imelda gave Jack her camera and asked him to take pictures as they milled around Grauman's Chinese Theater and by the stars and names along the Hollywood Walk of Fame. The family was carried away to the point of being giddy. They were truly in Hollywood.

It was late morning when Jack said to Imelda, "*Ich möchte Sie und Ihre Familie zum Mittagessen einladen. Wir gehen zu einen bekonnten Wurst Restaurant.* (I would like to invite you and your family to lunch. We are going to a famous sausage restaurant)."

"You are very nice," answered Imelda. The family got back into Jack's truck, and as they drove through different areas of Hollywood, he would explain the history to Imelda, who in turn explained it to her family. When Jack related the cowboy history of Gower Gulch, the family wanted to get a picture by the Gower Gulch sign; so he parked and took their picture beside the sign. Afterwards, Jack continued driving west on Sunset Boulevard, pointing to the many television and radio stations along the route. His intention was to take the family to a Los Angeles landmark at

La Brea and Melrose, known for its hot dogs. The family talked happily to each other as they looked at the many buildings on Sunset.

Jack came to a stop light and noticed he had pulled up at Sunset and Cherokee. *Sunset and Cherokee, Sunset and Cherokee,* he thought. *Why is that intersection familiar?* He kept thinking, *Sunset and Cherokee. I know I've heard that before, but where?* He then remembered the woman from Phoenix he had met in Oceanside.

Jack quickly looked right and saw a Catholic church. When he looked left, he saw a covered bus stop bench. *Unbelievable,* he thought. *There really is a covered bus stop bench at Sunset and Cherokee, and when in L.A. she hangs out here.*[13] Just as the traffic light turned green, Jack smiled and mused to himself, *How Hollywood is that— salvation on one side of the street and sin on the other side?*

When Jack arrived at the hot dog stand, the family left the truck and got into line. He joined them shortly after finding a parking space. Imelda explained the menu and they placed their orders. Jack also placed an order and paid for them all; then he left the family alone to enjoy their hot dogs and wandered through the stand, recognizing the autographed photos of American movie stars. When the family had finished eating, Jack led them back to his truck. Once he had made sure they were secure, he climbed into the driver's seat, and turning to Imelda he asked, *"Möchten Sie ein Foto von Ihrer Familie mit dem Hollywood Zeichen haben?* (Would you like to have a photo of your family with the Hollywood sign?)"

Before Imelda could answer, Erik blurted, *"Jawohl!* (Yes, certainly!)"

"OK," replied Jack.

He proceeded north to Franklin Avenue and then east to Beechwood Drive. Jack drove up Beechwood past the small local village stores, then went left on Ledgewood and continued until he came to a three way intersection. At that point, he headed straight up Deronda Drive and through the winding, narrow streets of the Hollywood Hills. He took the family to the top of Deronda Drive, where an open space between two homes provided a panoramic view of the Hollywood sign.[14] The family were almost beside themselves with excitement. Jack took a picture of the whole group with the sign prominently in the background. Then he took another picture, with the family looking around to stare at the sign. As Jack drove back down the steep winding streets, the family chatted among themselves and looked out the windows; it seemed as if they were trying to remember every house, tree and view they passed.

When Jack came to Beechwood and Franklin, he turned left. There was another landmark not on the family's list, so Jack decided to take them there. He drove left on Western Avenue and continued to Fern Dell, turning left again. He entered Griffith Park with the intention of taking the family to the Griffith Park Observatory. As Jack drove deeper in the hills of the park, the family began to look at one another, almost with concern. Robert said, "*Ich wusste nicht, dass Los Angeles auch einen Wald hat.* (I didn't know that Los Angeles also had a forest.)" They arrived in the parking lot and Jack escorted them to the viewing area in front of the observatory.

It was a breezy day so the view before them was crystal clear. The family stood in silence so as to absorb the view. Jack pointed to several hills in the distance. He explained to Imelda that they were looking at Santa Catalina Island, almost 70 kilometers away. Imelda relayed this to the family as they gazed across Los Angeles. The breeze pushed Imelda's hair in different directions to reveal the orange and reddish hues, and Jack thought some car manufacturer should use the shades of her hair for the colors of a hood ornament. Or maybe she could sell her hair to the New York Port Authority, who in turn could attach its brilliance to the flame held by the Statue of Liberty. Day or night, the flame would be illuminated. No floodlights would be required.

Jack left them alone as they entered the observatory, talking interestedly to each other. When the family had finished walking through the grounds, they returned to Jack's truck and he drove them back to the tourist area of Hollywood Boulevard. Jack hoped the several hours he had spent with them would be remembered by the family as a sign of goodwill.

Robert looked at Imelda and said, "*Frage diesen Herren ob er weiss wie man von hier zu Disneyland kommt.* (Ask this gentleman if he knows how to arrive at Disneyland from here.)"

Before Imelda could turn around and face Jack, Jack blurted, "You want to know how to get to Disneyland from here? That's amazing," as he thought about the same question at his interview. The family looked at Jack with astonished expressions on their faces, and he realized his comment had made them feel uneasy. Jack looked at them and said, *"Man sollte erst denken und dann sprechen. Ich spreche erst und denke spater. Nicht gut.* (One should first think and then speak. I speak first and think later. Not good.)" The family laughed.

Imelda came forward and said, "Thank you, Jack. You made our visit to Hollywood a great day."

Jack looked at Imelda and her family and said, *"Ja, ich kenne den Weg nach Disneyland. Ich werde ein Landkarte machen.* (Yes, I know the way to Disneyland. I will make a map)." Jack drew a map from Hollywood to Disneyland, hoping that his German was understandable. He handed the map to Imelda.

With a gleam in her large green eyes, Imelda smiled and said, *"Wir danken Ihnen herzlich.* (We thank you heartily.)"

"Danke schon," (Thank you very much,)" Jack replied as he walked away toward his truck. He opened the truck door, but before he got in he turned around to look at the family one more time. They were grouped together waving goodbye. Jack returned the wave while thinking, *Auf wiedersehen* (*Goodbye*), then he started the truck and headed east toward Downtown Los Angeles.

Jack visited jobs in the Miracle Mile and Hancock Park areas. He was continuing toward Downtown Los Angeles when it occurred to him that he had overlooked a job in the museum area of Wilshire Boulevard, so he turned around and headed west on Sixth Street. As he was driving on Sixth Street he saw a woman with long blonde hair, walking with the flow of traffic, her left arm extended and thumb up, evidently hitchhiking. Periodically she turned and seemed to yell toward the passing traffic. She continued on Sixth Street and stopped across from the Hungarian Revolution Monument.[15] Facing the oncoming traffic as Jack passed her, she yelled, "Help me! Will someone please help me?"

Jack made a quick turn on Park View, came up Alvarado and turned left on Sixth Street. As he pulled up to her, she had her head down and was sobbing. "Excuse me, miss, but I heard you asking for help."

She was taken aback that someone had actually stopped. She ran to the passenger side window and pleaded, "Will you please help me? I need to be at the Superior Court in forty five minutes."

Jack tried to quickly evaluate her and said, "I will help you but you must answer two questions truthfully. The first question is, Do you have anything illegal on you, drugs, drug paraphernalia, open liquor bottle, anything?"

"I swear to you I don't have anything," she said.

"OK. The second question," said Jack, "What is your real first name?"

"My name is Judy," she replied.

"All right, I'll help you. Get in," Jack told her.

She had a slender build and a naturally friendly face with freckles. Judy climbed into the truck, and as she put on the seat belt she looked at Jack and said, "I understand why you asked me if I have anything illegal, but why did you want to know my real name?"

"I don't like hanging out with strangers, so if I know your real name, I feel that I know you. Does that sound quirky?" asked Jack. Judy did not respond. Jack went on to say, "As the crow flies, the courthouse is not that far, but traffic could be thick this time of day. Do you live around here?" asked Jack.

"I live at the New Netherlands Hotel," she answered.

"The New Netherlands Hotel is in a dangerous part of town," exclaimed Jack. Judy looked away. A minute went by and then Jack asked her, "Do you mind if I ask you a personal question—and you don't have to answer? Why do you need to go to court?"

Jack's easygoing demeanor made her comfortable and she replied, "I need to appear for a parole hearing."

Jack was shocked and said, "You! You look too all American to be on parole. What did you do?"

Judy looked out the window as though ashamed to answer. She turned to face Jack and said, "I got caught in a drug sting buying drugs for my boyfriend. I had bought drugs for him before but the third time was the charm, not a good charm, as I was arrested." This time Jack did not respond.

Jack had driven several blocks before he said, "Judy, can I tell you something?"

"Sure, go ahead," she answered.

"Please do not be offended by what I have to say; it's not my intention to hurt your feelings. Your boyfriend has no respect for you. A true boyfriend would do what he could to keep you from harm's way and not encourage you to go into it. You are there to assist his needs, and if you get arrested, that's OK. You are expendable. He'll find another girl to help him if you disappear.

Judy answered quickly, "I know you're right, but I don't know what to do. We've been together so long. I feel, if I leave him, I am abandoning him at this low point in his life. I don't think I can do it."

Jack thought for a minute and came up with the following. He asked, "Judy, did you ever see *The Wizard of Oz*?"

"Of course," she replied. "Who hasn't?"

Jack went on to explain. "Do you remember the scene near the end of the movie, where Lion had received his dream of courage, Tin Man his dream of a heart, and Scarecrow his dream of a brain? Dorothy stood there with her dream of going home unfulfilled. Suddenly, the Good Witch appeared and told Dorothy she could have gone home at any time. The power to go home was always within her. She only lacked the belief. Dorothy returned home as soon as she believed that she could do so. Be like Dorothy and use belief to draw the power within you to move forward in your life. You can do what you want, but never let someone persuade you to voluntarily slip a chain, attached to their anchor, around your own neck." Judy sat there in wide eyed silence while Jack spoke, almost as a pupil listening to her professor. Jack reached into his pocket and pulled out a twenty dollar bill. "I want you to take this. It will be dark when you get out of court. Take a cab back to the New Netherlands. It's dangerous during the day and worse at night. There are no strings attached. You can use the money to buy drugs for your boyfriend or use it for your personal safety."

Judy hesitated but slowly reached out and took the bill. "Thank you very much. I am embarrassed that I am taking your money," Judy stated.

"Don't be embarrassed. I'm giving you the money with the best of intentions for you," said Jack.

They had driven several blocks, when suddenly Judy drew back sharply against the truck door, away from Jack. It was as if some powerful, invisible force had picked her up by the shoulders and thrown her into that position. "What's wrong?" yelled Jack. Judy sat in the corner with both hands cupped over her mouth. Jack pulled the truck over to the curb and said, "Are you OK?"

Slowly, her trembling left arm went forward with her index finger pointing at Jack. She removed her right hand from her mouth and said, almost in a whisper, "You're an angel."

"Pardon me?" was Jack's response.

With a little more confidence, Judy again said, "You're an angel."

"An angel? I've been called a lot of things, but *angel* isn't one of them. It's impossible that I could be an angel. If I was an angel, it would tarnish my image of Almighty God. He would certainly pick someone worthier than me," said Jack.

"But you *are* an angel," insisted Judy. Jack started to reply but she interrupted. "Stop. Listen to me. You must let me speak."

Taken aback by her forcefulness, Jack said, "Go ahead."

Judy took a moment to regain her composure and then continued. "You are an angel. I'm Jewish. In my tradition, an angel is someone who suddenly or mysteriously comes into your life and offers advice and comfort. That's you. Hundreds of cars drove by me but you stopped to help. You asked me for my real name. You wanted to know who I am. You gave me advice, which, as I listened, seemed to make a lot of sense. Then you gave me money for my safety. I am very thankful."

Jack did not know what to say. As they came closer to the courthouse, Jack looked at Judy and said, "Maybe I played the role of the good Samaritan. Maybe we have reached the same bottom line from two different Testaments." Jack stopped in front of the courthouse with ten minutes to spare. Judy opened the door and had started to swivel to her right to exit the truck when she suddenly turned back in her seat to face Jack.

"I want to remember you; so what's you're real first name?" asked Judy.

"My real first name is Joseph," replied Jack.

"Angel Joseph. I will remember you as the first angel to come into my life. Thank you for proving that angels really do exist and not just in the fairy tales of a Jewish grandmother. The next time I watch *The Wizard of Oz*, I will see Dorothy in a different perspective," said Judy. She got out of the passenger seat and shut the truck door behind her as she went on her way. Jack waited until she had entered the courthouse doors and then drove away.

"This has been quite a day," he remarked, as he reviewed the events in his mind.

Let's see, thought Jack, *I visited a Russian Orthodox church to remember the sacrifices of the Russian people during the Great Patriotic War. I escorted a German family through Hollywood, to make sure they would enjoy themselves. I found a bus stop bench used by a woman from Phoenix for prostitution, and then I learn I am an angel from a Jewish girl who needs a ride to a parole hearing for a drug bust. Man, wait until I tell Jane about this day. Normally, she has a glass of wine before dinner, but when I tell her about today, she may knock off the whole bottle.*

ANOTHER LOS ANGELES

A DRAMATIC INCREASE IN sewer and pipe lining projects been initiated for the Pico Union area of Los Angeles. Large new schools had also been approved for construction in this part of the city. Such improvements had brought a demand for all types of construction equipment, including equipment from Jack's employer. Jack visited a job site at Eleventh Street and Arapahoe. He thanked the job crew for using his employer's equipment and left company promotional items with them.

Jack drove up Arapahoe to the intersection of Olympic Boulevard with the intention of making a right hand turn on Olympic. As he came to a rolling right stop, he noticed a very attractive black woman, in a bright blue dress, standing by a chain link fence on his left. Before he made a complete stop, she scampered toward the truck saying, "Hey, baby, hold on, hold on." She ran up to the window and told Jack, "If you have fifteen minutes, I'll give you the best blow job you've ever had. I promise, in fact I guarantee, it will be the best blow job you ever had. You'll remember me for a long time if you say "Yes."

Jack replied, "I don't have the time or money and, besides, I'm married."

"Married?" she rejoined. "Baby, I won't tell nobody."

Jack said, "Do you mind if I ask you a personal question?"

"No, baby. What do you want to know?"

Jack asked, "Are you a local and here all the time?"

"Actually, I'm from San Francisco," was her answer.

Jack teasingly said, "San Francisco. Wow! You must have a lot of frequent flyer miles."

She kept her eyes fixed on Jack as she lowered her head and said, "Baby, now listen up good. I have a lot of frequent miles, but they're not for flying. You hear what I'm saying?"

"I hear you loud and clear and I believe you, I really do," Jack replied.

"Well, if you don't have twenty dollars for you to have a good time, do you have a couple of dollars to help me through a hard time?" she asked.

"Yeah, I do have a couple of dollars to help you," said Jack as he reached into his pocket. He retrieved several one dollar bills and gave them to her.

"You've got to be careful around here. Baby, this is a tough neighborhood. I'm not worried about me. I know how to take care of myself. I'm worried about you," she said.

Jack started laughing. "Let me guess: I have an innocent, almost naïve look about me. I've heard that before. So what do you think?" asked Jack.

She laughed in response and said, "Baby, there is something about you that makes me think I'm talking to a kid. It's been good talking to you. Baby, I have to go."

Jack replied, "I know what you mean. I have to go too. I hope all works well for you."

"Hey, baby, thanks for helping me. Maybe we'll meet again," and she turned the corner and walked away.

Jack continued on Arapahoe across Olympic Boulevard and turned right on James M. Wood Boulevard. As he slowly drove along James M. Wood, he realized another world existed in Los Angeles.

Jack was used to seeing green lawns and individual homes in his neighborhood. He now viewed gray concrete and crowded apartment buildings. Signs in his neighborhood always read Happy Birthday or Congratulations in the front yards of homes. Signs in this neighborhood were marked on walls in spray paint with cryptic letters, names and gang insignia. If he needed an oil change, Jack would take his vehicle to an oil center. Oil changes in this neighborhood were done in the front yard or on the street. Jack called the Auto Club when he needed a car to be towed. In this neighborhood, the police placed a "boot" on a car before they had it towed. Jack had trash picked up by a disposal company every Thursday. Here, trash was discarded in the streets and overwhelmed alleys. Trash in the alleys was utilized by vagrants and the homeless as improvised shelter.

Jack parked on James M. Wood between Lake Street and Alvarado. His employer had equipment in the area and Jack left promotional items with the contractor. Jack returned to his truck and was making notes in his log when he happened to look up and see two very attractive women moving in and out of the alcove of the corner store on Alvarado and James M. Wood. They wore high heeled shoes, skirts and bright colored blouses, which differed greatly from the neighborhood dress. As Jack looked at the two women, a car driven by a single male pulled up alongside the curb and was quickly approached by one of the women. She leaned into the open passenger side window and spoke to the driver. Shortly, a second car driven by a single male pulled over to the curb, but the other woman did not approach the car; she only glared at the driver. The first woman stepped back from the car, smiled at the driver, and returned to the alcove in less than a minute. At this point, both cars left, with Jack thinking, *What was that all about?* He concluded his notes, started the truck and continued east on James M. Wood.

As Jack crossed Alvarado, he was met with a sight that only could only be imagined. Prostitutes stood on the corners and walked along the street, seemingly with impunity from any authority. They were in all colors, shapes and sizes, exposing as much of their bodies as possible. Some of the women were young and very attractive, while others were ravaged by age and drugs. Jack could not believe his eyes. *This must be one of the best kept secrets in Los Angeles,* he thought. *It is almost as bad as Figueroa Street.* As he drove down the street looking to his right and left, he reflected, *This is like driving through some type of gallery. And I guess it is. It is driving through a gallery of gals.*

Jack stayed on James M. Wood, stopping at sites with his employer's equipment. After visiting multiple locations, he headed east on Seventh Street and turned right on Bixel. Jack rolled down the hill in his truck, coming to the stoplight at Eighth and Bixel. When he pulled up at the light, he noticed three homeless men on his left, on the grassy island between the street lanes. The three men, one black and two white, were dressed in an eclectic garb of what they had found or what had been given to them. They made a colorful trio as they panhandled amongst the cars at the light. Jack looked at the three of them and dubbed them *"Los Tres Amigos."* He continued straight ahead and entered the 110 Freeway going south.

Two weeks later, Jack returned to the area to follow up with customers. He stopped at a service station to get gasoline for his company truck and noticed a street vendor, across from the gasoline station, selling iced fruit. When his truck was filled with gas and paid for, Jack crossed the street and stood in line to buy a watermelon wedge. While waiting in front of the fruit vendor, he observed a guy with a blue L.A. baseball cap standing across the street. There was a single line of three or four men in front of him. The first man handed cash to the guy with the L.A. cap, as did the second and third man in line. *What's going on here?* thought Jack. *Maybe, he's the local bookie and is collecting bets or he's a numbers runner. Who knows? Maybe it's all legitimate.* Jack purchased the watermelon wedge and continued visiting job sites and offices in the area.

Late that afternoon, Jack attended a meeting conducted by the Los Angeles Unified School District on the upcoming school building programs. The meeting concluded around seven o'clock, and while driving on Seventh Street Jack again saw the guy with the L.A. cap, walking with two other men. *That fellow gets around,* thought Jack.

LOS TRES AMIGOS

JACK HAD TO return to the Downtown area many times as the scheduled projects began to be implemented. He left a major project at Alameda and Temple and then drove west on Temple to new school construction sites. He visited with project managers and construction superintendents. His employer's equipment was on these various sites, and he wanted to make sure that the company's service was first rate. He received favorable feedback from all locations and then left for the jobs in the Pico Union area. Jack's next visit would be at the multiple school construction sites at Third and Bixel. He visited those jobs and their trailers, and when he had finished seeing customers in that area, he drove down Bixel toward the 110 Freeway.

Jack arrived at the stoplight at Eighth and Bixel. He looked to his left and there on the grassy island between the lanes of Bixel stood *Los Tres Amigos*. As they gazed at him, Jack waved and the black amigo came running up to Jack's truck.

Jack told him, "I've seen you and the other two guys here before. I call you *Los Tres Amigos*, or The Three Friends, and that's a good thing. It's always good to have friends."

"Yeah, man," said the black amigo. "We are friends. We've been hanging together for a couple of years now."

"That's good," Jack responded. "You guys should stick together." Jack was digging in his pocket for a couple of dollars when he noticed one of the white amigos was holding a puppy. It looked like a pit bull mix, with a white body and brown patches. On a quick second look, Jack noticed an almost perfect brown circular patch around the puppy's left eye.

As he took money out of his pocket and handed it to the black amigo, Jack asked, "What's your name?"

"My name is Curtis," was the reply.

"Curtis, just out of curiosity, is your dog's name Petie?" asked Jack.

"He doesn't have a name yet. We just found him yesterday. Why Petie?" queried Curtis.

"Your dog has a brown circle around one eye," Jack answered. "Did you ever watch *The Little Rascals* series on television when you were a kid? Their dog had a ring around one eye and his name was Petie."

Slowly, a broad smile spread across Curtis's face as he said, "You're right. Now I remember Petie." He turned around and yelled across the street, "Hank, we're going to call our dog Petie."

"Whatever," replied Hank.

Momentarily, Curtis looked off into the distance as he stared straight ahead, perhaps looking at a place from long ago. He turned back to Jack with a tear running down his cheek and said, "Thinking about Petie brings back good memories of being a kid."

"You're right, Curtis," said Jack. "Thinking of Petie does bring back good memories. Anyway, here are several dollars to help you guys."

"Oh, man, thanks a lot," said Curtis. "We appreciate it very much."

Jack gave the money to Curtis and had started pulling away from the curb when he saw the guy with the blue L.A. baseball cap talking to people across the street. Jack quickly turned the truck back to the curb and said, "Curtis, who is that guy over there talking to those people—the guy wearing the baseball cap? I see him all over this area."

Curtis looked across the street, turned back to Jack and said, "That's Enrique. We call him Enrique the Tax Collector."

"Why's that?" asked Jack.

"He's part of the gang that runs this area. If you want to work around here, you pay rent for your space. He charges us ten dollars a week to stand here. I've heard that local businesses must pay rent to him and the gang."[16]

"How often does he come here?" asked Jack.

"Man, he's here every Wednesday. He's like a clock," answered Curtis.

"Thanks, Curtis. I've got to get going but I'll probably see you guys another day. Take care of yourselves and Petie," said Jack.

Curtis started laughing and said, "We will and thanks, man, for your help." Jack drove down Bixel and disappeared onto the 110 Freeway heading south.

Jack merged onto the 110 Freeway recalling Curtis's words: "He's here every Wednesday. He's like a clock." He thought, *If this guy is like a clock and he's at 8th Eighth and Bixel every Wednesday... I saw him somewhere else, but I don't recall the day or intersection. If I can find the intersection and remember the day and I see him again, then maybe I can triangulate his movements and circuit. Don't guess,* he reminded himself.

Jack arrived home and reviewed the family's day with Jane. After listening to Jane and getting the daily family update, Jack said, "I think I have stumbled upon an extortion ring."

"An extortion ring—what makes you think that?" exclaimed Jane.

"Well, I've seen this guy getting money from people in the Pico- Union district. We have a lot of equipment in the area and consequently I have seen him at various locations. I was talking to a homeless guy—"

Jane interjected, "Jack, how can you listen to a homeless guy? They're usually substance abusers or mentally ill."

Jack smiled and said, "Jane, you're a great person and I love you very much. Please don't sanitize, under the names of substance abusers, alcoholics, drug addicts, con artists and everyday bums. Do you remember the volunteer organization you joined to help the homeless and street beggars? Your group always offered to take these people to shelters and help them find jobs. They always declined or never arrived, even though they promised they would."

"That's true," answered Jane.

Jack went on to say, "The homeless guy's name is Curtis and he told me the gang guy's name is Enrique. They call him the Tax Collector. He's a member of a gang that controls the neighborhood. He comes by every Wednesday to collect rent from Curtis and his friends for standing at the intersection of Eighth and Bixel."

Jane hesitated and said, "So, what are you going to do, Jack?"

"I'm going to call Wilcox in the morning and run it by him," responded Jack.

"This 'part time job' is making me nervous," said Jane. "Your observation and tip on the crack house led to multiple arrests but I was scared. The dollar amount on the check was great but now you may be engaging a gang. Go ahead and call Wilcox. You've always used discretion and common sense. But please, be very careful," said Jane.

"Of course I'll be careful," Jack said laughingly, "It might be right up there with boar hunting."

"Great," said Jane.

AT HOME ON THE RANGE

J ACK RECEIVED A phone call at home on a Friday afternoon. "Hello," answered Jack.

"Jack, this is Richardson. How are you doing today?"

"I'm doing OK. What's going on?" asked Jack.

"Look, Cunningham and I are going to the rifle range in Azusa next weekend, and if it's OK with you, we thought we would come by your house and check out your World War II collection. Both of us remember you mentioning your collection at your interview. We want to know if you would like to go to the range with us?"

"No problem," answered Jack. "It'll be fun going to the range with you guys, and I'll definitely show you my collection before we leave."

"Cunningham and I will come by your house on Saturday around 10 a.m.," Richardson said.

"*Prima*," was Jack's answer.

"What was that?" asked Richardson.

Jack laughed as he answered, "*Prima*; it means `perfect' or `excellent.' I'll see you guys on Saturday."

Richardson and Cunningham arrived at Jack's house just after ten and knocked on the front door. Jack opened the door and greeted them both.

"We hope we're not intruding," said Cunningham.

"Not at all," Jack replied. "I'm glad you came by. So, you want to see World War II."

"Of course," answered Richardson.

"Follow me upstairs," said Jack.

Richardson and Cunningham followed Jack to a room on the second floor of the house. Jack went to the middle of the room and as Cunningham and Richardson entered he said, "Well, what do you think?"

There was stunned silence as Richardson and Cunningham gazed around the room. They saw posters, photos, the rifles of World War II, as well as hundreds of books, many autographed by individuals who had participated in the historic events of the war. They also looked at a display case containing items from the nations of World War II. Richardson then spoke, "Jack, this isn't a collection. This is a museum. I've been to the Imperial War Museum in London. I'll tell my friends, if they can't make it to London, maybe they should visit you."

Jack laughed and said, "I'm a history guy. Anyone who enjoys history is always welcome."

Jack answered the many questions Richardson and Cunningham had and explained various details as they walked around the room. Then Richardson said, "I think it's time to go."

Cunningham agreed. "You're right. We need to go. Jack, I want to come back here sometime. After seeing everything you have and listening to you about the Second World War, I now know if I can't find a professor on the subject, I can come to you."

Jack smiled and said, "I've been told that before. You're welcome anytime." Jack grabbed his rifle case, climbed into Richardson's car and the three of them drove to a shooting range east of Los Angeles.

They were lucky as they drove onto the range property. There was a break in the shooting. All three registered at the main office with the range master. Jack, Richardson and Cunningham selected available benches. Richardson and Cunningham selected benches 64 and 65. Jack picked bench 83 when he came into the office. "Jack," said Richardson with a smile, "what's the problem? Cunningham and I both took showers this morning. Why did you pick a bench so far down from us?"

"Oh, it has nothing to do with you guys. Benches 82 through 87 are for the 600 yard range. The 100 yard range is too easy. I always want to test myself. After you guys set up, would you mind documenting my shots?" asked Jack.

"Not at all," answered Richardson. "Let me know when you are ready."

"Thanks," replied Jack. Another fifteen minutes passed before the range master announced to commence firing.

Jack asked Richardson and Cunningham to observe his accuracy through a spotting scope. They followed him back to bench 83. As Jack set up his rifle, Cunningham asked, "What kind of rifle is that? It looks old or antiquated."

Jack laughed and said, "You're right. This rifle is old, as it has been passed down through my family. I guess you can say that this rifle and I are antiquating together."

Richardson and Cunningham smiled; then Richardson said, "Go for it, Jack. We'll monitor your shots. At 600 yards, you'll need a lot of guidance."

Jack calmly turned around to face Cunningham and Richardson, smiled and said, "I'll need more than your guidance. I'll need your prayers."

Jack sat by the shooting bench and pulled the hearing protectors over his ears. He placed the rifle butt against the recoil pad on his right shoulder. Then he sat at the bench and placed the rifle on the leather rifle rests. Jack took a deep breath, exhaled and slowly squeezed the trigger. He focused on the scope cross hairs above the bull's-eye on the target. He was quickly pushed back by the rifle's recoil, and even with the ear protectors Jack could feel the concussion.

Jack heard Richardson say, "Good shot, Jack. At 600 yards, you're about one half inch to the right of the bull's-eye." Jack turned around to thank Richardson, but Richardson just said, "Take another shot." Jack slowly turned around and aimed. Seconds later, he was again pushed back in his chair. Richardson, looking through the scope, said, "You're an inch to the left of the bull's-eye. That is great shooting."

"Hey, thanks," said Jack. Jack started cleaning the rifle barrel for additional shots as Richardson and Cunningham walked away from the bench.

"What do you think about his shooting?" asked Richardson.

Cunningham answered, "He was goddamn accurate, wasn't he?"

Richardson looked at Cunningham and said, "With a little more elevation, he could be knocking cantaloupes off fence posts at 800–900 yards. He's on the cusp of being a military sniper. Not to mention he's using a forty or fifty year old rifle."

As they walked back to their stations at the shooting range, Cunningham said, "Remember at Jack's interview it was mentioned by Franklin or someone, are we sure that we know everything about this guy?"

"I do remember that," said Richardson. "But everything we checked came back as true." Richardson started laughing.

"What's so funny?" asked Cunningham.

"We need to get with Franklin and you know who to make a change in our standard interview form," said Richardson.

"And that is?" queried Cunningham.

"We need to revise the form so as to ask all future candidates, Are you a good shot with a rifle? Are you a marksman?" said Richardson.

"Amen to that," replied Cunningham.

Jack had taken one additional shot, left the bench with rifle in hand and joined Richardson and Cunningham. "Thanks, guys, for monitoring my shots. It sure saves a lot of time not going back and forth between the rifle and the spotting scope," said Jack.

"That's all right," replied Cunningham. "You did some great shooting."

"I guess I was lucky," said Jack.

Richardson quickly responded, "No one is lucky to have that grouping at 600 yards. Jack, you're a very good shot."

"Thanks," answered Jack. "I thought I would join you guys at the 100 yard range." Jack, Cunningham and Richardson returned to the 100 yard benches. Jack put his rifle away. It was his turn to monitor the rifle shots of Cunningham and Richardson.

Richardson and Cunningham spent the next hour at the range, while Jack sat in the background and watched their target shooting. When Richardson and Cunningham finished shooting, Jack joined them in the sandwich shop. They laughed and joked about their shooting skills over lunch. They compared shooting to playing golf: you make an accurate shot at 200 yards; you feel that you are consistent when you take the next swing, but you are way to the left or to the right.

When lunch was finished, Richardson drove Jack back to his house in West Los Angeles. Jack got out of the car with his rifle in hand and waved goodbye. "Thanks, guys. I'll see you soon," said Jack.

"Our pleasure," said Cunningham. "It was a lot of fun today." Jack walked to his front door as Richardson and Cunningham drove off.

He found Jane standing in the kitchen. "Did you have a good time?" she asked.

"I did," said Jack.

"Good," said Jane. "Now you have more friends to go shooting with you."

MERENDAR CON ENRIQUE
LUNCH WITH ENRIQUE

JACK WENT TO the corporate office on Monday. He checked in with the dispatchers and had a brief meeting with the prez. Looking at the new contracts, he saw that more contractors had ordered significant amounts of equipment for the major projects west of Downtown Los Angeles. He noted the equipment delivery locations and left the office to visit and thank the various contractors.

Jack had called on several contractors in the area and, while driving west on Seventh Street, had to stop at the red light at Seventh and Bonnie Brae. As he gazed straight ahead, Enrique stepped onto the crosswalk in front of Jack's truck. Jack watched Enrique disappear into a restaurant at the corner of the intersection. He looked at his watch and noted the time. It was 10:00 a.m. on a Monday. Jack turned right on Bonnie Brae, parked on the right side of the street and placed coins in the second parking meter. *How strange*, thought Jack. *The guy walked right in front of me. I know his name and where he will be on Monday, Tuesday and Wednesday. In regard to his life, I am a phantom. I hover around and over him but he has no idea of my existence. It's time to join him.* Jack waited for the green light, crossed Seventh Street and entered the restaurant.

He found himself right behind Enrique in the buffet line. Enrique ordered fried bananas, prawns, rice and several Chinese dishes; then, after paying for his order, he joined three individuals at a corner table. Jack completed his order, paid the cashier and sat at table facing Seventh Street. Moments later, one of the men at Enrique's table began to speak.

"*Buenos dias, Enrique. Como le va el dia?* (Goodday, Enrique. How is the day going?)"

Enrique answered, "*Muy bien, Arturo. Aqui esta la colcciones para el dia por el momento.* (Very well, Arturo. Here are today's collections)." Jack remained facing Seventh Street but listened to the continuing conversation behind him.

Arturo went on to say, "*Yo puedo ver que es estado muy acupado y hacienda un trabajo muy completo.* (I can see you have been very busy and doing a thorough job.)"

Enrique replied, "*Todavía tengo un problema con el nuevo dueño de la lavandería. Ella se niega a pagarme.* (I still have a problem with the new owner of the laundry. She refuses to pay me.)"

Arturo told him, "*Ten paciencia, Enrique. Aun su ella no quere pagar seas cortesia. Ensenale a ella que usted es un senor razanable. Vaya a verla dos o tres semanas. Nosotros le vamos adar unos meses mas para que ella puedo juntar con nuestro plan. Despues de ese tiempo ella va aprender que es mucho mas barato de pagar a nosotros que estar siempre reemplazando las ventanas en frente. Entiende usted?* (Be patient, Enrique. Even if she refuses to pay, be courteous to her. Show her that you are a reasonable man. Visit her every two or three weeks. We will give her several more months to join our plan. After that time, she will learn it is cheaper to pay us than continually replace her front windows.)"

"*Yo intiendo* (I understand)," said Enrique.

"*Muy bien* (Very well)," answered Arturo.

Arturo counted the money Enrique had placed on the table and said, "*Toma este dinero porque esto es tu parte de la coleccion de hoy.* (Take this money as your part of today's collection.)"

"*Gracias* (Thank you)," replied Enrique, accepting the payment. Enrique left the restaurant when he had completed his lunch. Jack just sat there gazing at Seventh Street. A minute later, Jack got up from the table with his diet soft drink can in hand, got into his truck on Bonnie Brae and left the area.

When Jack arrived home that evening, as he entered the front door he said, "Jane, are you here?"

"I'm in the kitchen," Jane replied.

Jack approached the kitchen table, pulled out a chair, sat down and told Jane, "I've definitely found an extortion ring. I followed the guy, whom I mentioned to you previously, into a restaurant and overheard a conversation."

Before Jack could continue, Jane turned around and asked, "Is this the MacArthur Park area? I know you have been in that area a lot. Tell me the truth, Jack. Is that the location of the extortion ring?"

Jack hesitated momentarily, then answered, "Yes, it is." Before he could continue speaking, Jane started crying. "What's wrong? Why are you crying?" asked Jack.

"Why am I crying?" sobbed Jane. "Why am I crying?" she repeated. "That's the area where, several weeks ago, it was reported that a waitress in a restaurant made some gang members leave and they came back later and shot her to death. I love you very much and our kids adore you, Jack." Jane regained her composure and continued, "Jack, I'm not naïve. That part of Los Angeles is very dangerous. Maybe today you came face to face with the murderers."

Jack briefly thought about Jane's comments and said, "Don't worry. Everything I have seen is at a distance. They had no idea of my presence. I never faced them."

"Are you sure, Jack?" asked Jane. "We would be devastated if anything happened to you."

"I'll be just fine. I'm calling Wilcox tomorrow to let him know what I found," said Jack.

"All right," replied Jane, wiping her tears away. "Dinner is ready now. Would you please call the kids?"

Jack looked upstairs and yelled, "Hey, guys, dinner is ready." The three Avila kids came running down the stairs to join Mom and Dad at the table.

The next day during his lunch break, Jack stopped at a pay phone and called Wilcox. Jack's lunch breaks were always unpredictable due to customer demands.

"Wilcox," was the answer.

"Agent Wilcox, this is Jack Avila."

"What's going on Jack? I'm in a hurry. I'm on my way to a yearly conference," said Wilcox.

"I've confirmed the extortion ring I mentioned to you," said Jack.

"That's good," answered Wilcox, "but I'll be busy the next several days. Call Richardson and let him know what you found."

"OK," said Jack.

The next morning, Jack called Richardson's office.

"Richardson," answered the voice at the other end of the line.

"Agent Richardson, this is Jack Avila. How are you?"

"I'm doing great, Jack. How about you?" asked Richardson.

"I'm doing just fine," said Jack. "Agent Wilcox told me he was going to a conference and asked me to call you."

"No problem," said Richardson. "And this phone call is regarding what?" "I've come upon an extortion ring in the MacArthur Park area," said Jack.

"You told this to Wilcox and he directed you to follow up with me?" enquired Richardson.

"That's correct," said Jack. "I mentioned it to Wilcox some time ago, but I was not sure about it. I now have confirmation after overhearing a conversation. I reported this to Agent Wilcox, but since he was obligated to go to a conference, he said to contact you and let you know what I found."

"OK. So, what's the deal, Jack?" asked Richardson.

"I have come upon an extortion group in the MacArthur Park area," said Jack.

Richardson responded sharply: "Jack, you as an individual have identified an extortion ring? That's ridiculous. Who do you think you are?"

Taken aback by Richardson's comments, Jack composed his thoughts and replied, "It may be by accident but it's true. I had lunch with the guy——"

Before Jack could continue, Richardson snapped, "God dammit, Jack, what are you saying, you had lunch with the guy? What guy?"

Jack realized he needed to explain the situation calmly. "Agent Richardson, I've come upon this situation by accident and it is a long story, but I can prove to you what I have found."

Richardson interrupted again. "Jack, I'm going to meet you so that you can show me what the hell you're talking about."

"That's fine," said Jack. "Would tomorrow, Tuesday, around 11:00 a.m. be OK, at the intersection of Twelfth and Burlington?" asked Jack.

"Where is that approximately?" queried Richardson.

"It's in the Pico Union area, west of Downtown Los Angeles," said Jack.

"No problem," said Richardson. "I'm somewhat familiar with that area. OK, I'll meet you there at 11:00 a.m. tomorrow."

Jack was waiting in the neighborhood when Richardson arrived. Richardson got out of his car and said, "Jack, good seeing you. How the hell are you?"

"I'm doing OK, Agent Richardson. Thanks for asking," said Jack.

Richardson climbed into Jack's truck. He hesitated, then said, "Jack, I know there are times when I bark at you. It has nothing to do with you. Your assignment was to voluntarily drift around Los Angeles and let us know what you found. Like any organization, there are demands and requirements behind the scenes. Sometimes the pressure of those demands makes an easy going guy like me sound belligerent. Jack, look at me," said Richardson."OK, show me what you found. Your lead on the crack house was right on. I believe you when you say you have found an extortion ring. When you're ready, let's go."

"No problem," said Jack. "I mentioned yesterday about my lunch with the guy."

"You had lunch with an extortionist or some type of thug?" asked Richardson.

"Yeah. Actually, I was eating at a nearby table and overheard his whole conversation with another guy he was reporting to," explained Jack. "Apparently some woman isn't going along with their game, so they might start breaking the front windows of her *lavandería*."

"Her what?" queried Richardson.

"A *lavandería* is a laundry," said Jack.

"That makes sense," Richardson said.

Jack and Agent Richardson left the Twelfth and Burlington neighborhood in Jack's truck. Jack drove north on Burlington and turned right on Olympic. He drove into the service station at Union and Olympic and parked under the large tree so as to face the wall.

"Now, what?" asked Richardson.

"Our guy will be here soon. He is very predictable. Let's go," said Jack.

"Go where?" inquired Richardson.

"We're going to the market across the street. There is a great food court. You'll enjoy it," said Jack.

"OK, Jack, let's go," replied Richardson. As they walked through the stalls, he remarked, "Man, this place is something else!"

Jack laughed. "I thought you might get a kick out of it."

They stopped at a food counter and placed an order. In fifteen minutes they returned to Jack's truck, and as they sat down, Jack adjusted the rearview mirror to look upon the intersection behind them. Jack and Richardson were talking and enjoying their lunch when Jack happened to glance in the rearview mirror and saw Enrique come into view. "Our guy just showed up," said Jack.

Richardson turned around and said, "Which guy?"

"See the fellow with the black pants and the blue and yellow soccer shirt? That's Enrique."

"Yeah, I see him. Jack, get out of the truck and go buy something in the food mart. While you're in there, I'm going to take pictures through your partially open window. Get out now," ordered Richardson. Jack left the truck and went into the food mart. With Jack out of the line of focus, Richardson took multiple uninterrupted photos of Enrique. Most of the shots showed men coming up to Enrique and giving him money, with nothing being exchanged.

Jack returned to the truck, opened the driver side door, sat down and said, "Well, what do you think?"

"Based on what I saw and photographed, I think you are right. In fact, I am very confident that you are right," stated Richardson.

"So now what?" asked Jack.

Richardson calmly said, "Jack, you have done a great job again. Your observation is very correct and it is confirmed by my photos. Money being given to an individual with nothing being exchanged is very incriminating."

They watched Enrique for several more minutes as individuals walked up to him and gave him money. Suddenly Enrique started walking away.

"Let's go," said Jack.

"Where are we headed?" Richardson inquired.

"We're going to follow his route," said Jack. "Are you ready?"

"Sure, let's go," answered Richardson.

"Enrique will be in this general area. I'll drive up Union and turn right on Eighth Street. He'll visit some people there and then disappear. I haven't followed him from that point, but sometime tomorrow he'll be at Eighth and Bixel," said Jack.

"Jack, you sound very positive about this, don't you?" remarked Richardson.

"Yeah, I really do."

Richardson paused, then said, "I believe you, Jack. It seems you have evaluated this situation very well."

"Thanks. So what's next?" asked Jack.

"Take me where this guy will show in the next few minutes. You have tinted windows in the truck and I'll take additional pictures of him with the `company' 35 mm camera," said Richardson. As Enrique came up the street, Richardson took many photos. "That'll work," he said.

"Like I told you," Jack stated, "if you want or need additional shots, Enrique will be at Eighth and Bixel tomorrow."

"Very good," replied Richardson. Moments went by, and then Richardson said, "Jack, I'd like to ask you a question, if it's OK with you."

"No problem, just ask," responded Jack.

"Jack, you made an impact on all of us at your interview. Some of the things you said were funny but some of your other remarks made us stop to think and evaluate. What I'm trying to say is that each one of us remembered something you said. Did you remember anything we said?"

"Not at all," answered Jack. "I was nervous just trying to answer all the questions truthfully. But you know what's weird?"

"What?" asked Richardson.

"Over the years, I have had people tell me, `Jack, I remember when you told me this'; or some guy would say, `Jack, you gave me advice many years ago and it made so much sense, I've never forgotten it.' The irony is that I don't remember my specific comments until they mention it to me."

Richardson nodded his head as if in agreement and said, "Maybe, Jack, you're one of those guys who has great common sense and stands back from a situation and evaluates it based on logic and doesn't get emotionally involved."

"Maybe," said Jack. "I really don't know."

"Anyway," said Richardson, "you've done a great job."

"Thanks a lot," answered Jack.

"I'm going to pass these photos, along with your comments and my observations, to the LAPD," said Richardson.

"That's fine," Jack replied.

He drove Richardson back to the Twelfth and Burlington neighborhood. Richardson exited Jack's truck and as he climbed into his car, he turned around and said, "Keep up the good work, Jack."

As Richardson slammed the car door shut and started driving away, Jack called out after him, "Thanks, but don't thank me. It goes back to a homeless guy."

RETURN TO EIGHTH AND BIXEL

TWO WEEKS AFTER meeting Richardson in the Twelfth Street neighborhood, Jack returned to the area to confer with a general contractor and several subcontractors. The meeting lasted over two hours. When it concluded, Jack stopped and had lunch at a Mexican restaurant on Wilshire Boulevard near Good Samaritan Hospital. After finishing the meal, he paid the bill and tipped the waiter. As Jack left the restaurant, it occurred to him that he was not far from Eighth and Bixel and he thought, *Maybe Curtis, the amigos and Petie will be there.*

Jack turned right on Bixel from Wilshire and drove down the hill. He could see Curtis standing in the grassy island as he crossed Seventh Street. When he stopped at the red light at Eighth and Bixel, he could see that Curtis's left arm was in a cast. "Are you OK, Curtis?" asked Jack.

"Not really, man," answered Curtis.

Jack quickly turned right on Eighth Street, parked the truck and ran back to Curtis. As he approached, Jack could see Hank had a bandage across his forehead, a swollen, black left eye and stitches on his right cheek. Curtis said, "Some hoodlums came from South Central and rousted all of us sleeping under the bridge. They came through, taking anything they wanted. They had baseball bats and just started swinging. I got hit on the arm but I took care of myself. I landed a punch in the middle of one guy's face as he began to swing his bat. I felt a crunching sound as my fist hit his face and he started screaming. Maybe, I broke his nose. Hank got it worse, but the doctors said he'll be OK. Our buddy Tom is still in the hospital with broken ribs and a collapsed lung."

"I'm sorry to hear about that," said Jack. "Hey, what happened to Petie?"

"Petie is OK," replied Curtis. "He's tied up behind those bushes over there," and he pointed across the street.

Jack reached into his pocket and pulled out a ten dollar bill. "Take it," he said.

"Hey, man," said Curtis. "I know that you know we're living out here because we're doing drugs. That's why those punks from South Central came here, thinking we might have some money on us. Living here on the streets, you meet those people who give you help and those who rob or ignore you."

"You're right," Jack responded.

"Don't take this the wrong way," said Curtis, "but I need to tell you something. Look, man, I don't know your name and I don't want to know your name. I forget names as time goes on. But I'll always remember your face."

"How's that?" asked Jack.

"I'll remember you as the friendly guy who would come by and always helped. I'll always see your face when I look at Petie," said Curtis.

Jack started laughing. "Are you telling me that I have a dog's face?"

Curtis began to laugh. "No, man. When you mentioned *The Little Rascals* and that their dog's name was Petie, it brought back good memories. You need good memories when you're out here."

"I understand," said Jack. "Well, look, I got to get going. Maybe I'll see you on my next round."

"Maybe," answered Curtis. They shook hands, then Jack turned away and walked down Eighth Street. He climbed into his truck and headed west.

Jack continued driving west on Eighth Street until he came to a stoplight. While waiting at the light for pedestrians to cross over, he noticed a store on his left with plywood-boarded windows. The business was a *lavandería*. Not wanting it to be obvious that he was looking at the store, Jack drove around the block, came back to Eighth Street and parked farther down the road. Then he crossed the street so as to be on the same side as the *lavandería*, and as he walked by the store he made a mental note of the address. Jack continued to the end of the block, crossed the street and walked up the opposite side back toward his truck. When he reached the truck he jotted down the address of the *lavandería* on a piece of paper.

Upon returning home that evening, Jack called Richardson, hoping he could reach the agent before Richardson left the office. The phone rang several times; then Jack heard, "Richardson."

"Agent Richardson, this is Jack," he said.

"Jack, how are you doing?" asked Richardson.

"I'm doing just fine," Jack answered. "But earlier today I passed a laundry, or *lavandería*, with broken front windows. Maybe Enrique did it."

Richardson hesitated and replied, "Maybe he did."

"Here is the address," said Jack.

"Thanks, Jack," said Richardson. "I'll pass it on to the appropriate authorities."

OPERATION STREET SWEEPER

T WO WEEKS LATER, after Richardson and other officers of the NIB had reviewed Richardson's photos along with Jack's observations and comments, the NIB contacted the Los Angeles Police Department. Wilcox gave the final approval to transfer all information to the LAPD. LAPD reviewed all of the information in detail; then the organization put together a plan that would make Enrique, Arturo and their gang approach them.

LAPD slowly moved undercover officers into the area. They posed as street vendors, pedestrians and the homeless. Officers spread into the areas and intersections provided by Richardson and mentioned by Jack. Additional officers from the Eighth Street office moved into the surrounding neighborhoods. Whatever the disguise or ruse, all officers were eventually approached by Enrique, who told them they needed to pay "rent" for the sidewalk space. LAPD monitored their encounters with Enrique and his associates with photos and court approved recording devices. This documentation process lasted several weeks. It was determined that the coordinates to be used would be Bixel on the east, Pico on the south, Carondelet on the west and Wilshire on the north. Midmorning on a Wednesday, Operation Street Sweeper was launched.

LAPD swept into the designated area from all directions. They came in many guises. They arrived as street vendors, as plainclothes men, in "black and whites" and on bicycles. By the time the operation concluded, Enrique, Arturo and almost thirty other members of their notorious street gang had been arrested and charged on multiple counts, including drug trafficking, conspiracy, racketeering, assault and battery, and extortion. Later in the week, LAPD and other city dignitaries acknowledged the success of the operation, and their overall review and statements were documented on the evening news.

Wilcox was at home watching the late night news. He made notations as the television account concluded and then reviewed the situation. *Amazing,* thought Wilcox. *Richardson went with Jack and evaluated the situation. Jack provided info that led us to this investigation and, in turn, Jack says it all came about because of a homeless guy. We give all the information to LAPD, they do their job and the next thing you know, politicians are on television taking credit for the exploits of others.*

Wilcox was sitting in his chair just shaking his head. His wife walked by and said, "What's wrong?"

"Ah, honey, it's not a big deal. Sometimes it's hard to watch those who have no idea of the work and risk involved being the first ones to run to a microphone and take credit. Maybe, I'm just too tired. I think I'll hit the sack," said Wilcox.

His wife responded understandingly, "Tomorrow is another day and things won't seem so bad after a good night's sleep."

Before Wilcox entered the bedroom, he turned around to his wife and said, "I love you."

She smiled and replied, "I love you too."

NOWHERE, MAN

Southwest Excavating and Remediation was setting up for a job in East Los Angeles. The company had had a close association with Jack's employer for many years, and their management requested that Jack go to the location and become familiar with the job requirements. So Jack called and set up an appointment to meet the management team on site. Several days later, Jack arrived at the job site trailer and parked in a designated spot. He grabbed brochures and promotional items and entered the trailer to meet the management staff of the project.

"Jack, great seeing you," said Brian. "Will you be our rep on this job?"

Jack smiled and said, "It's good seeing you and the other guys too. Yes, I will be the rep on this job. It's like the project you had by Los Angeles International Airport a number of years ago. You were everywhere and I was everywhere trying to cover for you."

Brian smiled and said, "Jack, come with me and let me introduce you to the staff of this job." He escorted Jack to two offices within the trailer. First he introduced Jack to Mike. Mike was a longtime employee of the company and familiar with Jack from previous jobs. After they had exchanged remarks, Brian took Jack down the narrow hallway to a second small office. "Jack, this is Eddie," said Brian. Eddie got up from his desk and approached as Jack leaned forward to shake hands. "Eddie is here to help us with the neighborhood. He grew up here", said Brian.

"Good meeting you," said Jack.

"Same here," said Eddie.

Mike joined them and he went on to explain the situation. "Jack, this is going to be a fast and furious situation. We bid the job for twelve weeks but we know it can be done within eight. The incentive package calls for $10,000 per week under twelve weeks. We'll need you to be here to coordinate the movement of your company's equipment. Jack, you need to check in with us at least once a week. I know you have a very busy schedule, but we'll need you, if we are to achieve our eight week goal."

"It will be a great challenge," Jack replied. "It will be OK."

Jack returned to the job a week later. The equipment from Jack's employer was throughout the area. The project was moving at a frantic pace, just as described by Brian. Jack left a message for Brian with Mike: he would return in just two days as a follow up.

Jack entered the trailer two days later to find Eddie the only one inside. "Eddie, how are you doing today?" asked Jack.

Eddie hesitated and said, "I'm doing OK. What's going on?"

"Not much," responded Jack. "I just thought Brian might be around." Jack and Eddie exchanged small talk and then Jack inquired, "Eddie, excuse me for asking, but East Los Angeles is known for gang activity. What's going on around here?"

Eddie was momentarily taken aback and seemed to recoil from the question. He answered, "I'm a better man than I used to be."

"What's that mean?" asked Jack.

Eddie went on to explain, "I grew up in this neighborhood. As a kid, everything was great and as I got older, guys in the hood asked me to join the gang. They would talk trash to me when I came home from school, to taunt me to join the gang. They would have parties in the street and have girls all over the place to show me their power. The bottom line was that joining the gang was voluntary. If you never wanted to join, after a while they would leave you alone. So, what's your question, Jack?"

"I guess I don't have a question," answered Jack.

Eddie said, "I'll answer your question. I started running with the gang in my late teens. I had a good time with those guys, as if I was part of a large family. There were other times, when I look back, I'm not proud of, when I had to hurt somebody."

"Meaning?" queried Jack.

Eddie hesitated, recalling his past. "You heard me. There were times when I had to hurt somebody. Sometimes I had to hurt somebody real bad. One time, me and some of my crew saw some punks from a rival gang getting lunch in a restaurant. They had come across one of our family a week before. The main guy could have asked our homie, 'Who are you?' or 'Where are you from?' gotten the right answer and let him go. The punk decided to have two of his homeboys hold our guy while he punched him, over and over again. At that point, that guy lost the pass to walk away. He no longer had that option. Our guy was all by himself when he got beat up. Had we come across one of the other gang's homeboys and that homeboy answered the questions the right way, we would have let him go. When I was running with my brothers, payback meant against the guy who broke the code, not just any guy in the other gang. That way, only the guy that broke the code—even one of our guys who broke the code—knew he would be the target. It's not like that anymore. Now, just knowing the guy who broke the code can get you killed.

"Knowing the punk was in the restaurant, I looked around and saw a trash can and found an empty wine bottle inside the can. I waited with my homies. When he came out of the restaurant and was in the parking lot, we hit him hard. He didn't see us coming. I broke the wine bottle across the punk's face. The bottle just broke into a hundred pieces. I heard later that he lost some teeth, had a broken jaw and was blinded in one eye. After meeting a good woman and having a couple of kids, I decided to leave the gang. I couldn't go on living like that. I didn't want my kids to fear everyday life. I didn't want them to be someday in a parking lot and get attacked."

"Was that a problem, leaving the gang?" asked Jack.

"No," said Eddie. "The gang was a volunteer deal. You were free to go at any time. Just don't snitch and go on with your life."

"So what were the gang areas around here?" Jack inquired.

Eddie looked out the trailer window, extended his right arm toward the window and said, "Right there."

Jack walked up to Eddie and looked where he was pointing out the window and said, "Lincoln Park?"

"That's the line," said Eddie. He smiled and started laughing. "Jack, let me tell you something. I grew up in this area, in this neighborhood. If I go into Lincoln Park, I need to be careful. That's why I haven't been in

Lincoln Park for years. You know, Jack, you could walk across the park and nothing would happen to you. The bad guys would leave you alone. Even my guys from the past would leave you alone. They would see that you are someone just passing through and not some type of threat. If I walked through the park, some guys might come up to me and ask, 'Where are you from?' or "Who are you?' There are only two right answers."

"What are they?" asked Jack.

"If you are ever in a gang area and somebody asks you, 'Where are you from?' the answer is, 'Nowhere.' If someone asks you, 'Who are you?' the answer is, 'Nobody.' Those answers always worked in the past," said Eddie. "Answer the questions as I just described and my gang and other gangs would let you go. It was like admitting to the other gang that you were nothing. It was like a dog would roll over on its back to prove submission to a more powerful dog. Anyway, those answers worked when I was rolling with my crew. I'm not sure they'd work anymore with all the killing going on.

"This may sound stupid but I had an aunt who had a nephew in another gang. His side of the family and my side of the family would meet at her house on holidays. Her house was neutral turf. The whole family would have a good time. There was plenty of food, beer and shared stories about the past. He and I would talk about the good days growing up with our aunt. The next day, the truce was gone. I knew I had to look for his Bros and he knew he had to look for my Bros.

"There's a gang right up the street from here. They call themselves the Pee Wees. Someone convinced them that if they are thirteen or fourteen years old they can do any crime and not be charged as an adult. They all have guns and they scare me, as they threaten my family." Eddie went on to say, "Jack, when I listen to you talk to other guys in this trailer about your family, you seem to have everything lined up straight. It seems you have a plan. I'd like to ask you a question."

"Go ahead," said Jack.

"Now that I've told you about my past, do you think I'm a good man?" asked Eddie.

"Eddie, don't listen to all the talk," Jack told him. "I've had plenty of ups and downs as an individual and as the head of a family. You're a good man. You're trying hard like any man. You need to have a plan. I had an appointment with a customer a long time ago. He wasn't in his office when I arrived, so I just stood there and looked around. On his desk was a plaque. The inscription on the plaque read: `Life Is the Thing That Gets in the Way of All Your Plans.' Reality can come between you and the best of plans. When your immediate plan fails, you can't get discouraged and quit. Come up with another plan and keep going. You know what makes you a good man? You came to a place in life where you realized that your wife and kids were more important than you. They were more important to you than your gang life. Any guy can father a child, but only a man will be there to guide his child through life. We sometimes think that a coward is a soldier who abandons his position of responsibility during a battle. A true coward is a guy who abandons his responsibility with his wife or kids. That's why I call someone who leaves his wife or kids a *guy*. He's not worthy enough to be called a *man*."

Eddie stood there as if mesmerized by Jack's words. He then said, "After listening to you, I realize that I am a good man and a good dad."

"Eddie," said Jack, "you don't need me to tell you what you already do everyday. Anyway, I have to get going."

Eddie said, "Now I know why the other guys, I mean men, always want to talk to you."

Jack replied, "I'll be back next week. It's been good talking to you."

"OK. I'll see you later," said Eddie. They shook hands and Jack left for another appointment.

The next week, Jack returned and checked with Brian and Mike. "How are you doing on the job?" asked Jack.

Brian answered, "We're doing great. We're way ahead of schedule. The company you work for has been very instrumental in managing our costs. As of right now, we should finish the job four weeks earlier than projected."

"That's great," said Jack. "I'm glad we have been able to help you attain your goal. Is Eddie around?"

"No," replied Mike. "He worked all weekend so he has today off. He'll be back tomorrow."

Jack said, "Let him know I came by the office and said hi."

"I will," said Mike.

Jack left the office and returned to his truck. He had opened the door to get in, when he turned around to gaze upon Lincoln Park across the street. Jack thought to himself, *It's a beautiful day to go for a walk in the park*, and so he shut the truck door and walked down the slight incline to Lincoln Park. He crossed Mission Boulevard and walked through the concrete pillars to enter the park.[17] Jack decided to turn left and walk the circumference of the lake. He had gone only a short distance into the park when he was quickly spotted.

Three local cholos near a park bench were joking with each other. They wore white tank tops, khaki knee length shorts, and black sneakers with white sweat socks stretched upward on their legs as far as possible. Two were clean shaven and wore red bandanas. The third had a shaved head but sported a mustache and goatee. Tattooed around his neck was his gang affiliation symbol.

One of the cholos wearing a red bandana said, "Check it out. Who's the idiot walking around the lake? What's he doing?" The other two locals looked up to see Jack walking alone. All three silently watched him as he strolled around the lake.

The cholo with the shaved head said, "What's that crazy ass white guy doing? Maybe he doesn't know where he's at. Who knows? Maybe he is crazy or even dangerous."

The other two started laughing and one of them said, "Look who's calling someone dangerous." They all turned to again watch Jack continue on his walk.

"Let's go and introduce him to the neighborhood," said one wearing a red bandana.

"Leave him alone," said the cholo with the goatee. "We know he doesn't belong here. He's probably a tourist. Who knows, he might even be an undercover cop. Remember what happened to Chewy and Twelve Pack when they thought they would harass and rob some guy in this park. He was a cop, and all of a sudden it seemed cops were climbing out of the trees. Anyway, that guy isn't causing us any harm."

Jack kept on walking. He left the lake circumference and continued to the end of the park at Main Street. He turned right on Main and right, again, on Mission. Returning to the concrete pillars, he waited for the traffic light to turn green and then crossed at Lincoln Park. As Jack headed back toward his truck, he stopped and turned around to look at the park behind him. Then he resumed walking and was almost at his truck when Eddie's words came to mind, "You can cross that park and nothing will happen to you." As Jack approached the truck, he thought, *Eddie knows what he's talking about.*

A week later Jack returned to the job office. Brian and Mike told him, "Tell your employer you helped us make more on the incentive program than we anticipated."

"I will," said Jack.

Brian went on to say, "Eddie wanted us to tell you that he always liked talking to you. He's at our job in San Bernardino. He won't be back here. He wanted to make sure that we told you he always enjoyed talking to you. It was so important to him that he made us promise to tell you the next time we saw you."

"Tell Eddie when you see him that he's doing a good job at work and with his family. Tell him that Jack said so."

Brian said, "We will."

Jack smiled and said, "Do you promise?"

Mike answered, "We promise."

GET IT?

I T WAS A Thursday morning and Jack was looking forward to spending a day at the studios. He was scheduled to meet contractors and the facilities manager at a major studio in Burbank. The meeting revolved around the necessary equipment to remove an old underground diesel fuel tank and was likely to last several hours. After an extensive review of drawings and input from all those attending, the facilities manager proposed a plan. He would get back to the attendees with a final plan after the approval from top management. The meeting adjourned. It was 10:30 a.m. and Jack's next appointment that day was with a contractor starting a job at a major studio in North Hollywood. Since this meeting would not begin until 1:00 p.m., he decided now was a good time to get lunch.

Jack left the area of the Burbank studio by turning right on Pass Avenue and then left on Riverside Drive, heading in the general direction of his appointment in North Hollywood. At the intersection of Riverside and Lankershim, he saw a fast food restaurant and decided to get a sandwich.

He waited in line to order a chicken sandwich and a diet soft drink, and after collecting his order, he sat down at a table facing the window looking out on Riverside Drive. Outside the window was a young woman standing by the lamppost. She was wearing white sandals, baby blue pedal pushers and a white shell. Her most attractive feature was the very thick, curly blonde hair. She was a living example of "Curly Top." Jack assumed that she was a college student, with such a young face and her backpack. She gazed at the oncoming traffic as if waiting for a ride. Jack was looking out the window, when a car pulled over and took her away. *Oh, well,* he thought, *her ride finally arrived.*

He finished the sandwich and sat reading a construction magazine. A few moments later, the same car pulled up to the curb outside the window and he glanced up to see Curly Top jump out of the car, wave goodbye and stand again by the lamppost. Jack had just resumed reading the magazine, when another car driven by a single male pulled over to the curb and she got into the vehicle. *Wait a minute*, thought Jack. *Let's see if lightning strikes a third time in the same place.* He got a refill of his diet soft drink and sat at the table facing the window. Ten minutes went by, then the second car pulled over and the young woman with the curly hair got out and once more took up her position by the lamppost. Within minutes, a single male in a new sports car pulled to the curb and she disappeared for the third time. "Unbelievable," Jack said to himself. "They are everywhere." She was back at the lamppost in less than fifteen minutes. Jack left the table, thinking, *I've got to ask.*

He exited the restaurant and approached Curly Top. "Excuse me, miss, do you mind if I ask you a personal question? Are you out here working?"

"What makes you ask that?" she enquired.

Jack answered, "I was sitting at a table in the restaurant and noticed you coming and going."

"You've been watching me?" she gasped.

"Not intentionally. I was just eating lunch and saw you leaving and returning. I was at that table behind the window," said Jack.

She glanced at the window and the table beyond it; then she looked back at Jack as if to evaluate him. "You're right," she said. "I'm out here working."

"Are you a local?" asked Jack.

"No, not at all," she replied. "I was born in Reno, but when I was about twelve years old my dad took a job promotion, so we moved to Sacramento. I live in Las Vegas now."

"That's amazing. Do you drive over all the time?" he asked.

"No," she said with a grin. "I come over on a tour bus. It works out great. I don't have to drive. I get discount coupons for hotel rooms, restaurants and stores. It's a great deal."

"I'm impressed. You've thought it all the way through," responded Jack.

"Not really," she rejoined. "I learned this routine from my older sister when she was a prostitute."

"You come from a family of hookers?" exclaimed Jack.

"No," she answered. "My younger sister has no idea what I do or what our older sister did. Besides, my older sister is married now, has two kids and lives in Fresno."

"Miss, is it my imagination or does your family have a propensity to live in towns and cities that end in the letter *O*?" asked Jack.

She giggled and said to Jack, "*O*? No. Get it? *Oh no*."

"I get it," said Jack. "You're very clever."

"It's funny," she said, "I leave Las Vegas on a bus with guys who want to come here and go for a ride at an amusement park. I come here to take guys for a ride. Then I go back to Las Vegas with guys who want to gamble at a casino. With me, it's never a gamble. You always walk out the door a winner."

Jack asked her, "Where do you hang out in Los Angeles and in Las Vegas?"

"When I'm in L.A., I'm either here or farther up Lankershim. In Vegas, you can find me walking in the crowds on Las Vegas Boulevard. I usually start at Las Vegas Boulevard and Flamingo. I walk all the way to Sands; then I cross the street and walk along Las Vegas Boulevard back to Flamingo. I dress like a tourist so I don't stand out to the police. My regulars always see my curly hair in the crowd and pull over. I jump in their car and away we go."

"You have it wired," said Jack.

She hesitated for a moment, turned her head and said with a gleam in her eye, "I don't have to advertise. My reputation is well known. In fact, my reputation is spread by word of mouth. Get it?"

"Yeah, I get it," answered Jack. "By the way, should you ever change your profession you could probably make good money writing thirty-second ads for radio or television. You're very witty and have some great one-liners. Anyway, I'll leave you alone, as I have to get going."

As Jack walked away, she called after him, "It was nice talking to you and thanks for the compliments."

Jack went to his appointment at the studio off Lankershim, which ran well into the afternoon. Although they discussed the addition of many buildings to the property, the meeting concluded with no immediate plans. Leaving the studio, Jack got into his truck and headed for the exit. He turned left on Lankershim and right on Cahuenga to enter the 101 Freeway north.

As he headed home, Jack was thinking, *What will I say to Jane about the girl outside the restaurant? If I tell her, she is going to think the same as she did before, that I'm a hooker magnet, and wonder what I'm doing. If I don't tell her, I'm not being honest with her or myself and that's not right.*

He mulled it over while he drove, until suddenly the answer occurred to him: *I know! I'll do what Jane sometimes does with me. I'll wait until she is watching some program on television. Then, while she has her attention on the show, I'll mention my encounter with the girl. Later on, when she asks, "What were you saying?" my response will be, "I can't believe you didn't hear one word I said."*

That'll work, he decided, and he chuckled at the idea of being able to turn the tables on his wife.

THE GUY WITH THE MUSEUM

I T HAD BEEN almost eight months since the Pico-Union arrests. There had been no agency request for Jack. LAPD called the agency on a Tuesday afternoon asking for Wilcox. Wilcox was on vacation with his family, so the phone call was transferred to Richardson.

"Richardson," was the response on the telephone.

"Agent Richardson, this is Captain Fitzgerald with LAPD. How are you doing today?"

"I'm doing very well, thank you," replied Richardson.

There was a hesitation, and then Fitzgerald went on to say, "We need your help. There is a group or a gang selling drugs in Venice. They call themselves the Venice Beach Aryans or the Beach Aryans, or something like that. We roust them but they are always clean. We know they're dirty but we never find dirt on them. I'll be honest with you: there is an internal investigation going on. Maybe they are always clean because they receive a 'tip' from inside."

Captain Fitzgerald continued: "I can supply photos. One guy has an Iron Cross tattoo on his arm while his partner has a swastika tattoo on his neck. No matter what we do, these guys can smell us coming. There is someone else behind the scene."

"Send the photos to my attention along with your comments and observations," said Richardson.

"No problem," said Fitzgerald. "I'll fax the photos and info immediately."

Within an hour, Richardson had the faxed photos and information on his desk. He called Cunningham and asked Cunningham to come to his office.

"What's going on?" asked Cunningham as he entered Richardson's office.

Richardson said, "There's a gang or some group selling drugs in Venice. The LAPD cannot catch them in the act of possessing contraband. When LAPD does stop them, they are always clean. Here are photos and notes supplied by LAPD." He pushed the photos and information across the table toward Cunningham. Cunningham reviewed the notes and photos. As he was reviewing the information, Richardson remarked, "Does anybody come to mind regarding the name of this group, a swastika and Iron Cross tattoo?"

Cunningham slowly looked up at Richardson and said, "Yeah, a guy does come to mind. The guy we know with the museum."

"I'm thinking of the same guy," said Richardson. "Wilcox will be back tomorrow. I'm going to call Jack and set up a meeting when all four of us can meet." Richardson called Jack's home and left a message on his voice mail.

The next morning Wilcox returned to work and found a message from Richardson. He called Richardson. When Richardson answered the phone, Wilcox asked, "What's going on?"

Richardson replied, "We got a call from LAPD regarding a group selling drugs in Venice. Every time LAPD checks them, they are clean. They call themselves the Venice Aryans or Beach Aryans. One guy has a swastika tattoo and another guy has an Iron Cross tattoo. LAPD has sent us photos and notes. No matter what LAPD does, these guys never have anything on them. LAPD is running an internal investigation to make sure no one in their organization is providing information to these beach guys."

"OK, what's your proposal?" asked Wilcox. "Cunningham and I thought we should get Jack in here. After all, he is definitely a World War II guy."

"No problem. Go for it," said Wilcox.

The next morning, Jack returned Richardson's phone call. "Agent Richardson, this is Jack. I'm returning your call."

"Thanks, Jack. When can you come to the office?" asked Richardson.

"Well, I guess, I can come by the day after tomorrow. Ten in the morning would be good for me," said Jack.

"That's perfect," answered Richardson.

Two days later, Jack entered the building, presented his ID and was escorted to Richardson's office, where he found Wilcox, Richardson and Cunningham seated behind a desk.

"Good morning, Jack," said Wilcox as Jack entered the office.

"Good seeing you guys," said Jack as he took a seat.

Wilcox began speaking: "I was out a day last week when LAPD called and spoke to Agent Richardson. Jack, LAPD phoned this office looking for assistance. They sent photos and notes. If you look at those photos of the two individuals, you can see that one has a swastika tattoo on his neck and the other has an Iron Cross tattoo on his arm. They are selling drugs on the Venice boardwalk."

Suddenly Jack interrupted. "That's not an Iron Cross. That's a Balkan Cross."

"A what kind of cross?" asked Wilcox.

"His tattoo is a Balkan Cross," exclaimed Jack.

The three agents looked at each other and then Wilcox asked, "What are you talking about, Jack?"

"The Balkan Cross is the symbol the Germans used in World War II to identify their airplanes, tanks and vehicles," Jack explained.[18]

The three agents stared at him, and suddenly Richardson took charge.

"Listen, Jack. When LAPD called this office and explained the situation, my first phone call was to Cunningham. The first person we both thought of was you. We notified Wilcox and now all four of us are sitting here. Jack, we are looking at the right guy. I was told by Taylor that when you have a problem, you have a phrase you tell yourself. Jack, tell yourself that phrase and come up with an answer. Cunningham and I have seen your museum and Wilcox knows about it. Now, on top of everything we have said, we show you photos and you immediately identify some type of cross from the Second World War. Take these photos supplied by LAPD and study them. Let us know the next time your employer needs you to go to Venice. Should you meet those guys in the provided photographs on the

Strand, observe their activities from a distance. Do not contact or communicate with them. Anyway, that's it," concluded Richardson.

Jack got up from his seat on the other side of the desk and, picking up the photographs, turned to leave the room.

Suddenly, Richardson stood up and said, "Hey, Jack." Jack turned around to face him. "You have my full confidence and that of Cunningham and Wilcox. You have already proven yourself."

"Thanks," said Jack as he headed for the door.

"Wait a minute, Jack," said Richardson. "I've been practicing with Taylor."

"How's that?" asked Jack.

Richardson smiled and said, "*Machen Sie das Fenster auf.*"

Jack started laughing and responded, "That's exactly what I intend to do." Then he exited the room, walked down the hallway, took the elevator and was soon driving away on Wilshire Boulevard.

Later that night, Jack and Jane each had a glass of wine before joining the family for dinner. They reviewed their kids' activities throughout the day. None of the children had any problems to report. They had completed their homework assignments, so they were free to do what they wanted. Jack waited until all the kids were upstairs before he said to Jane, "I've been asked by the agency to observe some guys in Venice."

"What are we talking about?" asked Jane. "The agency has paid you well and I'm very proud of you regarding the drug bust in South Central Los Angeles and the extortion ring by MacArthur Park. It seems that their next request always gets more risky or dangerous."

"Not really, Jane," answered Jack. "There is some type of association between the Second World War and the guys in Venice. Wilcox, Richardson and Cunningham value my knowledge on the subject. That's why they asked me to observe these guys on the beach."

When the Avila kids had gone to bed, Jack approached Jane and said, "We are a great couple. How strange that you grew up in South Bend and I grew up in Los Angeles. We were two thousand miles apart as kids, but we were raised with the same outlook and values on life. I'm very lucky that I found you."

"We are both very fortunate," answered Jane. "You know what's weird,

Jack? When I think of past conversations with your friends when we were dating, the one comment that comes to mind was that you should have been a spy. Jack, are you a spy?"

Jack collected his thoughts and replied, "I'm not a spy, Jane. Maybe I'm an informant. The word *informant* has a bad connotation. The most important aspect that I have, by luck, is that I contributed to the downfall of bad guys."

VENICE

SEVERAL WEEKS HAD passed since the last meeting at the Wilshire Boulevard office, when Jack located several job sites in the Venice Beach area. He noted the locations off his employer's contracts and went to make sales calls west of the contracts' intersection. The first call was to Pacific Coast Construction. They were working on Washington, one block east of Lincoln. Jack parked his truck and walked up to the owner. "Frank, how are you? Thanks for using us on this job."

"No problem, Jack. Your company is always there and you always follow up. I know by your response that you appreciate my business," said Frank.

"We greatly appreciate your business," answered Jack. "So what's it like working by the beach?"

"Well, the beach is about two miles down Lincoln but unlike most beach communities, our first visit was from the police. They told us that there is a long established gang area down the street and to be aware of our surroundings. We knew we were working in a dicey area," said Frank.

"How did you figure that out?" queried Jack.

"It wasn't hard," Frank responded. "You could tell by the prostitutes in the area.""Are you serious?" asked Jack. "Here in one of the beach cities?"

"They are here every day," said Frank. "They are on Washington, east and west of Lincoln. There is also a pair working north on Lincoln in a shopping center. I recognized them. Last year, we had a job in north Long Beach and they were on Artesia Boulevard. I might be mistaken, but when we had that large job in Van Nuys a couple of years ago, I could swear they were working on Sepulveda or Laurel Canyon."

"It seems," said Jack, "that if they are milling around a shopping center, they are shopping for something other than groceries."

"I think you're right, Jack," said Frank with a smile.

"What's the deal? The Los Angeles area must be 'the happy hunting ground for hookers,'" said Jack. "They seem to be everywhere."

Frank looked at Jack and started laughing. "You know, Jack, you might be right." They spoke for several more minutes before Jack left.

He drove down Lincoln and parked his truck; then he walked one block and turned right on the Venice boardwalk.

Jack walked by the eclectic shops and the varied street entertainers. Muscle Beach was active with weight lifters pumping iron in the sun. The paddle tennis courts were full with players. Continuing his stroll down the strand, looking at the colorful shops, Jack heard music in the distance. As he got closer, it seemed the people on the boardwalk were hypnotized. Jack saw a band and approached them, thinking, *These guys are great. Everyone is mesmerized by their music. They must be the Pied Pipers of Venice.*

The drummer and main vocalist were black. The base and lead guitar players were white. The singer, with his long dreadlocks and great smile, kept the crowd captivated. The song featured two trumpet players, who walked around the band and then through the crowd, never missing a note. One trumpet player wore a USC football shirt, while his counterpart sported a UCLA basketball shirt. As Jack went by them, he thought to himself, *I guess these guys are here to hedge all bets made in Los Angeles.* Jack continued strolling the boardwalk, past shops and entertainers, for another hundred yards or so, before turning around; however, he did not see the individuals in the photos provided by the agency.

As Jack returned toward his original starting point, he passed the band, then taking a break. He approached one of the trumpet players and said, "You guys are great."

"Thanks," answered one.

"What's the deal with the shirts?" asked Jack.

Both guys started laughing and one of them said, "We've been friends since we were kids. I went to UCLA and he went to 'SC. I was in the UCLA band and he was in the 'SC band. We wear these shirts to spoof each other. It's more of a joke between us than a rivalry."

"Whatever the situation, you guys and the band were really good," said Jack.

"Thanks, man," said the guy with the USC shirt.

Jack returned to his truck and left Venice. He visited some additional jobs in the Palms and Mar Vista neighborhoods and was almost ready to leave the area, when he again studied the individuals in the photos and their tattoos. He thought to himself, *These guys have no known names, at least none given to me. They have identified themselves with tattoos. The tattoos definitely come from the World War II years. The swastika is a dime a dozen, but the Balkan Cross is unusual. Why would someone pick the Balkan Cross? Maybe they each pick distinctive symbols from the same era.*

As Jack was driving to his next stop in Culver City, he passed a tattoo parlor; so he quickly pulled over to the curb and parked the truck Entering the shop, he noted the available tattoos shown on the walls. An affable guy in his twenties, with a shaved head, nose ring and multiple tattoos, came from behind a curtain and approached the counter. "Can I help you?" he inquired.

Jack looked at him and asked, "Can you do all of these designs?"

"Yeah, no problem," answered the artist.

"I am amazed," said Jack. "You are a very gifted person."

"Thanks," said the artist, "but if I wasn't good, I wouldn't be in business."

"You have the right attitude," Jack remarked. "If you're not good at your job or profession, you will be out of business."

The tattooist replied, "I really look at myself as the owner of a small business. When I tell my buds that I'm working on my quarterlies, I'm talking about my quarterly tax payments. When they are talking about quarterlies, they mean the quarter horse races at the track in Los Alamitos. They still live like they are teenagers and expect someone else to just give them a job or the government to bail them out. I've moved on to prove what I can do," he concluded.

Jack went on to say, "You know, it is guys like you who are the backbone of America."

"Thanks," answered the artist.

"Can I get some advice from you?" asked Jack.

"Sure," the tattooist replied.

"I need to get a non-permanent tattoo that is durable and to know how to maintain it. What do you suggest?"

"I only do permanent tattoos," said the artist. "Bring me a picture or drawing of what you want. Based on what you want or what you show me, I'll recommend a guy who can help you."

"Thanks," answered Jack. "I know I'll be back soon."

Later that evening, Jack returned home and reviewed the day's events with Jane and the children over dinner. After the meal, the Avila kids left the table to finish their homework assignments and get ready for bed. Jane began clearing the table and washing dishes.

"Jane, can I help you?" asked Jack.

"No. Go do what you need to do," replied Jane.

"OK, I will," said Jack. Jack went to his World War II collection to search for a particular book. When he'd found it, he pulled the volume out from among others in the collection and looked through the pages until he located a certain emblem. He studied the emblem and thought to himself, *Whoever these guys are, if they know this emblem, they must know history. If they don't recognize it, I may have an edge on them.*

Two weeks later, Jack would return to the Culver City area to follow up with several contractors who were using his employer's equipment. After the last meeting, he drove to the tattoo parlor.

Jack entered the shop and was greeted by the same individual. "Good seeing you, again," said the artist.

Jack had previously made a close up copy of the emblem so as not to reveal the book. He responded, "Good seeing you, and I know you can help me. Can you duplicate this symbol?"

The artist studied the design, looked at Jack and said, "Hey, man, this is trippy. Is this one of those symbols from the 1960s, like sex, drugs, and rock and roll? I'm only in my twenties, but I've heard about those years. Wait," he said, "what was the word they used? Oh, yeah, I just thought of it. Wasn't the word *psychedelic*?"

While the artist was referring to the American 1960s, Jack was thinking of the turmoil of the European 1930s. "This symbol predates the sixties but not by much. It's amazing what can happen when a generation goes psychedelic on you. Can you or can you not copy this?" asked Jack.

The artist was momentarily taken aback, as he realized that Jack was referring to another place and time. He replied, "I know a guy who can duplicate what you have. He is a graphic designer by profession, and is very well known. He does henna tattoos. He can apply the tattoos so they look old or brand-new. Sometimes the studios use him for movies. He is very busy for Halloween and New Year's Eve parties. He's the guy you need. This is his phone number."

"Thank you very much," said Jack. "I'm sure I'll be back to visit you in the future."

Jack got into his truck and left the area.

Later that evening at home, the kids were studying in their rooms as Jane was preparing dinner. "How was your day?" asked Jane.

"It was a great day, but I want to tell you something," said Jack.

Somewhat startled by Jack's demeanor, Jane quickly turned around and said, "What do you want to tell me?"

"I'm going to get a tattoo," said Jack.

"A tattoo!" exclaimed Jane. "A tattoo," she repeated. "Great. I can't believe you came up with that idea." said Jane.

Jack chuckled and replied, "I'm thinking of getting a nonpermanent tattoo. The agency has asked me to contact some guys in the Venice area. They have World War II era tattoos. If I ever meet them, I could show them that I have something in common with them. You know, Jane, when it comes to the Second World War, I'm a hard person to beat."

"I know that piece of history has been your passion." Jane replied. "What is your plan, Jack? Why do you think those guys will respond to you?"

"I'm not sure they will. I'm not even sure I will ever meet them. But if I do meet them and they are World War II guys, I might be able to gain their confidence. Who knows, I'm probably a dreamer. Most likely I am," said Jack.

"You're not a dreamer," Jane remarked. "You have always been very realistic. You are a good husband and father, and our kids are lucky to have a dad like you." She started to leave, then turned around and faced Jack. "Follow your plan," she said. "When it comes to World War II, I know you know your history."

Jack just smiled at her and nodded. As he walked down the hallway, it crossed his mind, *Remember what General Eisenhower said, "Even the best of battle plans might have to be scrapped after the first shot is fired."*[9] The next day, Jack called the graphic artist and set up an appointment.

He met the artist at the artist's home in Mar Vista on the following Saturday. Jack showed him the emblem. "I can duplicate this with no problem. It will be a henna tattoo. It can last five to six weeks. When you take a shower, just protect the area and gently pat it dry. What is this?" asked the artist, looking at the emblem. "I can't recall seeing this type of design before."

"It's a long story and I'd rather not go into it. It's more mysterious that way."

"No problem," said the artist.

"How much will it cost?" asked Jack.

The artist laughed and replied, "The first one's free."

"Are you sure?" queried Jack.

"Yeah, it's OK. I can tell you're one of those guys who will be back," the artist stated.

Jack rolled up his left shirt sleeve and the artist began drawing. Forty-five minutes later Jack was wearing the emblem. The artist walked him to a large mirror so that he could see it for himself. "That's amazing," said Jack. "It looks so real, like it is a permanent tattoo. You are very good."

"I hear that a lot," answered the artist.

"You're right. If I need to have this done again, I will be back," said Jack.

The artist smiled and said, "I knew it."

Jack returned home in the afternoon and showed the tattoo to Jane. "That does look real," she said. "The guy did a great job. I don't know what it is, Jack, but just make sure our kids don't see it. They'll tell everybody and you and I will have to explain it to the world."

"Believe me, the kids will not see it. You're right that they will blab it to friends and strangers. I don't have the patience for that," said Jack.

The balance of the weekend went quickly. Monday morning had the Avila family, like most families in America, going in divergent directions. Jack was driving to work thinking about his new assignment, heading in the direction of Venice Beach.

MOTION BY THE OCEAN

JACK DROVE TO the corporate office on Monday morning. As usual, he had a meeting with the president of the company and checked recent deliveries with the dispatchers. He went through the company contracts to determine job site deliveries; then he left the office with an itinerary pointing toward the West Los Angeles, Palms and Venice Beach areas. After visiting the projects in West Los Angeles and Palms, Jack left for the sites around Venice Beach. He parked the truck off Venice Boulevard and started walking down the boardwalk.

Jack passed the beautiful beachfront homes and condominiums. He walked beyond Muscle Beach, the eclectic shops and beach performers. He was strolling down the boardwalk when he recognized the band from several weeks before. They were setting up to play. Jack saw the black lead singer with the dreadlocks, approached him and said, "I was here about a month ago and saw you guys play. You were great. You were playing a song that was heavy on trumpets. Two of the band members were playing trumpets during the song. Did you guys write that song?" asked Jack.

The lead singer started laughing and said, "No, man. People ask us all the time if we wrote a song. We go through old albums and find great songs. That's our gig. People our age have never heard these songs, so they always ask us if we wrote the song. We find a great song, research the sheet music, and then practice, practice, practice. We don't look the type, but we do our homework.

"The song you heard is 'Maybe the People Would Be the Times Or Between Clark and Hillsdale.'"

"That's the name of a song?" exclaimed Jack.

"Yeah," said the lead singer with a smile. "I don't remember the name of the album, but the name of the group was Love and the lead vocalist was a guy named Arthur Lee. Even the lyrics of the song lend themselves as a great beach song. We do all types of songs. 'I Love Music' by the O'Jays and 'What I Like about You' by the Romantics always gets them dancing here at the beach. We even do songs for ourselves."

"How's does that work?" asked Jack.

"Well, for example, we do a knockoff of the Beach Boys' version of 'Come Go With Me.' It's a song that you really can't dance to, and you know guys, they look for any excuse not to dance. So what happens, girls by themselves or in pairs or small groups come up and dance. They start swaying to the music. With loose fitting bikini tops and tight fitting bikini bottoms, I'm talking motion by the ocean."

"Sounds like to me," responded Jack, "if you get enough bikini clad girls swaying to music down by the ocean and they get the notion to put some emotion into their motion, it must cause a commotion, and for your band, that's great promotion."

The lead singer laughed and said, "That was good, man. I'm going to remember what you said. I'm telling you right now that watching the girls dancing right in front of our band is almost up there with amateur night at a strip joint."

"Now, that's saying something!" exclaimed Jack. He and the lead singer both laughed out loud.

The lead singer went on to explain, "We don't have a regular band. We play songs based on who is available and who shows up. The trumpet guys won't be here, but today is your lucky day."

"Why is that?" asked Jack.

"We will be doing 'Come Go With Me' later. I think it is the fifth or sixth song on the menu. We're almost ready to go. Hang around or come back in about thirty minutes. You'll see what I mean," said the singer.

"Thanks," answered Jack. "I'll be back in a while."

Jack walked down the strand. A street entertainer, wearing a turban and playing a remote guitar, skated passed Jack on inline skates as he sang a song. Jack then came upon an individual who took a running start, leaped over six beach chairs, between lit torches and split a piece of wood at the end of his leap. The crowd around him erupted in applause to acknowledge his feat. Another entertainer, farther down the way, casually looked at the crowd, telling jokes while juggling bowling balls, as his assistant lay on the ground below the swirling balls. *These guys are amazing*, thought Jack.

He continued on the boardwalk for a short distance but did not see the individuals he was looking for. So he turned around and walked back in the direction from which he had come, eventually returning to the band. The lead singer saw Jack approaching and yelled, "Hey, man, that was perfect timing!"

The band put down their various instruments. The drummer walked from behind the drums toward the front to be with the other band members. The base guitarist put down his guitar and picked up a saxophone, then he also approached the other members gathered around the microphones. Simultaneously, they broke into a doo-wop version of "Come Go With Me." As predicted by the lead vocalist, girls and women in bathing suits came forward and started dancing. They came in front of the band as individuals, pairs and groups, and they danced in front of the band, bodies swaying in all directions, as if freed from all inhibitions.

Jack watched the scene and thought to himself, *Maybe that guy is right. This may be right up there with amateur night.* He watched for another minute and then started waving his right hand as if to fan his face. *Maybe the ocean breeze has stopped, but for whatever reason, it's getting hot around here.* When the song stopped, the groups of girls and women immediately dispersed. Jack approached the lead singer and said, "You were right on the money. There was definitely motion by the ocean!"

"Thanks," answered the singer. "Come by anytime. You'll always be welcome."

"Thanks a lot," said Jack. He started walking away, when it occurred to him, "I'm not here to have a good time. I'm here to find two specific guys." He made another pass up and down the boardwalk, but there was still no sign of the guys in the photos, so he returned to his truck and left the area.

Jack dialed Wilcox's telephone number later that afternoon. The phone rang and he heard a familiar voice: "Wilcox."

"Agent Wilcox, this is Jack. How are you?"

Wilcox smiled upon hearing Jack's voice and said, "I'm doing well, Jack. How have you been?"

"I'm doing well also. Just letting you know that I have been to Venice a couple of times but I haven't seen the guys in the photos. I just wanted you to know that I have followed up, but have nothing to report."

Wilcox listened to Jack's explanation and smiled to himself. When Jack finished speaking, Wilcox replied, "Jack, we know that you are very conscientious. We have no doubts about your work for us."

"Thank you, Agent Wilcox," Jack replied. "I'll do my best."

"Jack, only return to the area based on your employer's business," Wilcox told him firmly. "Maintain your log and expenses. You may have more luck finding a needle in a haystack than those guys. There is nothing predictable, as far as we know, regarding their movements. If they alter their appearance, you might be right next to them and never put two and two together. Who knows? They might look exactly like the photos. Concentrate on spotting the tattoos. The tattoos will be the best identification."

A TRUE BELIEVER

JACK WENT TO a scheduled meeting the next morning in the Palms district. The meeting ended two hours later, after which he left and drove toward Venice. He visited his company's supplied job site and thanked that contractor for his business. He then drove two miles from the Palms district, stopped at a side street and replaced his employer's magnetic signs with the Agency supplied signs. Jack parked on Ocean and visited two more work sites. He talked with the superintendents about their respective projects and thanked each of them for using his company's equipment. Jack had walked about fifty yards down the strand, when he stopped in his tracks.

On his left were the two individuals from the photos. One had the swastika tattoo on his neck and the other the Balkan Cross on his arm. They were talking to a bushy red haired surfer type, who kept moving in all directions as if uncontrolled. He quickly grabbed something from the guy with the swastika tattoo, jumped on his skateboard and disappeared within the crowd.

Jack's adrenalin kicked in at the prospect of speaking to these two individuals. "I don't think I can do it," he said to himself, as he walked away, physically shaking. Jack continued walking past the varied restaurants and shops while thinking, *Get your composure. Other guys do it.* He turned right on a narrow street and made another right turn into an alley. Jack could not believe what he saw. Straight ahead of him in the alley was the bushy-haired surfer.

The surfer type looked like a marionette as he moved uncontrollably in all directions. His face and body were in contortions. Jack looked at him and thought, *He's tweaking badly*. It then occurred to him, *Don't think, just do!*

Jack quickly retraced his steps down the street and boardwalk. Spotting the two individuals sitting on a bench on the strand, Jack approached them and said, "How are you guys doing today?"

Taken aback, one of them replied, "Do we know you?"

"No, you don't," answered Jack. "I was walking by earlier when I saw you guys talking to a surfer type. By accident, I saw him later in an alley and, man, he was really tweaking."

The skinhead with the swastika tattoo replied, "What's that have to do with us? He was just passing by and asking for directions."

"Sorry, I made a mistake. I thought if you guys were dealing in meth, I could make a connection. I know a guy in central L.A. who could sell it if he had it." Before either one could respond, Jack continued, "You have a swastika tattoo, and you have a Balkan Cross tattoo———"

Before Jack could finish, the guy with the Balkan Cross asked, "What type of cross do I have?"

"It's a Balkan Cross," answered Jack.

"Whatever. I saw it in an old photo and it looked cool and different."

"I see your tattoos but I want you to look at my tattoo," said Jack, and he lifted the left sleeve of his shirt to expose his emblem. The two skinheads looked at Jack's emblem and said nothing. While they continued staring at the tattoo, Jack said, "This is the sign of a true believer," then he rolled down his shirt sleeve. "If you guys change your mind, let me know. I'm here on a Wednesday or Thursday once a month. I have lunch and drift around. You can always spot me. I wear a brown baseball cap. Catch you guys later," and he turned around and left. The two did not respond. Jack walked away thinking, *I don't believe I actually did it.*

Jack returned to his truck and drove several miles before pulling into an alley. He exchanged magnetic door mats; then he drove a short distance and pulled up to call Wilcox from a pay phone.

In less than a minute Jack heard, "Wilcox."

"Agent Wilcox, this is Jack Avila. I did it. I spoke to the guys at Venice. I saw them talking to surfer, whom I later saw in an alley and he was contorting uncontrollably and———"

"Slow down, Jack. Just slow down. You spoke to them. What did they tell you?" asked Wilcox.

Jack regained his composure and said, "I asked them about the surfer whom I had earlier seen taking something from the guy with the swastika tattoo and they told me that he had just asked for directions. Then I asked them about their tattoos and showed them my tattoo."

"What the hell are you talking about, Jack? What tattoo do you have?" asked Wilcox.

"You told me to use their tattoos as the best identification," responded Jack. "Since their tattoos are from the World War II era, I got a World War II era tattoo. It's not a permanent tattoo, but it made them think. They said nothing; they just looked at me."

As Wilcox listened to Jack, he just shook his head as he passed his left hand through his hair, thinking, *Sometimes you get exactly what you asked for.* "Now what?" asked Wilcox.

Jack replied, "I told them if they had any interest in dealing with me, I could be found in Venice once a month, having lunch on a Wednesday or Thursday. They could spot me wearing a brown baseball cap."

"What the hell does a brown baseball cap have to do with anything?" exclaimed Wilcox.

"It's a long story. I'll fill you in later," said Jack.

"OK," answered Wilcox. "I'll be looking forward to your explanation."

Unbeknown to Jack and Wilcox, the two skinheads Jack had spoken to were also reviewing their day, with a man named Faust. "How did the day go, Todd?" asked Faust.

"It went great, but Jeremy and I were approached by some guy who claimed he saw Brett, the meth dude, contorting all over after being with us. We told him that we did not know the guy and he had only asked for directions," answered Todd.

"That frickin' little marble head freak is always a problem!" yelled Faust. "He's so flagrant when we sell to him, and if we don't sell to him, I'm afraid he'll turn us into the cops. So what else about this guy who spoke to you? Don't tell me he is another undercover cop with the pushy tactics and the crummy World War II German medals. You guys followed my instructions, right?"

"Of course," answered Jeremy. "We wear plastic gloves, place the sale in an envelope, make one sale at a time and then get rid of the gloves. Isn't that right?" he asked, looking at Todd.

"That's exactly what we did," answered Todd. "This guy didn't seem pushy," he continued. "I got the feeling he came upon us by accident. He didn't ask a lot of questions. He spoke about our tattoos and then showed us his tattoo. He said something about being a believer or a true believer, or something along those lines."

"What type of tattoo?" asked Faust.

"It looked like darts," responded Todd.

"Darts?" Faust replied.

Jeremy added, "It did look like darts."

"Strange," said Faust. "Let me know the next time you see this guy."

"Will do," answered Todd. "Oh, by the way," said Todd, "He told us we could spot him by the brown baseball cap he wears."

"A brown baseball cap?" asked Faust. "That's interesting."

"Oh, one last thing," added Todd. "The guy said he knows someone in central L.A. who could sell meth if he had it."

Faust looked at Todd and said nothing. Moments later Faust said, "If you see him, follow him from a distance like you did the cops who approached you. Don't talk to him; just observe his movements. Who knows, he may never show up again."

Jeremy replied, "He told us he's usually here once a month on a Wednesday or Thursday."

FAKERS

JACK RETURNED TO the Venice boardwalk on multiple occasions. The assignment was becoming discouraging. Whatever the time spent and distance covered, the individuals with whom he had spoken did not appear again. He walked several hundred yards up and down Venice Beach. Even the occasional stopping at Muscle Beach or the paddle tennis courts revealed nothing. On this particular day, having decided to have lunch, Jack stopped at a restaurant at Ocean Front and Horizon and was taken to a table by a waiter.

Jack ordered lunch and just "people watched." Within several minutes, the waiter brought his order. Jack started to eat while watching the crowd pass. Three women were at the next table loudly speaking of their boyfriends and what they would be doing on the upcoming Saturday night. Sitting at the table was a white brunette, a blonde and a redhead.

Jack was about to take a bite from his sandwich, when he heard the redhead at the next table exclaim, "Oh, my God! Do you see what's coming? How many pounds of cottage cheese do you see?" The other women at the table started to laugh. Jack looked up to see an overweight couple holding hands, walking down the way. He could tell that they very much enjoyed each other's company. A minute later, the redhead made another remark. "Isn't Halloween several months away or am I mistaken?" The other women snickered. Jack observed a man with a birthmark on his face passing by their table. The redhead made additional derogatory comments as couples and individuals walked by them. Jack finished his lunch, paid the bill and tipped the waiter. He left his table and approached the table with the three women.

"Excuse, me," said Jack while looking at the red head. "I was just sitting at the table next to you three and heard your comments. If I could hear them, then so could the people you criticized."

The redhead momentarily looked at Jack, turned to her friends and said, "Why don't you go back and go under your rock?" as she and the other two women laughed.

Jack bent over and placed his hands on his knees so as to be eyeball to eyeball with the redhead. He said to her, "You three criticize the realities of others. Those people are real. The three of you sit here with fake hair color, fake eyebrows and fake boobs. You are each fake."

At that moment, the redhead exploded out of her chair and screamed, "Fuck you!" Then she dipped her right hand into her bowl of pasta and hurled pasta at Jack. The pasta landed on Jack's face and shirt. The redhead stood trembling in hatred with her right hand extended backwards and fist clenched.

Jack stood there facing her calmly. She had started to reach for the pasta bowl when Jack said, "Don't even think of throwing that bowl at me. Do you see the concrete wall on your right out there?" She hesitated, glancing to the right and seeing the wall in the distance. Then her attention came back to Jack as she heard him say, "If you throw that bowl at me, I'm going to pick you up and put you through that wall. I'll have plenty of witnesses that you instigated this confrontation." She looked around to see restaurant patrons, waiters and boardwalk tourists staring at her. When she turned to face Jack again, he said, "My words stung you, just like your words stung those who passed by. But more importantly, you have embarrassed yourself in front of all these people." She still faced Jack, her body trembling. Jack then said, "You know, miss, now that I see you standing in front of me, before you ever criticize anyone in the future, you may want to take into consideration the size of your ass. I say that because I have seen smaller highway patrol roadblocks." Jack's verbal arrow pierced her heart. She placed her face into cupped hands and cried uncontrollably. Jack backed away from her very carefully; then he turned around and walked down the strand. He regained his composure and set out for his assignment.

He looked for the guys with the tattoos. He had walked approximately fifty yards along the strand when he heard, "Jack. Jack Avila. It's me." Jack turned around to face Kathy Schilling, an old girlfriend.

"Jack, what happened?" asked Kathy. "You have pasta and red sauce on your shirt."

Jack started laughing and replied, "Kathy, don't you remember? I never had very good table manners."

Kathy said, "Come on, Jack. I knew you very well and you had excellent manners; you were courteous and always easy to be with. I know you are still the same."

Jack hesitated and said, "Kathy, it's very nice to see you."

Kathy also hesitated, then responded, "It's great seeing you, Jack. When I'm driving on Mulholland or on Pacific Coast Highway between Malibu and Santa Monica, I can't help but think of us, even though that was a long time ago."

Jack answered, "It was a long time ago, but it was a great time being with you. So where are you now?"

"I live in Manhattan Beach. I'm married and have two boys and a girl," Kathy replied.

"I should have known," Jack chuckled. "I have two girls and a boy just the opposite. As the crow flies, I'm not that far from you. I live in west L.A."

Kathy seemed at a loss for words, when Jack said, "Your husband is a lucky guy. He's married to a great person."

"Thanks. So is your wife," Kathy replied.

Jack smiled. "I'll remind her when I get home."

Kathy looked away and then back at Jack. "Jack, it was great seeing and talking to you. I need to get going. I'm looking for a gift for my son's birthday. He wants a shirt from one of the stores along the boardwalk."

Jack replied, "It was great talking to you. I'm glad you spotted me and said hi."

"Me too," said Kathy. She went on her way while Jack continued down the strand.

He kept looking for the skinheads with the tattoos. There was no sign of them, as Jack walked up and down the area. Dejectedly he returned to the truck and climbed into the cab.

Jack sat in the truck and thought, *How weird to run into Kathy. Man, if Jane finds out I met her, she'll be really upset. She still looks at Kathy as an invisible competitor, even after all these years.* Jack started the truck and turned on the radio. He recognized the song as an old instrumental being aired. Within moments of the song starting, a woman with a beautiful voice began singing. Jack had begun driving down the street, but upon listening to the lyrics he quickly pulled back to the curb. He looked straight ahead through the windshield, not to see where he was going, but to reflect where he had been.

Jack and Kathy had been quite the item and a great couple among their friends. Many of their friends thought Jack and Kathy were destined for marriage. They were always together at parties, theaters, visiting museums virtually everywhere. They would drive along Pacific Coast Highway and Mulholland Drive in Jack's two-seat white sports car that he had had when they were together. As time passed, the great passion that brought them together began to wane. It was no one's fault. Reality came between them and it was time for Jack and Kathy to move in different directions. The song ended with the disc jockey announcing the name as "Am I the Same Girl?" by Swing Out Sister. Jack looked at the radio thinking, *If I ever hear that song again, I need to change to another channel quickly.* Then he wondered, *What if Kathy heard the same song? Would she look at me, thinking am I the same girl in your eyes?* Jack was about to change the radio channel, when the next song was announced by the disc jockey as "Living in America" by James Brown. He thought, *That's better. Great song. Great performer. Great country.* As Jack drove down the street, listening to the song, he was unaware that he had been spotted by Jeremy and Todd. They were noting the company name and 800 telephone number on the truck's magnetic signs before quickly disappearing into the crowds of Venice.

Jack was driving on Washington Boulevard when it occurred to him, *What if those guys saw me talking to Kathy? If they ask her who I am, then everything I have done is meaningless, maybe even dangerous. Maybe I'm in over my head. Oh, man. What am I'm going to tell Jane when she sees the stains on my shirt? If I'm lucky, I'll walk through the door and she won't be home. If I walk through the door and she sees me, I've got to tell her what happened. If*

I tell her the truth, then I'm real. If I don't tell her the truth, then I'm fake like the three women on the boardwalk.

That evening when Jack arrived home, he parked the truck in front of his place as usual. He looked at the house and thought, *I'll be lucky if Jane isn't home.* He grabbed his wallet and got out of the truck. As he inserted the key into the door lock, he said to himself, "Here goes."

He opened the door and said, "Jane, I'm home." Silence. Again, while walking through the house, he called out, "Jane, I'm home." There was no response. He checked the door leading into the garage and discovered that her car was gone. Then he went through the rooms gathering laundry. He placed the clothes, including his shirt, into the washing machine, added detergent and started the washer. Jack thought to himself, *That was close. Someday when this assignment is over and she is in a lighthearted mood, I'll tell her what happened. She might even enjoy the story.*

The next day, Jack walked into the corporate office to review the company's contracts, when the president approached him and said, "Jack, could you come into my office? I need to speak to you."

"Sure," answered Jack. Jack entered the office and sat at a table with the president.

"Jack, what's going on in Culver City, Marina del Rey, Playa Vista, Venice and Playa del Rey? You're spending a lot of time in those areas."

"I have," answered Jack. "We have a lot of equipment in those areas. I can review all open contracts with you, if you like."

"Not a problem, Jack," the president replied. "I just wanted to hear your answer personally from you. I know you are always on top of the game and know your stuff. Keep up the good work."

"Thanks," said Jack, as he turned around and left the office.

THERE ARE BETTER MEN

THE NEXT MORNING, Jack called the agency and arranged to meet with Agent Wilcox at 10:00 a.m. When he arrived at the office, Wilcox was waiting for him.

"Good morning, Agent Wilcox," said Jack, as they shook hands. How are you doing?"

"I'm doing just fine, Jack. What's going on?" asked Wilcox.

As he took a seat across from Wilcox at the desk, Jack got straight to the point. "Agent Wilcox, I think it's time for me to leave, or at least to leave Venice. I've been going there for months now, and except for the one time I spoke to the guys in the photos, I've never seen them again. I told you I have to maintain a tattoo. During the times that I've been there I've been splattered with pasta, cursed at, and have met an old girlfriend."

"Wait a minute," interrupted Wilcox. "You've been hit with pasta and met an old girlfriend. It seems to me you're having a good time at the beach."

"It's not funny, Agent Wilcox," Jack responded. "My boss is asking me why I'm spending so much time in the area."

Wilcox was silent for a moment so as to gather his thoughts.

"Well, Jack, all I can tell you is that you have done a hell of a job since you've been here, and I say that not for us or the LAPD but for the people of Los Angeles. You have helped to take down some major players, and it's OK if you want to walk away. Just think, Jack: When you began with us, you originally came up with the idea of the assignment at the crack house, which resulted in the taking out of that operation. Next, your observations in the Downtown L.A. area led to the arrest and conviction of about thirty members of a notorious street gang. Then we asked you to try and contact some guys suspected of drug selling in Venice, and you were able to approach and speak to them. You have basically been able to achieve the same results as the LAPD and you're a one man show."

"So you won't look at me as a loser if I walk away from this assignment?" asked Jack.

"It's not a problem, Jack. I understand, and we'll talk again," Wilcox replied with a smile.

"Thank you, Agent Wilcox," said Jack as he stood up to leave. When the door of the office had closed behind him, Wilcox thought to himself, *I give that guy a lot of credit.*

The same morning Jack spoke to Wilcox, Todd and Jeremy also went to speak to a superior. They knocked on the door of a small house three blocks from the beach. A very large man opened the door and said, "How are you guys doing?"

"We're doing OK," said Jeremy. "We happened to see and follow the guy with the weird tattoo. This is the name of the company he works for and this is the phone number."

"That's great. What happened?" asked the large man.

Todd answered, "We saw him walking along the strand. We kept a safe distance and followed him back to a truck. He just sat in the truck for a couple of minutes and then took off."

"You guys did a great job. Stay here. I'm going to make a phone call and I'll be right back," said the large man as he left the house.

"Will do," Todd replied.

Wilcox was sitting in his office when, approximately two hours after he had spoken to Jack, a phone rang. Wilcox looked at the phone in disbelief. It was the one originally established to cover for Jack. The telephone had been in Wilcox's office for over a year and there had never been a call or a message. As Wilcox reached for the receiver, he saw "Pay Phone" on the caller ID screen and quickly looked at the scripted responses. He answered with the company name that matched the magnetic mats on Jack's truck.

The male voice at the other end said, "I saw your company truck in Venice today. I'm curious as to what type of construction work you do."

Reading from the script, Wilcox answered, "We do grading, primarily for large projects. We'll do smaller jobs based on specific requests. What are you looking for?"

The voice stammered, "Well, I'm, I'm not really sure, but I may have an upcoming job. Who is the guy you have in this area?"

Wilcox responded, "Our guy in that area is Jack Rogers. He's a good guy and knows construction."

"I'll keep you in mind," said the man and hung up.

Wilcox's heart was beating quickly as he thought, "A call from a pay phone, from someone who saw Jack in Venice and wanted to know his name. I'll call Jack later today."

While the large man was gone, Todd and Jeremy had been wandering through the house when they came upon a display case of World War II memorabilia. Todd was looking at the case and he suddenly yelled, "Oh, shit, Jeremy, check this out!" Jeremy ran over to the case. Todd yelled again, "Look at that. That's the guy's tattoo!"

"No shit! That's exactly it," said Jeremy.

The large man returned to the house, looked at Jeremy and Todd, and said, "I've got the lowdown on that guy."

Todd and Jeremy were beside themselves. One of them said burst out, "We found the guy's tattoo in your case!"

"What?" exclaimed the man.

"The guy's tattoo is in your case. That's it right there," said Todd.

The man reached into the case and pulled out the symbol. He sat in a large chair and looked at it more closely. "Are you sure this is his tattoo?" he asked.

"Of course it is. We told you it looked like darts and it does look like darts. So what's the deal?" asked Jeremy.

The man stared at the symbol. Then he looked up at Todd and Jeremy and said, "He told you something when he showed you his tattoo, right?"

Todd responded, "He said it was the sign of a believer or a true believer or something like that."

The man listened to Todd's answer and just nodded as he continued looking at the symbol. Looking up again at Todd and Jeremy, he said, "His tattoo is the lightning bolts of the SA [*ES–AH*], the *Sturmabteilung*.[21] Both of you guys come here and look closely within the circle. Do you see the *S* and the *A*?"

"Oh, yeah. Now that you point it out, it's as clear as day," said Jeremy.

The large man went on to explain: "The SA was the organization that provided security for Nazi speakers when their movement began. They would later become the street fighters against the Communists throughout Germany. The lightning bolts symbolized that they would strike hard and fast, anytime, anywhere. This guy is very knowledgeable, or just maybe he really is a believer. Did he say anything else?"

Todd and Jeremy just stood there for a moment; then Todd said, "He told us he is here on a Wednesday or a Thursday once a month, and we can spot him because he wears a brown hat."

The large man exclaimed, "A brown hat! This guy has a tattoo of the SA and wears a brown hat. The only thing missing is a brown shirt. The next time you see this guy, come and get me. If I'm around, I'd like to see him face to face."

"No problem," answered Jeremy.

Later that same night, Wilcox called Jack's home telephone number. Jack happened to answer the phone. "Jack, this is Wilcox, how are you doing tonight?"

"Fine, thank you, Agent Wilcox. What's up?"

"Jack, when was the last time you were in Venice?" asked Wilcox.

"Yesterday," answered Jack.

"Did you go anywhere else displaying our magnetic signs?" asked Wilcox.

"No," said Jack. "I was in surrounding areas but I only put the signs on the truck while going into Venice and took them off before leaving Venice. Why?" asked Jack.

"I had a phone call today. It was the first call on that special line we set up since you have been here," Wilcox related. "It originated from a pay phone and the caller asked what type of work our company did and our rep's name. He said he got the number from a truck in Venice. I gave him the company name and your name that we originally agreed upon. Do you get the message?"

"No, I don't," Jack replied.

Wilcox continued: "Somebody was checking on you. Maybe it was a legitimate inquiry or maybe a question from the guys you are looking for. Perhaps they are looking for you. The caller was very cautious. He wanted to know your name. He did not clarify his line of work or if our description of construction applied to him. I've been in this business a long time, Jack. I think the guys you have been looking for are now looking for you. Something you said made an impression on them." Wilcox paused and then said, "Jack, you've done a great job. I realize you have other responsibilities and we are very grateful for all your efforts. I can only ask you to consider returning to Venice two or three more times. That would place you in Venice another two or three months, at your discretion. If nothing happens, then I agree with you, it's time to punt. What do you think?"

Jack thought it over momentarily and replied, "OK, Agent Wilcox. I'll give it several more visits and that's it. I'll walk away knowing I did my best," said Jack.

DOKTOR FAUST

JACK DROVE TO Venice three weeks after the conversation with Wilcox. Five or six blocks before reaching the beach, he pulled into a narrow alley off Fifth Street between San Juan and Westminster. He had used this alley numerous times to switch out the magnetic signs. Jack left the alley and drove to Windward and parked in the public parking lot, paid the attendant and started walking down Ocean Front. There he met with the same disappointment: he did not see the two guys with the distinctive tattoos.

This is crazy, Jack thought to himself. *I shouldn't be doing this, but I gave my word.* Jack continued on Ocean Front, looking around with an increasing sense of frustration. He decided to have lunch at a restaurant near the end of Windward, and as he was being seated, Jack was spotted at the restaurant by Todd.

Todd quickly found Jeremy and said, "The guy with the tattoo is here." They ran to Muscle Beach and found their man. "He's here," yelled Todd over the chain link fence.

"The guy with the tattoo and the brown hat?" asked the man pumping weights.

"Yeah, he's having lunch right down from here," said Jeremy.

The man finished his reps, left the barbells and said, "OK, let's go."

Jack was sitting at a table eating lunch. His mind aimlessly wandered between family, job and future goals. He was used to passing shadows and conversations as he sat by himself. This day would be different. This day, just as described in Bram Stoker's novel *Dracula*, shadows took on substance and sat at Jack's table. He was startled as the chairs around him were suddenly pulled away from the table. He looked up to see the two individuals he had spoken to so many months before, but on his immediate right was a huge man. He was approximately six feet six inches tall, broad shouldered with large biceps and thighs and very tanned. His crew cut hair was gold due to sun exposure. "My friends tell me you have an unusual tattoo," said the large man.

Jack answered, "I consider my tattoo to be historical and not unusual."

"Can I see it?" asked the large man, seating himself at the table. Todd and Jeremy sat down in the other two chairs.

As Jack rolled up his sleeve and extended the upper part of his bicep toward the man, Jeremy said, "See, Faust, we told you it looked like darts." The large man glared at Jeremy and clenched his teeth, as Jeremy had revealed his name.

"Is your name Faust?" inquired Jack.

"My name is none of your business," retorted Faust.

"No problem," answered Jack. "I just thought if your name is Faust, like *Doktor Faust* in Goethe's play, then I could be Doktor Panzerfaust."[20]

Faust chuckled and said, "You know your stuff. Do you speak German?"

"A little," Jack replied. "Why do you ask?"

"You pronounced *Goethe* correctly in German," Faust replied. "Most Americans would say *GO-ETH*. Where did you learn German?"

"I learned German at Grandma's house," answered Jack. "I would absorb it as she spoke to me and my brother. I just know some basic stuff."

"That's good," said Faust. " You met my friends some months ago. What do you want to know?" asked Faust.

"I thought I saw your friends sell meth to a red headed guy with a skateboard," Jack responded. "By accident, I later saw the same person contorting badly in an alley. I know a guy who can sell meth if he has a source."

"What guy?" asked Faust.

"I go to an area near MacArthur Park and buy the big 'H' for a family member. He's too strung out to make the trip on his own. The guy I buy it from has asked me if I can get him meth to distribute in the area. That's why I asked your friends if they dealt in meth. I could be a courier between you and the guy near MacArthur Park. I'm in the construction business, so I go everywhere," said Jack.

"Can you take me there?" Faust asked.

"I can't because I have a company vehicle, and for liability reasons I cannot take someone else in case there is an accident; but I can meet you there," suggested Jack.

Faust looked at Jack coldly and said, "Maybe, I'll meet you there."

Jack quivered at Faust's expression and said, "That's not a problem."

"The bottom line is this," barked Faust. "We don't do anything illegal. We don't deal in drugs. I liked your tattoo. Catch you later," said Faust, as he, Jeremy and Todd quickly got up from their chairs, left the table and disappeared into the crowds of tourists.

Jack's heart was beating rapidly due to the adrenalin rush. *Wilcox was right*, thought Jack. *They* were *looking for me.* Jack got his check from the waiter, paid for lunch and walked from the deli to his truck, trembling.

While they were walking away, Todd asked Faust, "What do you think about that guy?"

"You might be right," answered Faust. "Think about it. He approached you guys once a long time ago. Cops are persistently coming back. He said that he occasionally came here for lunch. You found him having lunch. We know his name and the company he works for. He admitted that he is in the construction business. He had a valid reason why he couldn't take me to meet that guy near MacArthur Park, but he didn't hesitate about meeting me in L.A. I think you're right, Todd. He probably came upon you guys, by accident, because of that little red headed freak." Faust chuckled as they walked toward his house. "No one has an SA [*ES–AH*] tattoo," said Faust. He stopped midstride, looked at Todd and Jeremy and said, "Maybe he learned about the SA at his grandma's house."

After leaving the parking lot at Windward, Jack returned to the alley off Fifth Street. He swapped the signs and drove down Venice Boulevard. Stopping at a small retail center, he called Wilcox's direct line from a pay phone.

"Wilcox," Jack heard on the line.

"Agent Wilcox, it's Jack. You were right. I think they *were* looking for me."

"Slow down, Jack. What happened?" asked Wilcox.

"I was eating lunch in Venice when all of a sudden the two guys I had met before, along with another guy, sat at my table. The third guy was huge. He wanted to see my tattoo. Evidently the other guys had mentioned it to him. He wasn't surprised at the meaning of the tattoo. It coincides with the swastika tattoo and the other guy's Balkan Cross tattoo. Agent Wilcox, I just started talking. I made up one scenario after another. I'm not even sure what I said," said Jack.

Wilcox replied, "Jack, for those guys to come forward means that one or more of them have some degree of confidence in you. Something you said in your initial contact made an impression. Look back on that meeting. What comes to your mind? What do you remember?"

"The first question from the large guy was that he wanted to see my tattoo. One of the other fellows at the table called him Faust. I'm not sure whether that's his actual name or a nickname."

"We'll run that name through our inventory," answered Wilcox. "Now that I think of it, what is your tattoo?"

"It's a long story," said Jack. "When you're bored or have a lot of time on your hands, I'll explain the history."

Wilcox smiled and replied, "I look forward to that day. Until then, don't forget you may have those guys continuing to watch for you."

"After today, you're probably right," Jack responded. Then he hung up, left the shopping center and drove east on Venice Boulevard to the 405 Freeway. Entering the freeway, he headed north toward home.

Thirty minutes later, Jack entered his house and passed Jane as he went through the door. "How was your day?" asked Jane.

"I'm not really sure," replied Jack as he continued walking toward the living room.

"What's wrong?" asked Jane. "You're always positive and upbeat. For you to say you're 'not sure' scares me."

Turning to face Jane, Jack said, "The guys in Venice that Wilcox and the others asked me to contact came forward and spoke to me today. They wanted to know who I am. How funny that I usually ask people who they are. Today, I had to answer my own question. One of the guys was huge. He was tanned with a butch haircut. I was eating lunch by myself when suddenly these three guys sat at my table. They asked me about my tattoo and then took off."

"That's all they wanted to know?" Jane queried.

Jack stared at Jane and, not to alarm her, replied, "That's all they wanted to know."

MEET YOU AT THE PARK

TWO DAYS LATER Jack checked back with Wilcox. "Agent Wilcox," said Jack. "I haven't heard from you regarding the name Faust. Did you discover anything? I was curious."

Wilcox replied, "No, not a thing. The name Faust appears nowhere with a criminal record or on any wanted list. It's most likely a nickname."

"Oh, OK," answered Jack.

"Look, Jack, I'm on my way to a meeting. I'll call you back later today," said Wilcox.

"No problem. I understand," Jack responded. He thought to himself, *I'm dealing with guys who now know me but I have no idea who they really are or when they will appear. Am I putting myself and my family at risk? One or two more visits to Venice and that's it. Wilcox can give this assignment to someone else then. I'll walk away knowing that I did my best.*

Todd was on a skateboard going down Ocean Front, when he noticed an individual who Faust believed to be an undercover LAPD officer following Jeremy. Todd pushed hard on his skateboard and as he passed Jeremy, without looking at him, he said, "LAPD is behind you. Keep going. Don't make any deals," and he sped away. Jeremy heard the message but did not worry. He had no drugs on him.

No one approached Jeremy as he walked on down Ocean Front. Todd continued on his skateboard and stopped at a stand to get a soft drink. When Todd turned around to leave the stand, Toby, the meth freak with the wild red hair, was in his face. Toby started shouting, "Hey, man. I'll be out of stuff tomorrow. I've got to get my stuff from you or one of the other guys tomorrow. I'll meet one of you at the usual place."

"I'll see what I can do," answered Todd. Toby then disappeared. Todd quickly noticed people looking at him, as if they were trying to understand the conversation.

Todd got back on his skateboard and pushed himself down several streets. He jumped off the skateboard at a certain point and walked a circuitous route to Faust's house. He knocked on the front door but Faust was not home. Because of a prearranged plan, Todd went along the right side of Faust's house to the fourth rose bush, where he dug up a buried glass jar containing the key to Faust's house. Todd unlocked the door, replaced the key in the glass jar and buried it again by the fourth rose bush.

Over an hour later, Faust returned home to find Todd in the living room. "Is there a problem? Why are you here?" asked Faust.

Todd answered, "Remember the guy you thought was an undercover cop? I saw him today and I think he was following Jeremy. Then I was approached by Toby."

Upon hearing Toby's name, Faust screamed, "Goddamit! This is getting fucked up. Toby is a moving advertisement for drugs. I've always thought that fuckin' little dip shit will screw us up. This isn't working anymore. It's too hot around here. We need to get out."

"What should we do?" asked Todd.

Faust paused momentarily and said, "We should deal with Jack."

"Who's Jack?" Todd responded.

"You don't remember, Jack? You of all people should remember him," retorted Faust. "He's the guy you thought had darts for a tattoo. Maybe he can leapfrog us out of this area and we can deal with one person, instead of many people. We have reached a point where the more people we deal with, the greater the opportunities we'll get screwed. We know his name and the company he works for. I believe I have a question that will let me know whether what he has told me is true or not. When you guys see Toby, just disappear."

"No problem," answered Todd. "Jeremy and I will look for the guy—I mean Jack."

"Good, let me know. You know where to find me," said Faust.

Jack returned to Venice three weeks later on a Thursday. He did not know that Todd and Jeremy had been scouring Ocean Front every day looking for him. Jeremy spotted Jack walking alone, as usual, and ran to Muscle Beach. He saw Faust and shouted, "He's here! He's standing by one of the concrete benches near the beach."

"Let's go. Do you remember what to do?" asked Faust.

"I got it down," replied Jeremy.

Jack was checking his watch determining how much longer he could stay, when he noticed from the corner of his eye through the dark glasses that Faust and another individual were walking toward him. It was impossible not to see such a large man approaching. Surprisingly, Faust and Jeremy walked on past him, as Jeremy threw a small wad of paper at Jack. Jack picked it up and unfolded the paper. On it was a written message: "Meet us at this street intersection." Jack thought about the site and said to himself, "It's not far from here and it's in a public place. I'll walk there."

He walked to the coordinates and spotted Jeremy waving to him, directing him into an alley off Main Street. Faust was standing on the other side of a dumpster and said, "Jack, I want to meet you in the MacArthur Park area. Show me what you're talking about."

"I don't get it. Why do you want to go there?" asked Jack. "You guys told me that you don't do anything illegal. Are you trying to set me up? Are you trying to find my guy? Besides, I won't be back there for another month," said Jack.

"I can't wait that long!" screamed Faust.

"Hey, look," yelled Jack, "I have a real job. I meet my guy on a Friday every fifth week. If he would ever see me approaching with someone else, he'd disappear into the crowds. Why are you screaming at me? You don't do anything illegal. Do you remember telling me that?"

Faust looked away and then back at Jack and said, "Sometimes we need to do what we need to do. If I did anything to offend you, it was not intentional. My approach is always a business deal."

"What kind of business deal?" Jack asked.

Faust regained his composure and replied, "You're right, Jack. I did say that. I spoke to some guys I know and I may be able to get your guy some meth. I'll make money, you'll make money and he will make lots of money. Look at me as though you're making an investment. Before we go any further, I want you to show me the area where your guy works."

"That's not a problem," said Jack.

Faust pulled a pen and a piece of paper from his right hand pants' pocket and said, "How do I get there and meet you?"

Jack calmly replied, "Drive north on Lincoln to the 10 Freeway or drive to the 405 Freeway north to the 10 Freeway. Go east on the 10 Freeway and remain on the 10 Freeway until you reach the Hoover exit. Exit on Hoover and turn left. When you cross Venice Boulevard, veer to the right. You'll be on Alvarado Street. In less than a mile, you'll find MacArthur Park on your left. *Puedes hablar español?*" asked Jack.

"What was that?" asked Faust.

"Can you speak Spanish, just in case you get lost? Here's the deal from my end," Jack continued. "If I can make money, I'll meet you."

"The deal from my end is that if I like what I see, you and your buddy will make a lot of money," said Faust.

"OK," said Jack. "I'll meet you next Thursday at Wilshire and Alvarado on the lake side of the park between 10:00 and 11:00 a.m. Bring lots of change, as all street parking is metered. See you in Los Angeles," and Jack turned around and walked away.

Jack's heart was pounding as he returned to his truck and drove away. He had not gone far when he returned to the ally off Fifth Street and switched the magnetic signs. He drove onto the 405 Freeway going south, not realizing he should be going north. Jack's heart was beating so fast, he thought to himself, *I hope I have a strong heart, otherwise my heart is going to blow any second now.* Jack saw Hawthorne Boulevard as the next exit, when it occurred to him, *I can't believe I've been driving south all this time.* He exited on Hawthorne Boulevard and looked for a pay phone as he drove down the street. Spotting one, he quickly parked his truck and called Wilcox.

The phone rang several times and then Jack heard, "Wilcox."

"Agent Wilcox, it's Jack."

"What's up, Jack?" asked Wilcox.

"Agent Wilcox, you won't believe it," said Jack. "The guys in Venice approached me and told me I might be able to make money if I deal with them. The large guy I previously mentioned to you wants to meet me in L.A. at MacArthur Park."

Wilcox responded, "They came forward to meet you and set up this plan? That's unbelievable. They have never come forward before."

"I know," answered Jack. "They bought into some story I made up as I went along. After the guy mentioned meeting me in L.A., I had to improvise. I just kept talking."

"So, now what?" inquired Wilcox.

"I thought you might want to send somebody and take a picture of the guy," Jack replied.

"Where?" asked Wilcox.

"I told him to meet me at the intersection of Alvarado and Wilshire on the lake side of MacArthur Park," said Jack. "We are supposed to meet next Thursday between 10:00 and 11:00 a.m. The guy is huge, tanned and with a crew cut. Make sure you send someone who is scruffy looking, to blend in with the MacArthur Park atmosphere."

"Jack, I want to take this moment to personally thank you for reminding me how to do my job," said Wilcox.

"No problem. Anytime," answered Jack. "Agent Wilcox, I'm in the driver's seat. He has no idea what to expect. Anything I tell him about the area, he'll have to accept. Around that area, I know what I'm talking about."

"What did you mention to him? I want to make sure we send a 'scruffy looking guy,' Wilcox said, laughing. "I'm going to give our photographer a picture of you plus a physical description. Will you be wearing anything distinctive?"

"Yeah," answered Jack. "I'll be wearing a brown baseball cap."

"Go for it, Jack," said Wilcox. "After all this time, you know we'll be there for you."

"I know you will," Jack replied.

The following Thursday, Faust followed Jack's instructions and arrived at MacArthur Park. *This is a different world*, thought Faust as he drove through the area. He parked in the neighborhood Jack had suggested. Faust was placing coins in the meter when he turned around and exclaimed, "Oh, shit, it's you!" as he looked at Jack.

Jack laughed and said, "Yeah, it's me. Follow me and I'll show you the area. There's a lot of stuff going on here."

Faust and Jack walked toward an intersection, when Faust mentioned, "This is a lot different from Venice. I don't feel that comfortable here."

Jack turned to face Faust and said, "Remember, I asked you *Puedes hablar español?* For me it's normal." Jack escorted Faust around the park. "I buy heroin for my cousin right here," Jack explained, as he pointed to a water fountain in the park. "My guy pretends to be drinking water and gives me the stuff as I walk by. I place an envelope with the money under his right foot as he drinks and I just keep walking."

Faust began, "You place money under a guy's foot as you——"

"I told you how it works!" Jack interrupted. "You heard me." Faust did not respond as he and Jack continued down the street to an intersection. They were standing at the intersection among five or six brown guys, when suddenly the group very quickly dispersed in every direction like a spooked covey of quail.

"What's that all about?" asked Faust.

Jack calmly looked at Faust and said, "The police are in the area."

"How do you know that?" rejoined Faust.

Jack told Faust, "Step back from the curb and listen to me. There are gang guys on every corner or every other block. If one guy sees a certain signal or sees other guys disappearing from blocks away, he will in turn disappear. When guys on a particular corner disappear, their accomplices farther down on various corners will disappear. It makes for a great silent and invisible communication system. Wait here and you'll see what I mean." In less than two minutes, an LAPD black and white cruiser drove down the street. "See what I mean?" said Jack as he faced Faust. "I know this area very well."

"I'm sure you do," replied Faust.

Jack hesitated and said, "Faust, you know what else I've learned about coming here?"

"What's that, Jack?" asked Faust.

Jack replied, "If you're in the dirt long enough, you'll become dirty."

Faust stared at Jack as if taken aback by the remark. Slowly, Faust nodded his head up and down and answered, "You're right, Jack. I guess we've become dirty. It wasn't the way I started but it's the way I've become."

"I've been up front with you and shown you the area," said Jack. "You asked me and I delivered. Perhaps we'll meet again," and he walked away.

"Wait a minute, Jack," said Faust. "Maybe we can work with each other."

"How's that?" asked Jack.

"If you have five thousand dollars, you can make a lot of money," said Faust.

"Are you kidding?" answered Jack. "If I took my savings and sold stuff, I might be able to come up with five grand."

"Look," said Faust, "If you buy five grand's worth of stuff from me, you can make an easy thousand dollars by taking the stuff from Venice to this spot. Your guy can buy what I'll supply for six thousand dollars and when he dilutes the quantity per bag, he'll make twelve to fifteen thousand on the street. Everybody wins."

"You mean I can make a thousand dollars just for driving down the freeway?" asked Jack.

"That's right," said Faust. "You can raise your end the more your guy becomes reliant on you as a supplier. It will work out."

"I'll see what I can come up with," Jack stated. "If I come up with the money, then what do I do?"

Faust replied, "Check with your guy if that makes you comfortable; but I guarantee, if he's looking for meth, in short order he'll be making a lot of money and so will you."

"No, that's OK. I believe you," answered Jack.

"When are you back in Venice?" asked Faust.

"I'll be in Venice next Thursday around lunchtime," said Jack.

"That's great," Faust responded. "Park your truck in the public parking lot near the end of Windward. Go to the paddle tennis courts and wait. One of us will meet you there."

"OK," said Jack.

He followed Faust back to where Faust had parked his car. As Faust got into his car, Jack said, "My job takes priority, but I'm planning on being at the paddle tennis courts next Thursday."

"Good, Jack. Someone will meet you at the courts," answered Faust. Jack watched Faust drive away. Then while he slowly walked back to his truck a surreal feeling came over him as he realized he could see the future before it happened.

Jack climbed into his truck and sat there thinking, *The trap is set. Unless something changes, Faust, Toby and Jeremy are doomed.* He reflected on his World War II studies and thought, *How many generals have seen the great trap before it happened?* It then occurred to him, *There is no trap here. There is nothing here. There is no plan. There is no commitment. The situation has not even been relayed or discussed by any of my superiors. It is based on a random conversation with a tentative plan for next Thursday. Jack, you need to inform General Wilcox.*

ARE YOU SURE THAT YOU'RE SURE?

JACK CALLED AGENT Wilcox late that same afternoon. A feeling of calmness came over him as he dialed Wilcox's number. The phone rang several times, and then Jack heard the familiar reply: "Wilcox."

"Agent Wilcox, it's Jack. How are you doing today?"

Wilcox replied, "Jack, I'm doing just fine. And you?"

"I'm OK. I just wanted to let you know that I've got the deal. The Venice guys will sell me meth next Thursday, if I have five thousand dollars."

Wilcox jumped out of his chair and exclaimed, "Jack, are you sure? Are you positive? Are you sure you understood? Don't fool yourself or me about the conversation."

Jack calmly replied, "The guy told me to bring the money and park in the public parking lot at the end of Windward and wait by the paddle tennis courts. Someone will contact me there. It seemed pretty straightforward."

Wilcox again asked, "Jack are you sure that you're sure? When I make a phone call to my boss and we call LAPD, a tremendous number of resources will be mobilized. We will be calling LAPD to let them know what's going down. You need to come to our office at your next opportunity, as soon as possible. We need to coordinate you with LAPD."

"No problem," said Jack. "And yes, I am sure. I can come to your office on Saturday."

"Saturday will be perfect. It will give us almost a week to prepare," answered Wilcox. "We'll get the game plan down and we'll get the money for you." Wilcox immediately checked through his log and notes until he found the name Captain Kessel with LAPD. *That's him,* he thought. *That's the guy.*

Wilcox dialed the number. There was no answer on the direct line, so the call was forwarded. After several more rings, a female voice answered, "Can I help you?"

"Yes, this is Agent Wilcox with NIB. It is imperative that I speak with Captain Kessel," said Wilcox.

"Captain Kessel is in a meeting and will be unavailable for another several hours. May I take a message?"

Wilcox exploded. "No! You tell Captain Kessel to leave his meeting and come to this telephone. Tell him Agent Wilcox is on the phone. He asked us for help and the situation is coming down now. I'll wait another several minutes. Tell him I'm on the line. If necessary, I'll come to your office and barge into his meeting."

"One moment, please. I'll go into the meeting and tell him the urgency of your call. Please hold," she said.

Wilcox suddenly heard a voice say, "Kessel."

"Captain Kessel, this is Agent Wilcox with NIB. We spoke seven or eight months ago regarding the drug ring in Venice. We have a guy who will be making a deal with them next Thursday. They intend to sell him meth. These are the guys who have evaded you for a long time. The deal goes down next Thursday by the paddle tennis courts in Venice. I want to make arrangements with you that all of your officers will have a photo of our guy. Is it possible for you to come to my office this Saturday, to meet our guy and coordinate what everyone needs to do? I also have pictures of the supposed ring leader.

"That's great! Absolutely, I'll be there," said Kessel. "This is an opportunity that has been a long time coming. Give me your address and direct phone number. What time on Saturday?"

"I'll get back to you on the time," answered Wilcox, and he gave Kessel the requested information.

"You must have quite an agent to have penetrated those guys."

Wilcox paused and said, "Yeah, he is quite the guy, even by our standards. Thanks for responding so quickly."

"No problem," answered Kessel.

Wilcox quickly called Jack at home. "Hello," answered Jack.

"Jack, this is Wilcox. What time on Saturday can you come by my office? I have a captain with LAPD coming to my office on Saturday to coordinate everything with you."

"How about 10:00 a.m.?" Jack asked.

"That's perfect," answered Wilcox. "I'll tell the guy from LAPD this Saturday at ten."

Jack went to the NIB office on Saturday morning and was met at the door by Richardson. "Jack, I've been studying the photos taken of you and the guy you met at MacArthur Park. What's the deal with the brown hat you're wearing in the photos?" he asked. "It doesn't match anything else you're wearing."

Wilcox then chimed in, "Yeah, what is the deal with wearing the brown hat?"

Jack looked stoically at Richardson and Wilcox and said, "For the main guy, it means a lot. He thinks it matches what I'm wearing in my soul."

Wilcox and Richardson turned to look at each other. "So what is in your soul?" asked Richardson.

Jack hesitated, looking at the two agents, and said, "I sometimes struggle with myself. I always try to do the right thing. There are times when my best intentions might not bring about the best results. It is important to realize that today's decisions will have long term implications. The long term implication may be detrimental.

Should I contribute to a decision that will be detrimental years from now, I hope other individuals will come forward in the future to rectify the situation. Right now, I have lied and deceived individuals to accomplish what I believe is good. Does the end result override the means? In this case, I believe it does. Maybe I can prevent these guys from ruining another life. You ask what's in my soul. Of course, to always help and support my family. That's obvious. To randomly help and support people unknown to me would not be obvious. Isn't that the great reward, knowing what you have done with no outside recognition and carrying that knowledge within you? How can I look at myself if I stand by and watch evil overtake good?"

Wilcox and Richardson looked at Jack and said nothing. Then Richardson said, "Goddamit, Jack, you are a philosopher! I understood everything you just said. From your previous discussions on philosophy, I gained the confidence to recognize a duck when I see one. Thank God you didn't say something to undermine my confidence in recognizing a duck!" Richardson, Wilcox and Jack started laughing.

Jack went on to say, "Agent Richardson, I know someday I will receive honorary doctorates in philosophy. If you are still into ducks at that time, I will bestow upon you a degree in the name of Doctor Quackenbush, or, if you prefer, Doctor Quack-in-Bush. I will also grant to you the highest degree possible based on my doctorate. That will be *summa cum laude* with hollandaise sauce. Think about it. No degree, or for that matter, no written proclamation, could be rated higher."

"That's perfect. Let me know the thesis to attain that degree. I'm not so concerned with *summa cum laude*, but I love hollandaise sauce," answered Richardson.

Wilcox was not laughing when he said, "Look, you two. We're here to discuss something more important than hollandaise sauce." At that moment, there was a call on the intercom to Agent Wilcox. "Great, send him in," said Wilcox. Officer Kessel entered the room.

Wilcox greeted Kessel at the door and introduced him to Richardson and Jack. "Officer Kessel, this is our man, Jack. He has worked hard for a long time to gain the confidence of the drug guys in Venice. They want to meet him in Venice next Thursday and make a deal."

Officer Kessel turned to Jack and said, "Congratulations. You have penetrated what some undercover officers could not penetrate."

Jack hesitatingly answered, "Thanks."

Wilcox then said, "We need to review these photos."

Wilcox passed copies of the photos to all attending the meeting. The ones that received the most attention were the pictures of Jack and Faust at the corner the park. "Unbelievable!" exclaimed Jack. "This is a photo when Faust first arrived. The guys standing on the corner are in this photo. Man, you are good!" Jack turned around to face Wilcox and Richardson. "Your guy must have been right next to me," said Jack.

Wilcox calmly replied, "Our guy was right behind you taking a lot of pictures and listening to your explanation. Do you remember telling Faust why the guys on the corner went in every direction?"

"Of course," said Jack.

Wilcox then gave Captain Kessel a photo of Jack's truck with the NID supplied magnetic signs. "This is the truck Jack will be driving," Wilcox said.

Captain Kessel intervened at this point in the conversation. "Jack, it is imperative that you wear the same clothing you are wearing in this photo, including that brown hat. These pictures will be supplied to multiple LAPD officers. We want to make sure that our officers distinguish you from the bad guys. Jack, there will be a lot of firepower there. Obey every directive made. You will be placed on the ground, hands behind your back. You will be handled roughly—the purpose being that there is no apparent informant. I want to confirm that the meeting place is the paddle tennis courts near the parking lot at the end of Windward. Is that correct?"

"Yes, it is," answered Jack.

"Well, everything will be put directly into motion. We will have undercover officers moving into the area from early to midmorning. Jack, let me emphasize that you wear the exact same clothing you are wearing in the photo. Here is a checklist of everything you need to do and expect. Take a few minutes and review it. Let me know if you have any specific questions while we are all here," said Captain Kessel.

Jack reviewed the list and said, "It all seems very straightforward."

"OK, Jack, this is my phone number," Kessel stated. "Call me approximately ten minutes before you arrive. This is my partner's phone number as a backup."

"Jack, you need to come by this office on Thursday morning to get the money, or if that's not possible, let me know where we can meet," said Wilcox.

"You know, Agent Wilcox, I have a feeling the morning will go by very quickly. Can I meet you and Agent Richardson in the Venice area?" asked Jack.

"That's not a problem. Where do you want us to meet you?" asked Wilcox.

"I'd like to meet you guys in the alley off Fifth Street between Westminster and San Juan," answered Jack.

"Richardson and I will meet you there," Wilcox responded. "How about 8:00 a.m. to give you plenty of time? Richardson and I were going to be in the general area anyway."

"Why's that?" asked Jack.

Wilcox smiled and replied, "When it all comes down, I want to make sure that Richardson and I are the first to congratulate you."

Jack looked at Wilcox and said, "I want to thank you guys for your support and encouragement."

All were still seated in the room, when Wilcox looked at Jack and said, "Are you OK with this? This is the time to speak up if you don't want to go through with it. Nothing will be said one way or the other. We can't demand that you continue."

Captain Kessel interjected, "Jack, based on this scenario, when you leave the alley, we'll have an undercover officer following you from a distance. He'll follow you down Windward so as to not betray his presence. Just like Agent Richardson's question, are you OK with the overall situation?"

"I'm OK. It's been a long time and I'm ready," answered Jack. At that point the meeting was adjourned and everyone went on their way.

GOING SOUTH

THE NEXT FEW days went by quickly for Jack, filled with the normal routines of his job. On Wednesday evening he arrived home and, greeted the family as usual. He reviewed homework assignments with the kids and then the children went their own ways while Jane prepared dinner. Jack entered his bedroom and picked out the clothes to match those in the photograph, placed the clothing on an ottoman and returned to the kitchen.

Jane said, "You're awfully quiet tonight. That's very unusual. What's wrong, Jack?"

"Nothing's wrong. I'm just tired," answered Jack.

"No, you're not. There's something else going on. What is it?" asked Jane.

"Tomorrow is the day I make the deal with the drug guys in Venice. I didn't tell you sooner because I didn't want you to be scared or not sleep at night. I'm a little nervous but I have to go through with it. LAPD and NID will be there. It's all arranged. If all goes according to plan, the guys in Venice will be going south real soon," said Jack.

Jane absorbed Jack's words intently. Her eyes welled with tears as she started to cry. "I'm scared, Jack. I know how much time you have put into this effort. I guess I never thought this day would really arrive but now it's here. Please be careful," said Jane.

"Of course I'll be careful. There will be a lot of guys there to protect me," Jack replied.

"I'll feed the kids now and we'll eat later," said Jane.

"Sounds good to me," responded Jack.

Jack reviewed the checklist while the kids ate dinner. When the children had finished their meal, Jack asked them, "How was school today?"

Tom answered, "You know, Dad, nothing new. The same old stuff."

"That's exactly right," chimed in Joanie. Tom and Joanie left the room.

"I had a great day at school," exclaimed Suzanne.

"You did?" Jack said. "What made it a great day?"

Suzanne replied, "We've been studying the American Revolution. I can't believe how smart and brave those guys were."

"What guys?" asked Jack.

"The Founders who signed the Declaration of Independence and the volunteers who fought with George Washington," answered Suzanne.

"The guys you mentioned were very smart and very brave," responded Jack. "Their ideas and bravery live with us today in our Constitution. Their ideas and bravery were recognized two hundred years ago and will be recognized two hundred years from now."

"That's amazing how you said that," Suzanne exclaimed.

"I guess you get that from my side of the family," Jack said, laughingly.

"What does that mean?" asked Suzanne.

"I am easily amazed," replied Jack. "You said it was amazing how I made some remark. When you are amazed, it makes you stop and wonder. When you stop and wonder, it makes you stop and think."

Suzanne stared at Jack and replied, "You know, Dad, you're amazing. Listening to you has got me thinking."

"Well, it's getting late. Why don't you save your thinking for tomorrow at school and hit the sack?" said Jack"

"OK, I will," answered Suzanne.

She had started going upstairs, when Jack said, "Suzanne." She stopped and turned around to face him. "Mom and I are lucky to have kids like you three," said Jack.

Suzanne replied, smiling, "We're pretty lucky that we have parents like you and Mom," and she went on up the stairs.

Jack returned to the kitchen and set the table. When Jane had finished cooking their dinner, she turned to face Jack and said, "Come over and help yourself." Jack picked out the various vegetables and pieces of chicken

Jane had prepared and placed them on his plate, then he walked over to the table and sat down to join her.

"So, what's going to happen tomorrow? Why am I so scared and nervous when you seem to be so calm, almost stoic. Do you know something I don't?" asked Jane.

"Jane, there will be a lot of police officers in the area. They will be watching me from the moment I enter the place. Agents Wilcox and Richardson will be there to make sure I'm OK. The most calming idea is that the transaction is in an open public area. It's not like I have to meet them in some remote region of the desert," said Jack.

"That makes me feel better, but I'm still not sure I'll get a good night's sleep tonight," said Jane.

"I'm not sure I'll get a good night's sleep either," responded Jack. "Oh, well. We can randomly talk to each other during the night when we can't sleep, but I'm confident it will all work out."

"OK, then. If you're confident, then I am too," answered Jane.

When dinner was finished, Jane cleared off the table while Jack swept the floor. When he had finished he turned to Jane and said, "I guess I'll go and get ready for bed."

"Isn't it a little early?" Jane asked.

"It might be. Remember the saying 'Early to bed, early to rise, makes a man healthy, wealthy and wise." Jack glanced back at Jane and said, "Tomorrow I need to be wise."

"You will be, Jack. You usually are," Jane replied.

Jack started laughing when he said, "Well, Jane, you know I've had my share of screw-ups. I think tomorrow, though, will work out just fine."

The next morning Jack got out of bed at 4:30 a.m.

"Why are you up so early?" Jane asked.

"I don't know. I feel like I'm leaving for a hunting trip," replied Jack. "The adrenalin is already pumping."

"Slow down, Jack. You're not leaving for a hunting trip," said Jane.

Jack looked at her and said, "Well, in a roundabout way I *am* going on a hunting trip."

Jane looked at Jack but said nothing as she got out of bed and left the room. Jack showered and dressed. When he entered the kitchen, Jane had coffee brewing. She poured a cup for him and for herself. "You know, Jack. I slept well last night. Just knowing you were confident, and the plan that was developed around you seemed to be so complete," said Jane.

"The plan is complete. It will work just fine. In fact, I'm excited to see the plan as it unfolds. I'm on the side of the guys doing the 'right thing.' Anyway, it's time for me to get going. I love you very much and I'll see you and the kids later today." Jack hugged Jane and then left the house.

He drove to the office, as on any other day, to review upcoming jobs and current contracts, making notes of these on a sheet of paper. The purpose was to list any new contractors and review the jobs of longtime company customers.

That same morning LAPD was making arrangements throughout Venice. Male and female LAPD officers posed as tourists, holding hands as they visited the varied shops along Ocean Front. Several LAPD officers were disguised as custodians as they cleaned the beach and swept the boardwalk. One LAPD officer, who was a member of a world-famous club in Hollywood, pretended to be a street performer, astounding those who passed by with his card magic. Two other undercover officers, in an adjacent alley, pretended to be homeless. Despite their location and disguise, they all had photos and descriptions of Jack.

Jack headed for Venice after leaving the corporate office. Before arriving in Venice, he replaced his employer's magnetic signs with the agency's signs. He drove to the alley off Fifth Street between San Juan and Westminster and waited.

Forty-five minutes later, two vehicles came down the alley. Agents Wilcox and Richardson got out of their car. "Jack, how the hell did you ever find this place?" asked Wilcox. "I had to enter the location twice in my GPS."

Jack smiled and said, "I told you in my initial interview that I get around."

Wilcox said, "Jack, I brought the five thousand for you, as agreed," and he handed Jack a roll of fifty one hundred dollar bills.

"Thank you, Agent Wilcox," said Jack, taking the money.

At that point, another individual came forward from the second vehicle. It was Captain Kessel. "Good morning, Jack. LAPD is ready if you are ready. All officers here have your photo from MacArthur Park, and I'm glad you're wearing the same clothing today that appears in that photograph. Do you have any other questions for me or what LAPD will be doing?" asked Kessel.

"No. I'm ready," answered Jack.

Captain Kessel then said, "Jack, when you leave the alley you will be turning right to head toward Windward. When you leave the alley and turn right, you will pass a pickup truck with faded red paint and dents on both sides of the body. The truck will be driven by one of our undercover officers. He will follow from approximately one to two blocks behind you. He knows where you're going, so he will remain at a distance, just to make sure you are protected from behind. When you enter the designated parking lot, he will park his truck on some street at his discretion and walk along the boardwalk. When the signal is given, he will be with the other LAPD officers to make the arrests of the drug guys here in Venice."

Jack looked at Captain Kessel and Agents Wilcox and Richardson. "I want to thank you guys for supporting me," he said. "I have put a lot of time and effort into this endeavor, and I know you have also put a lot of time and effort into supporting me. I'm a history guy and I feel that later today will be decisive."

Agent Wilcox looked at Jack and said, "Jack, we have no doubts that you are a history guy. Because of that, we knew you had the situation well calculated in advance."

"Well, I guess it's time for me to head down the road," said Jack.

Wilcox replied, "Yes, it is; but just remember, Richardson and I will meet you at the end of the road. See you there."

"I will meet you there," said Jack as he shook hands with Wilcox and Richardson.

Jack climbed into his truck and drove down the alley and turned right. He quickly passed the faded red truck. As Jack reached the street corner, he looked into the rearview mirror to see the pickup truck pull away from the curb and follow him. He noticed the truck drifting farther behind as he drove down Windward.

Jack arrived in Venice. His heart was beating so hard that he thought, *Relax, go forward and just do it.* He parked the truck in the lot at the end of Windward and paid the lot attendant for two hours of parking. Then he walked to the paddle tennis courts. All the LAPD officers, in their various disguises, recognized Jack from their supplied photos. Jack had been standing by the paddle tennis courts for almost an hour, when from his right Toby and Jeremy passed him and said, "Follow us."

Jack followed them back to his truck where he found Faust leaning on the driver's side door. "What's with this removable sign? You can remove it anytime. So what's the deal?" asked Faust.

"You're right," answered Jack. "The company I work for always wants to know what our competitors are doing. They tell us to remove the signs so our competitors and their customers will not see us. That way we learn what they are doing. Does that make sense?"

Faust stared at Jack and said, "That makes sense. Did you bring the money?"

"I did. This is almost all of my savings. Here it is," said Jack, and he gave Faust the roll of one hundred dollar bills.

Faust counted the money. He looked at Jack and then handed him a large plastic bag with many small bags inside. "Let me know how it goes. Your guy will always rely on you," he said.

Faust had walked a short distance, when LAPD came from every angle between the parked cars. Officers screamed, "Everyone on the ground now!" Faust turned to face the officers only to be met with additional orders to obey and realized that three semiautomatic pistols were pointed at his torso and head. "Down now!" screamed the officers. Faust was forced to the ground by several officers. His hands were held behind his back and handcuffs were placed on him as he unleashed a sea of obscene expletives. Toby, also on the ground, started crying. Jeremy said nothing as his hands were placed behind his back and handcuffed. Jack was face down on the concrete next to them in handcuffs as well. One officer had his foot on Jack's back to make sure there would be no problem.

After Toby, Jeremy and Faust had been taken away, Wilcox and Richardson approached LAPD. Wilcox identified himself as part of the NID and said to an officer, "We'll take responsibility for him."

"No problem," said the officer. Jack was released from his handcuffs.

"Jack, you did a hell of a job," said Wilcox. Jack did not look at them or respond to their comments. He just looked straight ahead. "Are you OK?" asked Wilcox.

Richardson then said, "Jack, talk to us. What are you thinking?"

Jack still stared ahead. Slowly he turned to face Wilcox and Richardson and said, "Who would ever think that knowing the history of the Nazis or their movement would ever produce something good?"

"Jack, your knowledge of the Second World War established a bond or similarity with the main guy. It made him trust you," said Richardson.

Jack looked at Wilcox and Richardson for a moment before responding: "I'm in the construction business. I associate with people who improve the lives of others. Faust is in the *de*struction business. He associates with guys who destroy the lives of others."

Wilcox said, "Jack, I'll get with you later. You need to do a debriefing with us and LAPD. There will also be the issue of testifying in court against these guys sometime in the future."

"That's not a problem. I need to get going," Jack answered.

"Go ahead. You should be very proud of yourself," said Wilcox.

"Damn right," added Richardson. "You should be very proud of yourself."

"Thanks, guys. I'll see you soon," said Jack as he walked away. He went back to his truck in the lot and drove away. Returning to the alley off Fifth Street, he placed his employer's signs on the truck, changed his clothes and returned to Venice Beach. He parked on Venice South and placed coins in the meter. Then he walked toward the beach, hands in his pockets, and sat on a bench facing the ocean. As he watched the breaking waves, he thought to himself, *Jack, don't be proud of yourself. Pride compounded too many times can lead to arrogance. How many times throughout history has arrogance contributed to self-inflicted humiliation and downfall?* Jack was staring at the waves, when General Beaufre's words "Victory is a very dangerous opportunity" crossed his mind. [22] Jack thought to himself, *Don't you ever forget General Beaufre's words. Victory presents the opportunity to lure oneself into believing that strategies and policies of the past will automatically work again in the future. Jack, always approach a new situation from the stance of humility. It will make you assess the situation more carefully and research it more thoroughly. Always remember that times change, situations change and, most importantly, opponents change. Never underestimate the opponent. If you do underestimate the opponent and you are taken by surprise, you will catch holy hell from Frederick the Great—and you don't want that!*

Jack walked slowly back to the truck. He climbed into the cabin, grabbed the phone and called home. After several rings Jane answered the phone and said, "Hello."

"Jane, it's me. Everything went great. It's all over. The Venice guy's were arrested earlier today."

"Oh, my God!" exclaimed Jane. "I'm so glad to hear your voice and know that you are OK. So what happened?"

"You know, Jane, right now I'm still operating on adrenalin. Do you think there are a couple bottles of wine in the house?" asked Jack.

"I'm sure we have a couple of bottles," replied Jane.

"Good. Pick out two bottles—one for you and one for me. I'll review what happened today with you later when I get home," said Jack.

"Jack, that is so great. I'm so proud of you," she responded happily.

"Jane, don't be proud of me, and I'll explain that when I get home," Jack said.

Jane smiled at her end of the telephone. "All right, Jack. I won't be proud of you. I'll just think of you as the great dad and husband you are."

GOING NORTH

TWO WEEKS LATER, Jack and Jane were making preparations to leave for a well deserved vacation. Jack drove the three children to his mother's house in the San Fernando Valley. He helped the kids unload their suitcases from the car and carry them to their respective rooms. While the kids were unpacking their cases, Jack approached his mother and said, "Thanks, Mom, for watching these characters. Jane and I appreciate it very much."

"Jack, it's never a problem. I always enjoy being with them. You both know that. Besides, they like my rules better than they like yours," Jack's mom said with a laugh.

"That they do," Jack replied. When the kids eventually came into the living room, Jack told them, "I better not hear of any problems when I get back."

"Aw, come on, Dad" said Joanie. "We're never a problem for Grandma. She's a lot of fun and lets us do what we want almost. There's around-the-clock ice cream and gum drops. Who's going to complain?"

Jack started laughing and said, "You're right. Grandma hasn't changed over the years. I love you guys very much," and he hugged Tom, Joanie and Suzanne. "Thanks, Mom," said Jack as he gave her a hug. "I love you very much and thanks for always helping us."

"You and Jane have a great time in San Francisco and don't worry about us. We're going to have a great time here," said Jack's mom.

"Thanks again, Mom," said Jack as he headed out the door. He got into the family car and made several stops on the way home to get water, snacks and other items Jane had requested.

Jack was walking out of a market, when he noticed a man in his mid-thirties with an unusual looking dog. The guy was looking away from Jack, reaching for a newspaper, when Jack asked, "What kind of dog is that?"

Without turning around and facing Jack, he answered, "A Wheaten Terrier."

Jack was not sure he understood and said, "What kind of terrier?"

The man suddenly turned around and with an annoyed look on his face said loudly, "A Wheaten Terrier."

"Oh, OK," Jack replied, slightly taken aback.

Jack arrived home and started putting suitcases in the car. Jane grabbed some additional items, got into the car, and off they went. They had decided to take Highway 101, the scenic route to northern California. They would follow the El Camino Real and pass the Spanish missions.

Jack and Jane stopped in beautiful Santa Barbara, parked the car and walked along State Street. Jane enjoyed the boutiques and the trendy shops, and while she was in the stores, Jack stayed outside and "people watched." Later they found an outdoor restaurant and ordered lunch. While waiting for their order, Jack said, "I saw this guy with an unusual looking dog when I left the market this morning. I asked him what kind of dog it was and when he answered, I didn't quite catch the name. Then when I asked him again, he responded as if I was bugging him."

"Well, Jack, maybe you were bugging him," answered Jane.

"Well, if I was bugging him, that's his fault," said Jack.

"Now, how do you figure that, Jack? You're the one asking the questions," Jane asked.

"If he had a recognizable breed, I wouldn't have to ask him what type of dog it was. He probably hears that all the time. Think about it. How often do you see a pad of steel wool with four legs and a tail?" said Jack.

"Here comes lunch," said Jane. "Drop the dog story."

"OK," said Jack.

Jack and Jane enjoyed their lunch and afterwards resumed walking along State Street. Finally, they returned to their car and entered Highway 101 heading north. Driving along the beautiful coastal highway, they passed the towns of Buellton, Solvang, Santa Maria and San Luis Obispo. In Paso Robles Jack pulled off the highway to get a soft drink for Jane and himself, and then they continued traveling north. After only nine miles, he suddenly turned off the highway at the San Miguel exit.

"What are we doing?" asked Jane.

"I want to show you something," said Jack as he made a right turn off the exit ramp. He followed the road and pulled into a dirt lot across from the local bar.

Jane looked outside the window and said, "Jack, this is just a dirt field. I'm sure you didn't bring me here to look at dirt."

"Of course not. This is where Uncle Val and I meet Ed Willis on the boar hunts," said Jack. "I wanted to show you so that the next time we go boar hunting, you'll know where we meet Ed."

"I'm just giving you a hard time," answered Jane, laughingly. "You know I'm glad that you and Uncle Val and your buddies enjoy the hunting trips. Now I'll always be able to visualize the place where you guys meet."

"I want to show you something else," Jack said.

"Well, OK, I'm ready. Show me," said Jane.

Jack drove a short distance and announced, "Here we are."

"What's this?" asked Jane. "It looks like an old building that's ready to collapse."

"This is Misión San Miguel Arcángel or Mission Saint Michael the Archangel. It was founded by Padre Lasuén in 1797. I contacted the rector, Father Thompson, and told him that I wanted to visit the mission on our way to San Francisco so that I could show it to you."

"Let's take a closer look," said Jane.

Jack parked the car in a small lot and opened the car door for his wife. They crossed the mission courtyard and headed for the church. Entering the church, they looked around at the paintings and statues. "Amazing," said Jack. "Padres like Lasuén had no idea where they were headed, but they just kept going. I remember my dad telling me, a long time ago, to 'be like them.' Jack grabbed Jane's hand and said, "Come on, let's go." They walked toward the rectory door. Jack knocked on the door and waited.

A minute went by before a Catholic priest opened the door. "Father Thompson?" asked Jack.

"I am," answered Father Thompson.

"Father Thompson, I am Jack Avila and this is my wife, Jane," said Jack.

"Jack and Jane Avila, it is a pleasure to meet you. Please come in." Father Thompson and Jack had exchanged some small talk when Father Thompson said, "I want to thank both of you for your generous contribution to our rebuilding program." Jane gasped. Jack had never mentioned anything to her about a contribution to the mission. She fumed inwardly with embarrassment but said nothing.

"No problem," answered Jack. "I'm glad we could help."

"Oh, by the way, we honored your request," said Father Thompson.

"I know," said Jack. "I saw it when we entered the courtyard."

"I'll go look at it," said Jane, and she left the room.

"Your contribution came at the right time. I was about at my wits end when your contribution arrived. We have tried various fundraising activities but it is very difficult for missions in rural areas or off the beaten path. I was getting discouraged," said Father Thompson.

"Don't get discouraged," responded Jack. "Look, Father Thompson, when I have a problem or need to be creative I tell myself, *Machen Sie das Fenster auf*, which is German for 'open the window,' like open the window to your mind. No matter what my situation, I tell myself that phrase, take a deep breath, think about the dilemma, and eventually I come up with a solution. It always works."

"I like that phrase. It sounds rather snappy. What is it, again?" asked Father Thompson.

"*Machen Sie das Fenster auf*," replied Jack.

"Let me find a pen and paper. I want to write it down." Father Thompson left the room. He returned and sat at his desk. "OK, Jack, what is the spelling?" he asked.

Jack started saying the letters, "Capital *M* as in Mary. Hey, Father Thompson, it must be an appropriate phrase if it starts off with *M* as in Mary!"

Father Thompson looked up from his desk, smiled at Jack and said, "Indeed."

Jack continued spelling out the phrase, letter by letter, while the rector carefully copied it down. When he had finished, he repeated the phrase, "*Machen Sie das Fenster auf.*"

Father Thompson reviewed his notes and slowly said, "*Machen Sie das Fenster auf.* Is that accurate?"

"That's perfect," answered Jack. "Well, Father, it's been a pleasure talking to you. Jane and I are going to San Francisco for a getaway vacation. We need to get going,"

"Very well," Father Thompson replied. "I am most grateful for your contribution and the opportunity to meet you and Jane."

"Thanks, Father," said Jack as he left the rectory.

Father Thompson closed the door when Jack left the room and turned around to go to his desk. He looked at his notes, repeating, "*Machen Sie das Fenster auf. Machen Sie das Fenster auf.*" He was about to sit down when he noticed the rectory window was closed. He thought to himself, *Machen Sie das Fenster auf. Open the window*, and he walked over and opened the rectory window. A strong breeze made the curtains flutter. Father Thompson took in a deep breath and thought, *This is very refreshing.* He looked out the open window to see Jack and Jane standing in the courtyard.

After leaving the rectory office, Jack approached Jane in the courtyard. Jane turned to him and said, "I'm so mad at you right now, Jack, I could almost slap you."

Unruffled, Jack inquired, "What's the problem? Why are you so mad?"

"You didn't tell me that you contributed money to this mission. I think that was deceitful not to tell me until we were here," said Jane.

"What are you talking about, Jane? I brought you here to surprise you. It would be deceitful if we hadn't stopped here and I had never mentioned it to you. Besides, do you see what is waving in the wind right above you?" asked Jack. Before Jane could respond, Jack continued, "I also donated the Spanish flag at the top of the flagpole. I wanted to add historical authenticity to this site."

"I don't care what you added," snapped Jane. "You took a part time job to help our kids get through college someday and then you give part of it away. How much did you donate?"

"I'm not going to tell you right now," said Jack.

"No, Jack. I want to know right now," demanded Jane, raising her voice.

"I don't care what you want to know right now. I'll tell you when we get back to the car," responded Jack.

"Why do I have to wait?" asked Jane.

"Because I don't believe yelling is appropriate on mission property," Jack answered. Jane huffed and quickly turned away.

Jack reached the car while Jane opened the passenger side door and got in. He sat down in the driver's seat and asked, "OK, Jane. What do you want to know?"

"I don't like surprises," Jane yelled.

"What do you mean, you don't like surprises? Of course you do," Jack replied calmly.

"No, I don't," Jane snapped.

"OK, then on your next birthday, when I hand you a gift wrapped in decorative paper with a ribbon and a bow, just before you open it, I'll tell you what's inside; that way you won't be surprised."

"Don't be a jerk," Jane said.

"Don't get mad at me when I make you reflect upon your own words," Jack rejoined.

"Jack, just leave me alone for a while," said Jane.

"No, problem," he answered.

Jack returned to Highway 101 and started driving north again. Jane kept looking out the window to her right, away from her husband. There was no conversation. Twenty miles later, Jack said, "You know, Jane, giving me the silent treatment never works. In fact, I enjoy it. I know the longer you're quiet means the longer you're evaluating what I said."

"Shut up, Jack," said Jane, as she continued looking to her right.

"OK, Jane, you win. I'll shut up. But while you torment yourself, I'm going to enjoy the drive through beautiful countryside." Jack suddenly said, "Jane, look at the deer in the field." She still sat looking out her side window. Jack started teasing her. "Jane, they are over here, on my side of the road." She kept her eyes focused to her right. "Too bad," said Jack. "We passed them." Jane did not respond. Jack went on to say, "You know what I think, Jane? Deer are everywhere, but right before the hunting season they disappear. I wouldn't be surprised to learn that they use their large numbers to get great group rates and vacation in Miami during the hunting season."

Jane did not look at Jack. Staring out her window, she shook her head. "Jack, just be quiet," she said.

Jack replied, "OK, I'll be quiet and turn on the radio." Jack switched on the radio and quickly realized the song playing was "Little Lies" by Fleetwood Mac. "Uh-oh. We don't want to listen to that song, do we, Jane?"

A moment later, Jane shrugged her shoulders and turned to face Jack. "I guess I jumped off the deep end when Father Thompson mentioned the donation. I initially felt insulted that I was not included. I know that you are a great dad and husband—and, I might add, a great 'history guy'—and would never intentionally hurt my feelings. As you would say, 'Think it all the way through,' but I didn't. I'm sorry I got angry with you," Jane said.

"Jane, that's OK," replied Jack. "You know when you get mad at me I don't listen to you anyway."

"Well, I guess sometimes that's a good thing," remarked Jane.

Jack said with a smile, "Let's just enjoy the drive." He found an oldies radio station along the central coast, as they drove further north, and turned up the volume so they could enjoy the song that was playing.

At its conclusion, the disc jockey announced, "That was 'You Can Do Magic' by America."

Jack turned to Jane and said, "That was a really good song. I don't know anything about the band, but they named themselves after a great country."

"They did. We're lucky we were born in America," exclaimed Jane.

"That's for sure," Jack replied, "We are very, very lucky."

Sie müssen sich immer errinern,
Wenn Sie ein Problem haben,
Machen Sie das Fenster auf.
Machen Sie das Fenster zu Ihrer Phantasie auf.

You must always remember,
If you have a problem,
Open the window.
Open the window to your mind.

ENDNOTES

(1) Hernan Cortes

(2) Hernando de Soto

(3) Juan Ponce de Leon

(4) Junipero Serra

(5) Fermin Lasuen

(6) Juan Crespi

(7) Bernardo O'Higgins

(8) The Gordian Knot

(9) Carl Philipp Gottilieb von Clausewitz

(10) Frederick the Great

(11) The false street markings

(12) The Diagram given to Wilcox

(13) The covered bus stop bench at Sunset and Cherokee

(14) The Hollywood Sign from the top of Deronda Drive

(15) The Hungarian Revolution Monument

(16) Monikers of the 18th Street Gang

(17) The Pillar entrance to Lincoln Park

(18) The Balkan Cross

(19) General Dwight D. Eisenhower

(20) Panzerfaust

(21) The lightning bolts of the SA

(22) General Andre Beaufre

Blitzkreig (This final footnote entry has no numerical reference. It is an extension relating to the last several sentences in the General Andre Beaufre description.)

1. Hernan Cortes (1485-1547)

In 1518, Hernan Cortes was appointed by Cuba's governor, Diego Velazguez de Cuellar, to lead the third expedition to the Mexican mainland. Its purpose was to explore and secure the interior of Mexico for colonization. The expedition was recalled at the last moment but Cortes ignored the order, and the Spanish expeditionary force, consisting of 500 men, several pieces of artillery and 13 horses, landed in February 1519 on the Yucatan Peninsula in the Mayan territory. In March 1519, Cortes formally claimed the land for the Spanish crown.

Stopping in Trinidad to hire more soldiers and obtain more horses, Cortes proceeded to Tabasco, where he won a battle against the natives. From the vanquished people he received twenty young indigenous women, all of whom he converted. Among these women was La Malinche. Malinche knew the Nahuatl (Aztec) language and also Mayan, thus enabling Cortes to communicate in both. Quickly learning Spanish, she became a very valuable interpreter and counselor, and through her help Cortes learned from the Tabascans about the wealthy Aztec Empire.

In July 1519 his men overtook Veracruz. In Veracruz, Cortes met some of Moctezuma's subjects and asked them to arrange a meeting with their ruler. Moctezuma repeatedly turned down the meeting, but Cortes was determined. Leaving a hundred men in Veracruz, Cortes marched on Tenochtitlan, the Aztec capital, in mid-August, along with 600 men, 15 horsemen, 15 cannons, and hundreds of indigenous carriers and warriors. On the way, he made alliances with native tribes such as the Tlaxcalans and the Tonoacs.

The Tlaxcalans were a hardy and industrious people. They had never been conquered by the Aztecs and Aztec allies. They attacked the Spanish with large numbers of warriors on several occasions; however, the Tlaxcalans were defeated in every battle, due to the Spaniards' use of muskets, crossbows and artillery, along with their terrifying cavalry. The Tlaxcalans had never seen a horse, as the horse had disappeared from North America thousands of years before, and to these people the horse was a supernatural creature.

The Tlaxcalans sent emissaries to Cortes. They saw in the Spanish a vehicle to topple the despised Aztecs, while Cortes viewed the Tiaxcalans as the large force of allies he would need as he continued inland.

The Tlaxcalans guided the Spanish to Tenochtitlan, and on November 8, 1519, the Aztec emperor, Moctezuma, peacefully welcomed Cortes into the great city. Moctezuma deliberately let the Spanish enter the heart of the Aztec Empire, hoping to get to know their weaknesses so as to crush them later. He gave them lavish gifts in gold, which enticed them to plunder vast additional amounts of gold.

Learning that Spaniards on the coast had been attacked, Cortes took Moctezuma hostage in his own palace as a precaution, requesting him to swear allegiance to Charles V.

Meanwhile, the governor of Cuba had sent another expedition, comprising 1,100 men led by Panfilo de Narvaez, to arrest Cortes for insubordination. The ships arrived in Mexico in April 1520, and when the news reached Cortes, he left 200 men in Tenochititlan and marched to the coast, where he defeated Narvaez despite his numerical inferiority. When Cortes told the defeated soldiers about the city of gold, they agreed to join him.

During his absence, Cortes's men had attacked and killed Aztec nobles in the main temple. Then, upon his return in late June, Cortes found the Aztecs had elected a new king. Shortly, thereafter, the Aztecs besieged the palace housing the Spaniards and Moctezuma. Cortes ordered Moctezuma to speak to his people from a palace balcony and persuade them to let the Spanish return to the coast in peace; but during the rebellion Moctezuma was stoned to death by his subjects and Cortes decided to flee to Tlaxcala. Much of the treasure looted by Cortes was lost (as well as his artillery) during this panicked escape from Tenochtitlan.

With the assistance of their allies and reinforcements arriving from Cuba, Cortes's men finally prevailed. Cortes designed and commanded a siege of Tenochtitlan. Newly constructed ships, with musketeers on board and some vessels carrying small artillery pieces, sailed the lake to prevent supplies from arriving in the city by canoe. The causeways were blocked by Spanish soldiers, cavalry and thousands of Indian reinforcements. During the fighting that ensued, many inhabitants fled the city and the Aztec forces were severely worn down.

A key element in the fall of Tenochtitlan was the manipulation of local functions and divisions by Cortes. Numerous battles were fought between the Aztecs and the Spanish army, which was composed of predominantly indigenous peoples; but it was the siege of Tenochtitlan that was the final, decisive battle that led to the downfall of the Aztec civilization. When Tenochtitlan fell in August 1521, it ended the rule of the Aztecs in central Mexico.

This marked the conclusion of the first phase of the Spanish conquest of Mexico; and with the help of their new allies, the Spaniards would soon spread their influence to all parts of the country.

2. Hernando de Soto (1496-1542)

Hernando de Soto was a Spanish explorer, who sailed to the New World in 1514. During this time, he was greatly influenced by Juan Ponce de Leon, who discovered Florida, Vasco Nunez de Balboa, who discovered the Pacific Ocean, and Ferdinand Magellan, who circumnavigated the world. An excellent horseman, leader and tactician, he would serve as an officer with Pizzaro in 1530 in the conquest of the Incas in Peru.

In 1540, de Soto explored through modern day Georgia, South and North Carolina, Tennessee and Alabama. Along a river in southern Alabama, de Soto was led into Mabila, a fortified city, where his army was ambushed by the Mobilian tribe, under Chief Tuskaloosa. The Spanish repelled the attack and burned the town to the ground.

In the spring of 1541, de Soto would continue exploring west through Mississippi, Arkansas, Oklahoma, Louisiana and Texas, and on May 8, 1541, he and his troops arrived at the Mississippi River. They were the first Europeans to see the area described by Native Americans as the Valley of the Vapors, which is known today as Hot Springs, Arkansas.

Beyond his explorations, de Soto left other traces of his presence. It is believed the horses that escaped from his expeditions contributed to the wild mustangs and Indian ponies of North America. Hundreds of years later, Lewis and Clark would describe native Indians and their horses. The Eurasian swine brought with de Soto as a food source were ancestors of the current Razorback hogs of the southeastern United States.

De Soto died of fever on May 21, 1542, in the Indian village of Guachoya, near the present town of McArthur, Arkansas.

3. Juan Ponce de Leon (1474-1521)

Juan Ponce de Leon was a Spanish explorer and military officer, who sailed with Columbus in September 1493 on the second expedition to the New World. In November, the fleet arrived on the island of Hispanola, which several years later would become Ponce de Leon's base.

In 1508, he was given permission to explore the island of San Juan Bautista, now known as Puerto Rico, where he created the first settlement.

In 1512, Ponce de Leon was granted the authority to explore for lands north of Hispaniola, and on March 4, 1513, he set out with three ships and 200 men, sailing northwest along what are now known as the Bahama Islands. Continuing west for several days, the fleet landed on what Ponce de Leon believed to be another island and which he named La Florida, in recognition of the verdant landscape and because it was the Easter season, which the Spaniards called Pascua Florida (Festival of Flowers). It was the Florida peninsula.

Ponce de Leon returned to Florida in 1521 on a colonizing expedition. However, soon after landing, he was injured in an attack by Calusa braves and later died from his wound. His body was laid to rest in the Cathedral of San Juan Bautista in Old San Juan, Puerto Rico.

Pedro Menendez , following in the footsteps of Ponce de Leon, sighted land on August 28, 1565, along the northern Florida coast. It was the feast day of Saint Augustine of Hippo. He came ashore and named his settlement Saint Augustine. Saint Augustine is the longest continuously occupied European-founded city in North America. It was

founded 21 years before the British settlement at Roanoke and 42 years before Santa Fe, New Mexico, and Jamestown, Virginia. Only San Juan, Puerto Rico, is older than Saint Augustine.

Martin de Arguelles was born in Saint Augustine in 1566. This is the first recorded birth of a child of European ancestry in what is now considered the continental United States. The first recorded birth of a black child, in the Cathedral Parish Archives, is in the year 1606. The country's first sanctioned free community of ex-slaves was established in Saint Augustine in 1738, in an area called Fort Mose. The first Underground Railroad originally went from north to south, from the British colonies in the north to Spanish Florida in the south.

Francisco Menendez was a black slave in South Carolina but escaped to Saint Augustine. He was proclaimed a free man and was appointed the head of a black militia. Menendez evacuated Fort Mose when Florida was ceded to the British in the 1763 Treaty of Paris. Fort Mose, where Menendez was a military leader, is recognized as a National Historical Landmark.

4. Junipero Serra (1713-1784)

Junipero Serra was born Miguel Josep Serra i Ferrer. He took the name "Junipero" in honor of Saint Juniper, a follower of Saint Francis. He entered the Order of Friars Minor in 1730.

Father Serra traveled to North America in 1749. In 1768 he was appointed superior of fifteen Franciscans for the Indian Missions of Lower California and became the "Father Presidente." In 1769, he accompanied Governor Gaspar de Portola on an expedition to Alta (Upper) California; then in 1770 he moved to the area which is now Monterey and founded Mission San Carlos Borromeo de Carmelo. He relocated the mission to Carmel in 1771.

Seven other missions were founded under his presidency: Mission San Antonio de Paua, Mission San Gabriel Arcangel, Mission San Luis Obispo de Tolosa, Mission San Juan Capistrano, Mission San Francisco de Asis, Mission Santa Clara de Asis, and Mission San Buenaventura.

Father Serra is buried under the sanctuary in the church of Mission San Carlos Borromeo in Carmel, California, along with Padres Fermin Lasuen and Juan Crespi.

5. Fermin Lasuen (1736-1803)

Padre Lasuen was born Ferminde Francisco Lasuen de Arasqueta. He was ordained in the Franciscan order in 1752. He volunteered to work in North America and arrived in Baja California in 1768. He was appointed the second Presidente of the California missions in 1785, upon the death of Junipero Serra.

Padre Lasuen personally established nine of the twenty-one Alta California missions: Santa Barbara, La Purisima Concepcion, Santa Cruz, Nuestra Senora de la Soledad, San Jose, San Juan Bautista, San Miguel Arcangel, San Fernando Rey de Espana, and San Luis Rey de Francia.

6. Juan Crespi (1721-1782)

Juan Crespi entered the Franciscan Order at age seventeen. He came to America in 1749 and accompanied missionary explorers Francisco Palou and Junipero Serra.

In 1769, he joined the expedition of Gaspar de Portola to occupy Monterey. Padre Crespi authored the first written account of actual interaction between Franciscan friars and the indigenous population after his expedition traveled through the region known today as Orange County, California in July of the same year.

He would later serve as the chaplain of the North Pacific expedition of Juan Jose Perez Hernandez in 1774, and his diaries provided valuable records of these expeditions.

7. Bernardo O'Higgins (1778-1842)

Bernardo O'Higgins was the son of Ambrosio O'Higgins, a Spanish officer born in Ireland, who became governor of Chile and later viceroy of Peru.

Bernardo was sent to London as a teenager to further his studies. While in London, he became familiar with the ideas of the American Revolution. He returned to Chile and joined a nationalist group fighting against the Spanish.

Bernardo would lead military offensives, along with Jose de San Martin, until Chile achieved independence in 1817. Chile became an independent republic in 1818. Bernardo was the second Supreme Director of Chile, from 1817 to 1823.

8. The Gordian Knot

Legend had predicted that whoever could undo the knot would be destined for greatness as the king of Asia.

When Alexander, king of Macedonia, entered the town of Gordium, he requested that he be shown the knot. He was led to a small ox cart by some of the townspeople. The knot, which held the yoke to the shaft, had no visible beginning or end. As Alexander evaluated the knot, his officers and additional townspeople gathered around him. We do not know how Alexander untied the knot. One account claims he sliced it with his sword, thus producing the ends of the knot. Another explanation is that Alexander pulled out the pin holding the yoke to the shaft, causing the knot to unravel.

Alexander and the Macedonians would defeat King Darius and the Persians at the ensuing Battle of Issus. Alexander would then advance through modern day Lebanon, Syria, Israel and into Egypt. He would transform Egypt from a country that had looked within itself for thousands of years into a country that would look out at the world at large. Alexander founded and designed the great port city of Alexandria. He would eventually leave Egypt and spread his influence through Persia, Afghanistan and as far as India. Alexander launched himself into history. As predicted by the untying of the Gordian Knot and its prophecy of greatness, he would be known through the ages, not as Alexander, King of Macedonia, but as Alexander the Great.

9. Carl Philipp Gottlieb von Clausewitz (1780-1831)

Carl von Clausewitz was a Prussian soldier and military historian. He is regarded as one the foremost military theorists. His book *Von Krieg*, or *On War*, is studied to this day at military academies around the world. The writings in *On War*, include the following ideas:

War belongs to the social realm

Strategy belongs to the realm of art

Tactics belong to the realm of science

The methods of "critical analysis"

The dialectical approach to military analysis.

10. Frederick II of Prussia (1712-1786)

Frederick II, or Frederick the Great, is considered the father of the modern Prussian state. A member of the Hohenzollern dynasty, he ruled as King of Prussia from 1740-1786.

Also a brilliant military leader, during the Seven Years' War when Prussia stood alone, Frederick opposed and defeated the combined armies of France, Russia, Austria, Saxony and Sweden.

He demanded detail from government officials and the military.

Frederick was a proponent of enlightened absolutism, and for years he corresponded with Voltaire. He promoted religious toleration, and although officially a Protestant, he supported the retention of Jesuit teachers after their suppression by Pope Clement XIV. He was interested in attracting a diversity of skills into Prussia whether from Jesuit teachers, French Huguenots or Jewish merchants and bankers, particularly those from Spain.

Frederick was an admirer of George Washington and sympathetic to the American Revolution. His decision to no longer allow the Hessians to cross Prussian territory eliminated additional Hessians troops as mercenaries for the British.

Friedrich Wilhelm von Steuben was a Prussian military officer, who served as Inspector General of the Continental Army under General George Washington. Frederick supported von Steuben's effort to teach military drill and discipline to the Continental Army. France would later commit eight German regiments under their control to fight with von Steuben and Washington.

The town King of Prussia in Pennsylvania, which exists to this day, was named for Frederick the Great.

11. Jack's utility street markings

12. The diagram given to Wilcox

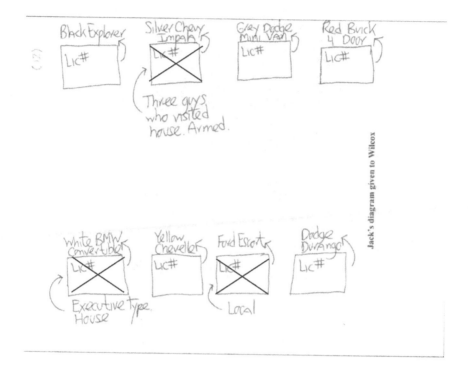

Jack's diagram given to Wilcox

13. The covered bus stop bench at Sunset and Cherokee

14. The Hollywood sign as seen from the top of Deronda Drive

15. The Hungarian Revolution Monument at 6th and Parkview

17. The Pillar Entrance to Lincoln Park at Mission and Lincoln Park

18. The Balkan Cross

The picture above is a copy of Robert Taylor's print, "Ace of Aces." It depicts Erich Hartmann and his wingman in their Messerschmitt Bf109 aircraft, with the Balkan Cross prominently displayed. Erich Hartmann is the highest scoring fighter pilot in aviation history. He was credited with 352 aerial victories during the Second World War.

*Ace of Aces by Robert Taylor, copywright, The Military Gallery,
Ojai, CA. "Ace of Aces by permission of the Military Gallery"*

19. Dwight David "Ike" Eisenhower (1890-1969)

Dwight David Eisenhower served as the Supreme Commander of Allied Forces in Europe, Western Front and became the 34th President of the United States.

After the successful Japanese attack at Pearl Harbor, Eisenhower was assigned to the General Staff in Washington with the responsibility of developing plans to defeat Germany and Japan.

General Eisenhower was appointed Supreme Allied Commander of the Allied Expeditionary Force in February 1944. On June 5, 1944, he ordered the commencement of Operation Overlord, the largest military amphibious operation in history. In the early hours of June 6, 1944, American, British, Canadian and other Allies would land on the beaches of Normandy, France. He would command American generals Omar Bradley and George Patton, British field Marshall Bernard Montgomery and French general Charles De Gaulle, as the Allied forces swept across Western Europe. Eisenhower was ordered to stop 100 miles west of Berlin due to political agreements previously made with the Russians.

The Russians would lose over 100,000 soldiers in the battle for Berlin. Overall German losses in the defense of Berlin are unknown.

20. Panzerfaust

The Panzerfaust or "armored fist" was a German anti tank weapon of the Second World War. It consisted of a small disposable preloaded gun, dispatching a shaped charge warhead. The American anti tank weapon equivalent was known as the Bazooka, although it had a different design and propelling warhead mechanism.

Development began in 1942. The body was a tube of low grade steel, approximately three feet long. Attached to the upper side of the tube were a simple rear sight and trigger. The edge of the warhead was used as the front sight. It had a practical range of 180-200 feet. The warhead was loaded with enough explosive to destroy the heaviest tanks of the War. The Russian T-34 and IS-2 tanks could not sustain the explosive power of the Panzerfaust, in the close quarter combat situations, for the Battle of Berlin.

Jack Avila, in his initial meeting with Faust at the restaurant in Venice, asked Faust, if he was Faust as in Goethe's Doktor Faust. Jack then asked if he could be Doktor Panzerfaust, aka, Doctor Bazooka.

21. The Lightning Bolts of the SA

22. General Andre Beaufre (1902 – 1975)

General Andre Beaufre entered the military academy at Ecole Speciale Militaire de Saint Cyr in 1921. There, he met Charles de Gaulle, an instructor at the school.

General Beaufre was serving in Algeria when Germany defeated France and he was arrested by the Vichy government. When released, Beaufre quickly joined the Free French Army.

After the war, Beaufre wrote a book titled "1940: The Fall of France". He stated "The collapse of the French Army is the most important event of the 20th Century". Beaufre went on to explain if the French army had maintained the same fortitude they displayed in World War I, there would have been no German conquest of Western Europe; French resistance would have made it impossible for Hitler to attack Russia in 1941; there would have been no Holocaust, and most likely no Communist takeover of Eastern Europe.

The French were instrumental in the introduction of the airplane and tank in the First World War. They did little to improve aviation and tank tactics between the wars. The Germans did not have tanks in the First World War and the effect of being attacked by tanks was not lost upon them. They worked hard between the wars on tank development and tactics.

Blitzkrieg (Lightning War)

General Heinz Guderian, the father of modern warfare, wrote a book titled "*Achtung-Panzer!*" (Attention-Tanks!), which was published in 1923. Guderian advocated a new type of warfare. It called for the close and coordinated use of airplanes, tanks and infantry. When implemented on the battlefield, his concept became known around the world as *Blitzkrieg*, or Lightning War.

Germany attacked Poland on September 1, 1939, and Polish armed forces were obliterated in two weeks. In 1940, all Western forces were defeated in several months and the British were forced to evacuate the Continent at Dunkirk. The *Blitzkrieg* concept brought significant results during the initial stages in the invasion of Russia,

The Germans attacked Russia on June 22, 1941, under the code name Operation Barbarossa. The operation was named after a German prince who lived centuries earlier; he was nicknamed Barbarossa by the Italians because of his red beard. Five Russian frontier armies were destroyed on the first day of the attack. By June 30, the Germans were half way to Moscow. The fast moving German forces captured 450,000 Russian troops at Kiev. Four Russian armies consisting of 43 divisions ceased to exist. At Smolensk, another 300.000 Russian troops were captured and two Soviet mechanized corps destroyed. The Crimean Peninsula and its main city, Sevastopol, were considered a Russian fortress but would fall to the German onslaught. Leningrad was surrounded and remained under siege for 900 days. After only months of war, the Russians had sustained millions of casualties. The German offensive of 1941 would not be halted until the Battle of Moscow.

With the Germans in the suburbs of Moscow, the Russians counterattacked. Their successful counterattack was launched on Friday, December 5, 1941. The Russian offensive would eventually push the Germans west, away from Moscow.

Two days later, in the morning hours of December 7, 1941, Japanese naval forces struck the American Fleet at Pearl Harbor, Hawaii. The military and industrial might of America would weigh heavily in the balance for the Allies and the eventual outcome of the war.

About the Author

Jon J. Esparza grew up in the Los Angeles harbor towns of Wilmington and San Pedro. He graduated from the University of Southern California with a Bachelor of Arts degree in International Relations and holds a master's degree in Business Administration from Loyola Marymount University. He is employed by a construction supply company in Los Angeles. Hobbies include hunting, fishing, military history and, especially, World War II.

Made in the USA
Las Vegas, NV
16 May 2021